To Nancy +
Bill
from
Ed F.

Brazzi And Company

Brazzi And Company

❖

Ed Fiorelli

Library of Congress Control Number:		2011905306
ISBN:	Hardcover	978-1-4568-9994-3
	Softcover	978-1-4568-9993-6
	Ebook	978-1-4568-9995-0

This book was printed in the United States of America.

To order additional copies of this book, contact:
Xlibris Corporation
1-888-795-4274
www.Xlibris.com
Orders@Xlibris.com
96424

For Maria, who knows why.

Contents

Brazzi's Thing

Brazzi didn't know the stiff. That was as it should be now that he'd come up with his new way of doing business. In the old days he had known all his clients, as he called them. Only once, under his old way of operating, had he dealt with a stranger. He'd seen the obit in The Hoople Herald, found that the dead guy's family were newcomers who had moved into one of those new tract homes at the edge of town. Some itinerant builder, already indicted, had bought the swampy land cheap, then quickly, quietly, efficiently filled it in, laying some concrete slabs and putting up a sign announcing "Hoople Homes, where Quality Lives." Rounding up a tribe of Mexicans, the fellow set them loose on the site, and within a few weeks, even counting foul weather, everything, including a few scrawny shrubs, was soon in place for John Q., the Poor Slob. So Barnum was right, and Brazzi didn't feel sorry for the sucker-buyers. If the stiff was among them, so be it, no sympathy. Besides, it wasn't good business to be soft-hearted. If he had learned anything in jail it was that a soft heart was a living carcass for the vultures. First and foremost Brazzi was a businessman. And business is business. And Brazzi saw that it was good.

It hadn't always been. Before he latched on to this better system, his method was hit and miss. He always started with the obit, of course. That was a given. Once he'd learned that So-and So had kicked off, he noted the day and time of the funeral and waited across the street from the church as the procession started up, the hearse leading the way. He followed in his own car, bringing up the rear, the stiff's parade meandering among Hoople's narrow lanes, halting briefly, in a last goodbye, at the dead guy's house. Then it was straight to the bone yard.

But Brazzi didn't bother making that trip. Pulling up near the stiff's place, he waited respectfully, patiently, for the coming of that second sense which told him it was safe to conduct business. A crowbar inside a suitcase was his credentials, his letter of introduction, his sample case, his resume, his interview and his paycheck. Sometimes he would go to the back, begin prying open a window. Sometimes rose bushes would snare his ass, sometimes a dog would snarl, drooling and clawing at him from behind the glass. More than once a neighbor would yell from across the way, "Can I help you? What are you doing there?"

"I'm looking for Mr. So-and-So."

"From the back window? My God, man, Mr. So-and-So just died."

"I guess I'll come back at a better time."

"You will like hell. I'm calling the cops."

And so Brazzi would scuttle the project, another case of unfinished business.

For sure, things were changing now. Lots of funeral homes were doing away with the hearse's salute at the stiff's house. Maybe they were catching on. In any case, that part of the business was getting stale. There was, too, the noisome problem of being recognized in a small town like Hoople where everyone knew what you scarfed down for breakfast, where you gobbled up lunch and when you farted in comfort at the dinner table.

Besides, the market was becoming unstable, opportunity dwindling. Only a few Hoople-ites obligingly croaked every week, so the pickings were getting too thin for a man like Brazzi who enjoyed the finer things, like a pair of clean briefs or the nightly specials at Gimpy's Elite Motel and Diner. Nobody's fool, Brazzi realized that following up funerals was played out; he had to come up with a new wrinkle. And come up he did, in spades. His thing now was working just fine. Instead of scanning the obit from The Hoople Herald, Brazzi went to the library, conning the dead pages from the big city paper where the stiff's picture smiled back at you, always real classy and professional, the biographic details rich in revelations like "he was fond of toads" or "he enjoyed his grandchildren and playing pinochle with his niece." The dead guy must have been a big-enough deal, well-off and all, to have had his obit done in the first place.

Take this stiff, for instance. Brazzi didn't know the guy from Adam, but he sensed with all the intuition of a born man of business that the stiff was just his meat, just his thing: "Financier." the obit called him. "Bon-Vivant." "Raconteur." Brazzi didn't know what the hell a "bone vie-vant" was, and the other word stumped him, but he knew that a financier was a man of means, means his widow, means the wake, means plenty of mourners, means lots of handbags, means big business. The thing was as plain as day, brilliant in its direct simplicity. You dress nice, you get into your car. You drive twenty, thirty miles where nobody knows you, you go to the wake, as posted in the paper, you sit quiet and respectable and you wait. Sometimes you smile and talk sociable with the suckers, all the while watching the women get more careless with their bags as time drags on. Sure, there's always the possibility that a couple of old skanks will take their stuff with them when they go up to the coffin. But they don't count, just chump change. It's the widow you want, or maybe the daughter or next of kin. Sooner or later they leave their bags on the chair or the grieving couch and that's when you swoop in, scoop up your haul and get the hell out. There's no guarantee that the widow will have a lot of cash in her bag, but the odds are good enough in your favor that there'll be something of value. The last old broad had a fifty dollar bill and a check made out to cash for two-hundred bucks. Anyhow, that's the risk incurred by all freelance speculators. You may even be able to snatch two or three bags at the same time if a few grievers decide to console each other and go up together, clutching each other like little kids for the first time about to meet scary old Santa Claus. Brazzi often entertained himself with the spectacle of these black-garbed matrons approaching the coffin. Italians, they were the worst, some even throwing themselves on the stiff, shrieking their intentions of following him soon hereafter, as if promising to catch the next bus. And so here we are.

A pink stone fountain topped with weeping angels stood among silk topiary as Brazzi, dressed in his only jacket and tie, walked into the lobby of Lemming and Styx Funeral Home. The place was crowded and he could hear the ordered, respectful buzz of conversation coming from a large room to his right marked "Chapel A."

Inside, he took a seat in the empty back row, noting the casual glances in his direction. The stiff was laid out in a fine-looking box, all ebony and silver, probably worth as much as ten years' rent for Brazzi's one room suite at Gimpy's. It didn't take long to spot the most promising client sitting in the front row. Aside from the black lace doily atop her head, there was no look of mourning about her. She was around sixty, he guessed, wearing a spring green dress, a sunburst brooch on her collar, gleaming even in the pink-tinted light of the parlor. Two women sat next to her, one at each arm. By the way they clutched their bags Brazzi knew this was going to be tough, but all he needed, he told himself, was patience.

Patience and a calm, compassionate face. It was his face, he supposed, his look of warm, friendly reserve, that brought to his side a woman about his age. Dressed in black, she had been wringing a handkerchief into a limp, soggy rag. She took a seat beside him, but continued to look ahead at the mourners who had gathered about the stiff. Brazzi knew the game. This woman was waiting to strike up a conversation. Seeing him alone, herself probably unattached, she was one of those who preferred the funeral parlor to the personal column: SWF, attractive, seeks company of SWM, for companionship, etc. She was, for Brazzi, an occupational hazard and he was willing to go along with this temporary diversion in the interest of business.

"Doesn't he look grand?" she began, nodding her head in the direction of the stiff.

"You bet," said Brazzi.

"They do wonders nowadays. He looks better now than he ever did."

Brazzi kept his eyes on the client with the doily and the brooch.

"Did you know him well?"

"What was that?" said Brazzi.

"Were you friends?"

"Just business."

"Oh. And are you in bonds?"

"In bonds?" said Brazzi. "Not now, no. I was, for about five years, but that was up the river. Upstate."

"I can't get over how wonderful he looks."

For a moment neither spoke. Brazzi's attention was so rapt with Mrs. Doily-Brooch that he didn't notice when the woman put her hand on his arm, at the same time leaning into him with a confidential leer.

"Well," she said. "I guess that old saying's true."

"What?"

"'Never judge a book by its cover.'"

"Don't read much, except the paper," he said, moving his arm.

"He looks so good all laid out," the woman said. ""You'd never guess what a rat he really was."

"The world's full of all kinds of rats", Brazzi observed.

"Yes, and he was certainly one of the biggest. I happen to know the whole story. Believe me when I say I'm not exaggerating. See that brooch?

"What brooch?" Brazzi pretended to look around the room.

"His widow," she was pointing with her head.

"You're going to tell me it's fake, right?"

"Let me tell you something. That brooch you call a fake cost twenty-five thousand dollars."

She pronounced each syllable of the sum in a deliberate, careful whisper, as if it were a coded signal, as if Brazzi were deaf and forced to read lips.

Brazzi subdued a low whistle.

"Yes," she went on. "And that was cheap. A cheap price to pay for a guilty conscience."

"Twenty-five thousand dollars." Brazzi's mind was revolving the figure; messaging it, creating permutations for it that were almost pure forms of arousal. What sums must the widow be carrying in her bag? Enough, maybe, for him to retire. The blue plate special at Gimpy's, with seconds and lots of gravy everyday of the week, including Sundays, loomed in prodigal visions.

"Nobody's perfect," Brazzi affirmed. It was the one statement in his grammatical arsenal that approached the level of philosophy.

"Excuse me," said the woman. "But that's exactly what us women would expect a man to say. 'Nobody's perfect'. That woman up there is a saint. The things that creep did to her. Are you married?"

"That *is* a swell brooch," he said.

"Everybody knew he was fooling around. He had at least six, seven women on the side. He was never home. Those trips to Guatemala. They weren't just to inspect the coffee beans."

"Maybe that's why the old guy has a smile on his face," said Brazzi, looking from the brooch to the stiff.

"You can joke about it," the woman said. "But his affairs embarrassed us and hurt her"—nodding at the widow—"especially his latest fling. Nineteen! A cosmetologist. She does my nails."

"Poor guy!" said Brazzi.

"And he thought he could make up for it all with a brooch."

"Twenty-five thousand bucks," said Brazzi. "That's a lot of making up."

The woman put the rag to her eyes. "The things you men do to us poor women. Did you say you were married?"

During all this time the widow didn't move from her seat. But now she got up and to Brazzi's growing excitement laid her bag on the chair as she walked to the coffin. He thought he detected a strange look on her face. He was at a loss to figure it out, but all that mattered to him at this point was the bag. It would be almost impossible to snatch it while her two Furies were still installed there, seated on her left and her right.

"She's a saint," the woman continued. "All this time she kept her cool. Not once did I hear her complain or curse him out. 'Divorce him' we told her. 'Take him to the cleaners.' 'I'll have it my way,' she said to us. 'You leave it to me.' 'It's not natural, you being so calm,' we said. 'I know what I'm doing ' she said. 'I'll take care of it.' 'What does that mean? What 're you going to do?' But she didn't say anything after that."

"And after that she got her brooch, right?"

"Men!" the woman said, and walked away.

It was almost closing time. Tomorrow was the funeral; it was now or never. It would take no more than five, six seconds to make it to the chair, swipe the bag and run like hell through the side door. He had parked his car two blocks away, but he was in good enough shape to reach it in a minute or two and be on the road before anyone knew what had happened. Twenty-five thousand bananas!

As if on cue, the mortician glided in, bidding everyone pay last respects for the night, and for good. By now only a few mourners remained and one by one approached the stiff. The woman who conversed with him was still there, and as Brazzi held back he smiled to himself. The woman was probably waiting for him, expecting to go out afterwards, maybe for a few drinks. Fat chance. He'd be half way to Gimpy's before she could ask again if he was married.

The two Furies had risen and were making their way to the coffin. That was good. But Brazzi noticed that strange smirk on the widow's face at the same moment she was putting down her bag. Now was the time. He turned to leave, and just as the widow herself faced the coffin Brazzi lunged forward, grabbed her bag and ran straight for the door. He was out and running; running so fast as not to hear the shouts and never looking back to see the stunned expression on the faces.

He was in his car in two minutes and on his way. He felt good. Business was picking up and he was getting better at it each time. He drove without stopping, finally pulling into his space at Gimpy's just in time to see Mr. and Mrs. John Smith signing in with no luggage. The elevator had broken down again, but he was too excited to have waited for it anyway. Taking the stairs two at a time, the handbag under his arm, he quickly unlocked his door and threw himself on the bed.

For the first time he hefted the bag, sensing that it seemed lighter than when he first copped it. That could be a good thing. Cash, lots of it, in big bills, would weigh practically nothing. He could certainly handle that. Brazzi's excitement grew as he opened the bag and began rummaging through it, impatiently emptying the contents onto the bed. His heart leapt when he saw, tumbling out amid lipstick, keys and feminine odds and ends, a shiny blue box. Not some crummy cardboard box you got from Louie the Fence, but a snazzy, classy box, like the kind from Tiffany's; the kind of box just the right size for that sunburst brooch. His fingers could hardly control themselves as he pried off the lid. His eyes widened. A sickening turn of his stomach confirmed something cold and soft lying amid cotton wadding. He felt himself fighting off nausea as he stared down at a shriveled pair of decomposing balls.

*   *   *

Brazzi At Breakfast

(second in a series)

Everything was going well for Brazzi until that morning when a maggot dropped into his coffee. He had barely emptied the third packet of sugar into his cup and was beginning to stir it with his finger when something rudely splashed into the brew. He had just time enough to see the pale vermiculate thing curl into its death dance before coming to rest, stretching out peacefully on the black, steaming surface.

At first he thought it was a grain of rice from last night's dinner at Woo Chong's Famous Celestial Bamboo Palace. They always give you a whopping container of rice with your take-out order. He had gone there in extravagant celebration of his finest achievement yet: the snatching of a handbag from a wake in progress in parlor C of Lemming and Styx Funeral Home. When he opened the bag in the security of his vehicle —Brazzi called it the company car, even though he was the only employee and the car was an '82 Volvo—he discovered among the usual items of keys and cosmetics a wad of fifties. Laying out the bills on the seat beside him he slowly counted until he reached nine. Four hundred and fifty smackers! Quite a haul, coming as it did from a beat-up old satchel of a thing, but then again he was in this business too long to be surprised by anything.

Anything, of course, except a maggot dropping from the ceiling, spoiling his Mr. Coffee morning. The unexpectedness of the event made him look up. The light fixture was dirty but he could clearly see through the clouded glass the squirming silhouettes of a few larvae busily crawling out to the edge. Even as he watched, two or three maggots slithered out of the space between the cracked ceiling and the fixture and dropped onto his table. Still another defiantly plopped into his cup.

16

For a moment he considered scooping the bodies from his coffee and drinking it down; no sense wasting good coffee, not to mention the last three packets of sugar. He would have to stop in Wendy's and quietly stuff his pockets with more. On second thought, though, why not go to hell with yourself? Four hundred and fifty bucks was reason enough to loosen up once in a while. Besides, his breakfast was already ruined by the thought that old lady Pitts lived just above him and today was the first of the month. He always paid her on time; the rent was cheap and he liked her because she never asked any questions, never made small talk, never tried to be friendly in a nosy sort of way. She was perfect—nothing but a human P.O. Box thrusting out its palm once a month, not ever thanking him but always reminding him firmly to close the goddam door on his way out.

This morning, though, he would have to talk to her, tell her about the maggots, even offer, half-heartedly, to get rid of them; after all, he couldn't have a team of the critters worming around his coffee cup every damn day during breakfast. He walked over to the sink, moved aside the empty containers from Chong's—the plastic fork still inside—and cleared the drain. Then he poured out the coffee, shaking his head in disgust. He cast a forlorn glance at the ceiling, watching another maggot fall, and then walked out into the landing.

There he bumped into Madam Goulagrossa who occupied the room next to his. "Bumping" was the right word, Brazzi reflected, for Madam Goulagrossa was a walrus of a woman with the biggest butt he had ever seen. Her flesh spurted around her entire body, forming a kind of shelf in support of her spandex circumference. He liked Madam Goulagrossa because she was adept in the art of survival, as Brazzi understood the term. He had once dreamed a dream in which he was a little boy playing with toy cars, rolling them off a cliff, discovering that the cliff was Madam Goulagrossa who laughed and laughed as the cars plunged off her shelf. In a variant of that dream he saw himself driving his matchbox Porsche around a narrow mountain pass, suddenly careening off the cliff which once again was Madam Goulagrossa's shelf. Brazzi didn't know what the hell the dream meant, but he understood the impression Goulagrossa had made on him and in his waking hours would come to appreciate the service good old Pitts had rendered.

It was the old lady who had introduced the two to each other, her only act of personal communication except for the rent business every first of the month. She took no checks, wanted to be paid in cash promptly before noon and silently issued a receipt while hastily showing the tenant out. And so it was that they had met that first time at the landlady's door. Afterwards, Madam Goulagrossa invited Brazzi to her place. Ordinarily he would have refused the invitation, not in the habit of making friends and distrusting offers of hospitality. But Madam Goulagrossa impressed him not only with her girth but by the way she had seized his arm and forcibly dragged him to her den.

"This is nice," said Brazzi, at a loss to say anything else. He looked at the couch, sagging and spotted, at the dingy drapes over the lone window, at the rumpled bed in one corner and at the pink dinette table with the cracked leatherette chair he had once considered picking up at the Salvation Army Thrift Shop. When he went back to get the set it was already gone, and later he was glad that if he couldn't have it, at least a fellow survivor could.

"It's O.K." Madam Goulagrossa said. "It'll do for now. Want a beer?"

"What kind you got?"

"What is this, Hannigan's Pub? I got beer. You want it or not?"

As they sat on the couch Brazzi sensed the beer was the only thing that was cold and he feared Madam Goulegrossa was trying to seduce him. He realized that he could easily crack a rib or suffer a fractured skull in her embrace and the thought gave the beer a bitter taste. He choked as he drained the bottle.

"I like you," she said. "Want me to do you?"

Brazzi tensed, ready to bolt, when Madam Goulagrossa rose from the couch, walked over to the pink dinette table and gestured for him to approach.

"Sit'" she said. "I'll give you a reading. No charge."

Madam Goulagrossa pulled out a chair and splayed herself into it, her flesh spilling over the sides like fresh lava flow.

"Now then," she began, squirming herself into a comfortable position. "Let me see your hand."

"Which one?" said Brazzi as he took a seat opposite.

"Your strongest, most active."

"I'm a southpaw," said Brazzi.

"Your left hand, then. That's a good sign. Lefties are fab. I'm a leftie myself."

Brazzi surrendered his hand and Madam took it, scowled.

"It's dirty," she said. "Where've you been, my man?"

Madam Goulagrossa wiped his palm with her sleeve, scratched about its surface with her index finger. "This is your life line. See this wide curve starting by the crux of your fingers? You're a man of great vitality, lots of get up and go. And this. This is your Apollo line. I don't find an Apollo line in every hand, but here it is in yours, clear as the sun. Your Apollo starts high in your palm. You'll have great success."

"I'm pretty good at what I do," said Brazzi. "I guess my hands don't lie."

"Happiness and achievement, it's all there. And here's a star, this little squib in the middle. See how it lies in the upper mounts of Apollo? A large fortune awaits you. It's unmistakable. I've never seen a palm so rich in good things to come. Even your Mount of Jupiter—over here, at the base of your index finger—even your Mount is especially well-developed."

"Well," said Brazzi. "I expect to make it big one of these days. You're not putting me on, are you."

"My standard fee for a reading is ten bucks," said Madam, aggrieved. "I try to sprinkle in some bad news along with the good. Folks get suspicious if it's all good. But with you, I'm sincere. And anyhow, I didn't charge you, did I? I said I liked you."

"That's O.K.," said Brazzi, looking at his palm admiringly. "I can understand all that. When a guy has a strong Apollo and a big Jupiter and it's all in his hand, that's pretty impressive."

Impressive too, was Madam's skill. In the days to come Brazzi often wondered if her readings were the real thing. After all, he had come into some good fortune, 450 smackers, to be exact. Yet his deeply painful knowledge of the world, his many cruel recollections of all those times he got screwed, curdled his optimism. Chances are she had latched on to something good. Like him, she had determined to play it out. In any case, he admired her ability to thrive, to make a go of it, and was pleased to see her this morning as he bumped into her en route to old lady Pitts.

It turned out that Madam, too, was on her way to the landlady. Brazzi was tempted to tell her about the maggots. But her greeting forestalled his remark.

"Rent day," she said. Her eyes were bleary and she was wrapped in a terrycloth bathrobe that bristled with pulls and loose threads along the sleeve. As if in answer to Brazzi's critical stare she hugged her robe tightly. "I like to sleep in. But on rent day I get up early to settle with that old bastard."

"It kind of ruins my day, too," said Brazzi.

"Yeah, you know, it would be nice once in a while just to get a 'hello' or a 'thank you'. I don't even say a smile. That'd be too much to ask. I knock on her door and I hear her scream 'What!' and then she comes out wearing an old housecoat and a sour puss. She don't say anything and I don't say anything. Just hand over the cash, swipe at the receipt and leave. Ten seconds, that's it. The old bastard."

"I don't smile much myself," said Brazzi.

"I kinda noticed that, my man. It's none of my business but why don't you loosen up? It wouldn't crack your face."

"She must have loads of money."

"Who, Pitts? I'm not surprised. But I wouldn't want any of it. Not if I have to live that way. No friends. No life."

"I'll take money anytime," said Brazzi. "Friends only screw you. And money can buy you any kind of life."

"That reminds me. Remember that reading I did for you? How've things been going? Good, I'll bet."

"Not bad," said Brazzi. "I'm doing O.K. Made a few bucks last night."

"I hardly ever see you, my man. What is it you do, anyway?"

Brazzi knew he had to be careful. Friends were fine, but at a distance.

"I am a enter prenoor. I work on spec."

"Well," said Madam Goulagrossa. "I guess you're entitled to your privacy. But as little as I see of you, I see even less of old lady Pitts. At least you get out. I've knocked on your door a few times but you were never in. Thought we might have a couple of beers. Now that I think of it, maybe you just didn't bother answering."

"I work nights, at least till nine or so. That's when the funeral parlors close."

Brazzi knew he had made a mistake. But he settled at ease when Madam Goulagrossa appeared not to notice.

"I haven't seen Pitts for weeks," she said. "In fact, not since last rent day."

"Maybe she took a vacation. With all that money."

"The only vacation she takes is watching the travel channel. But I doubt the old fart has cable. No. I've got a feeling something's wrong."

"I guess you could read that in her palm," said Brazzi. "Except that it's always crossed with our rent money."

By this time the two had reached the landlady's door.

"You want to knock, or should I?" said Madam G.

"You knock," said Brazzi. "You can get the abuse."

"We're both in for it," said Madam G., knocking.

They stood in the hall without speaking, expecting to hear a bellowing 'What!', but after knocking again Madam Goulagrossa looked at Brazzi and exclaimed, "Huh!"

It was at this point that Brazzi remembered to tell her about his breakfast maggots.

"They were all over the place," he was saying. "On the walls, the floor, even in my eggs bennydick."

Madam Goulagrossa wasn't listening. Her eyes widened in surprise as she turned the knob and the landlady's door opened for them. A sickening, cloyingly sweet odor filled the place. Brazzi gagged. He watched as Madam Goulagrossa quickly scanned the room before making for the kitchen. He lagged behind, even in his nausea having the presence of mind to look for something small and valuable that he could pocket. He heard her yell, "Oh my God!" and found himself standing beside her. The body lay at their feet. The landlady was lying on her side, in a fetal position, the smell so strong here that Brazzi's eyes began to water. His first thought was that he could skip this month's rent.

"You wait here," Madam Goulagrossa said. "I'll be right back."

Brazzi could feel the floor vibrate as she stomped out, but in the next instant he looked around and began to open the cabinets, stepping over old lady Pitts to reach a drawer that looked promising. Dead bodies were not novelties to him. They were part of his business; he had learned to draw comfort from their stillness; they minded their own business as they let him do his. Of course, the stiffs he had seen were all well-dressed, as if for a formal occasion, while this corpse on the kitchen floor was still in her ragged housecoat and smelled bad. But as he had told Madam G., he worked on spec, and this was as spec as you could get.

He had just managed to snatch a roll of quarters from an ashtray near the toaster when Madam Goulagrossa returned. She had changed into her spandex gear and was putting on a pair of large, yellow rubber gloves as she rushed in.

"Can't do anything in my bathrobe," she said, as if in explanation. "And I don't want to catch anything, know what I mean?"

With difficulty she knelt beside the body.

"Poor thing," she said. "Dying all alone like this."

"We all die alone when you get right down to it," said Brazzi.

Madam Goulagrossa began brushing off the maggots, first covering the landlady's head with a dishtowel. Carefully she prodded the body.

"She must have been dead since last rent day," she said. "The maggots probably slipped in between the flooring. I'll bet she tripped on this scatter rug. See, it's all crumpled up by her feet."

"How about her pockets?" said Brazzi.

He did not wait for Madam Goulagrossa to respond, but quickly swooped down and rummaged through the pocket facing out. "Nah!" he grunted, coming up empty except for a besnotted hankie.

"Try the other one," he said.

Madam Goulagrossa gently turned the body, exposing the other pocket. She flicked off a few maggots, then reached in. Her glove was too big to fit, so she quickly pulled it off and plunged in her bare hand. To Brazzi's delight she pulled out a number of crumpled bills. He could make out at least a couple of Grants. Jacksons were good, too. And Franklins, of course, though the only time he had ever seen one was when Jimmy the Bookie croaked and some guy, standing by the coffin, placed a hundred dollar bill on the pillow, muttering, "So long, pal. This squares us." It would have been sweet, snatching that Franklin, but there were too many eyes and too many tough-looking dudes for Brazzi to try anything. When all was said and done, a Grant was the best, small enough not to raise eyebrows but fat enough to give a man the comforting feel of status and respectability.

"How much we got?" he asked.

He watched as Madam Goulagrossa pulled off the other glove and began to uncrumple the bills.

"I count nine hundred."

"That's four-fifty apiece."

Madam Goulagrossa looked at Brazzi. She thrust the bills into her own pocket.

"Fifty-fifty," insisted Brazzi.

"Not so fast, my man. I got to think about this."

"What's there to think about? You get four-fifty and I get four-fifty."

Madam Goulagrossa slowly rose to her feet.

"That's an awful lot of money," she said.

"An awful lot of readings for you."

"You're right," Madam Goulagrossa said. "A lot of palms."

"Well, then", said Brazzi, holding out his arms. "Where's the problem?"

"Reading palms is one thing. But this . . ."

"You called it right, remember? You said I had a great Apollo and a big Jupiter. And now here's the cash to back it all up."

Madam Goulagrossa shook her head.

"I don't rob dead people, my man. And you're not going to do it, either. I'm surprised at you."

"Listen," said Brazzi, sensing he had nothing to lose. "Old lady Pitts won't miss it. Who's going to know? Besides, some of us make our living from dead people. It's none of your business, anyhow."

"It's anybody's business when you like somebody. I already said I like you."

"How about three hundred, then?"

Madam Goulegrossa shook her head again. "How about calling the cops?"

"No cops," said Brazzi. "I don't have no truck with cops. They're worse than friends."

"There's a phone over there on the wall. Tell them we found our landlady and some money and that we'll be waiting here for them. Or do you want me to do it?"

"You do it," said Brazzi. "My heart won't be in it."

"Cheer up, my man. When all this is over we'll go to my place and have a beer." As he watched her talking to the cops Brazzi reflected on how the day had begun and how his breakfast was ruined. He should have guessed that after such a bad start the only thing he would wind up with, aside from the rent, would be a lousy roll of quarters.

*   *   *

A Matter Of Instinct

(third in a series)

Examining his face in the bathroom mirror Brazzi detected the eruption of a pimple and carefully squeezed it between forefinger and thumb. He was suddenly repelled by the memory of his grandmother pinching him that way on his cheek, proclaiming him a "gooda boy". She hadn't intended to hurt him, but her gesture of affection nonetheless brought a tear to his eye. No matter how gentle he was with himself now, however, he couldn't help being upset. His face always broke out when he was distraught and the realization now that the cops were just in the other room asking questions about the dead body was more than his complexion could bear. Next to Nana's maternal violence, the presence of cops was a pandemic of acne. Besides, he had managed to grab only some lousy change from the kitchen counter while Madam Goulagrossa was checking out the body of old lady Pitts. When she found 900 dollars in the pockets of the corpse's grimy robe and decided to call the cops instead of splitting the cash fifty-fifty, he felt his guts churn, what his grandmother would have called "agita".

He heard the cops finishing their interview with Madam Goulagrossa and knew that they'd be in now to question him. As long as they stuck to the issue of the dead landlady Brazzi was sure he'd be able to fend them off. They couldn't possibly connect him with that fellow snatching all those handbags in a series of funeral parlor gigs. The cops on TV had called the guy a "perp", the local papers tagged him a "lowlife", but what the hell did the cops or the press know about his daring, his athletic skill, the bold, genius-like planning required to bring off such capers? Even the head undertaker at Lemming and Styx Funeral Home had been grudgingly impressed.

He tore off a piece of toilet paper and daubed the pimple on his cheek. He rolled off a few more sheets and stuffed them in his pocket. Then he hitched up his pants and walked into the living room where two cops were sitting on the couch waiting for him. The body of old lady Pitts was still lying on the kitchen floor where he and Madam Goulagrossa had found it. One of the cops stood up and motioned Brazzi to sit. As he took a seat the other cop rose and stood with his hands in his pockets, jingling his change.

"How are you, officer?" said Brazzi, not really giving a damn, but taking Madam Goulagrossa's suggestion: "Act nice," she'd said.

"It's 'Detective', said the first cop. "Detective Horney. That's 'Horney' with an 'e'".

"O.K.", said Brazzi.

"And this is Detective Cucuzzi." The cop jingling his change took out one of his hands and offered it to Brazzi who took it, shook it and gave it back. The first cop threw his partner a narrow-eyed glance in silent reprimand. Detective Cucuzzi quickly began scribbling notes in his little pad.

"I understand it was you and your lady friend who found the body, is that right?"

"She's my neighbor," said Brazzi. "I don't have a girlfriend."

"Your neighbor, then."

"We've never even held hands."

Brazzi realized that technically he was lying. But that was only if he counted the time Madam Goulagrossa read his palm which he regarded as an act of professional courtesy and not, God help us, a genuine case of female affection.

"Right," said Detective Horney, jotting down his own notes in a new pad.

"I work alone, as a matter of fact." Brazzi had to be careful. He was upset, agitated, not thinking clearly, giving away the store. Calm down, he said to himself.

Reaching into his pocket, he fingered another piece of toilet tissue and poked at his pimple.

"Let's get to the issue here," said Detective Horney. Brazzi noticed that the cop was wearing one brown and one black shoe and wondered why nobody had noticed.

"When you and . . . your neighbor . . . found the landlady, she was on her side just as she is now, right?"

"Isn't that what Madam Goulagrossa told you?"

"I'm asking *you*. Was she on her side, just as she is now ?"

"Yeah, I guess so."

"Are you sure about that?"

"Whatever my neighbor said is okay by me."

Detective Horney glanced knowingly at his partner.

"You didn't touch her at all, is that what you're saying?"

"Why would I touch a dead person?" said Brazzi, remembering what Madam Goulagrossa had told him. "I might catch something. I swear on a stack of Bibles, I have absolutely nothing to do with dead people. I never, never, never do any business with stiffs."

"I'm gonna ask you again, guy. Did you move the body?"

Brazzi looked towards Madam Goulagrossa who was nonchalantly sitting in the kitchen, thrumming her fingers on the table.

"We have reason to think the body's been turned or shifted."

"Why would you think that?" said Brazzi.

"We found maggots all about the corpse, but none on the side facing up, as if they'd been brushed off. Also, her robe is freshly wrinkled on the outside, as if only recently being turned up from the floor and the weight of the body."

Brazzi didn't know what to say. He had always thought cops were stupid bastards, redeemed from congenital idiocy only by a plodding stubbornness; at this point he wasn't able to make up his mind about these two.

"Besides," Detective Horney continued, as if lecturing. "The position of the corpse is unnaturally compromised. No one falls and lays like that. Isn't that right, Detective Cucuzzi?"

Cucuzzi had been making jottings on his little pad and now looked up.

"Right!" he said, sweeping his hand to his brow, half wave, half salute.

"It defies gravity."

"Well," said Brazzi. "I don't suppose old lady Pitts picked out her spot before she kicked off. She's not thinking of making a compromise. It's not like she told herself, 'This is a bad spot and my position's all wrong but I think I'll drop dead here anyway.'"

Detective Horney didn't share Brazzi's sense of humor.

"We don't know that she dropped dead. Not by a long shot," he said, looking squarely at Brazzi. "The M.E. will tell us that. She's been dead at least a few weeks, I'd say. Meanwhile, I've got another one for you. Your neighbor told us the old lady had some money on her. How much was it?"

"Madam Goulagrossa gave you the money, didn't she?" Brazzi said.

"Yeah, but how much was it. That's what I'm asking."

"I don't remember. Whatever she told you. Like I said, I don't touch dead people."

"You're not cooperating," said Detective Horney. "I could if I want take you and your girlfriend in right now. You two had to move the body to get at the money, and that's a crime. Tampering with evidence. A felony. You'd pull at least a year."

"She's my neighbor, not my girlfriend," said Brazzi.

"I don't like you," said Detective Horney. "What do you think, Detective Cucuzzi?"

"I don't like him, either," said Detective Cucuzzi. "Or her. Ask him again."

"I'm asking. How much money did you find in her pockets?"

"We came to pay her the rent. Me and my neighbor just happened to meet in the hallway in front of her door."

"How much, goddammit?"

"The door was unlocked, like we told you. We went in, found the body. Called you."

"Let's take the son-of-a-bitch downtown," said Detective Cucuzzi.

"I told you, officer"—the voice was Madam Goulagrossa's, wafting from the kitchen, calm, polite, insistent. "We turned over to you all the money we found, every penny."

"Yeah. We don't rob from dead people," said Brazzi, recalling Madam Goulagrossa's righteous avowal. Like the cops, she would never in a million years connect him with that perp, that lowlife, that scumbag who pinched handbags from wakes.

"What you're telling us then, is that you took the trouble to go through the dead woman's pockets but never counted the money, is that right?"

"We don't see dead landladies very often," said Brazzi.

"We were both pretty shaken up," explained Madam Goulagrossa, looking at the body. "Poor thing."

Both detectives made a few jottings in their pads. Detective Horney abruptly snapped his closed. "What do you think?" He looked to his partner.

"I think they're holding out. We don't know how much they kept for themselves."

"Tell you what", said Detective Horney. He turned to Madam Goulagrossa, but was addressing both. "I don't want to have to search you. A trip downtown, turning everything inside out, wasting your time and ours, the embarrassment. We're only doing our jobs . . ."

"Yeah. We don't appreciate you guys making things tougher than it already is," Detective Cucuzzi observed.

"We have a problem here," Detective Horney continued. "You say you handed over all the money, but you don't know how much. You didn't count it. You were upset."

"Big time," said Brazzi, daubing at another pimple.

"O.K. I believe you."

"I don't," said Detective Cucuzzi. "I say we take 'em in."

"There's your problem, see? My partner and I need to agree. Now what? Do we believe you, or do we do our jobs and hold you?"

"You can do your jobs by believing us," said Madam Goulagrossa.

"It doesn't work that way. Detective Cucuzzi and I have too much experience. We've got to go by that. And by our instincts. What we sense and what we feel. We work and act as a team."

Horney tucked his pad into his pocket, leaned against an end table, folded his arms and stretched out his legs. Suddenly noticing his mismatched shoes he quickly pushed himself erect.

Detective Cucuzzi broke the pause. "Maybe we should give them a break, Cosmo," he said.

"You think so?"

"Yeah, maybe."

Detective Horney brought Brazzi back to the kitchen where Madam Goulagrossa sat at the table, the body only a few feet away.

"I'll tell you," he began, urging Brazzi to sit by putting his hand on his shoulder. "It's not everyday that Detective Cucuzzi lets go of his instinct and gives in to his heart. But what the hell." He sighed. "Look. I'm going to leave the money in this manila envelope. I'm putting it on the table right in front of you. My partner and I are going to the next room to compare notes. Only take us a minute. My guess is you'll remember how much there was in the old lady's pockets and add it to what's already in the envelope. Do it before the M.E. gets here. Fast."

The cops turned their backs, went into the next room.

"I feel sick," said Brazzi. It was bad enough that Madam Goulagrossa had caught a hard case of scruples and decided to hand in the money; worse now to be face to face with it again and have to give it back a second time. Worst of all, to add his own dough, specifically the roll of quarters he had snatched from beside the toaster on the dead landlady's counter. The whole experience made him want to puke. He ran into the bathroom and leaned over the bowl. Nothing came up and he had to settle for a cursory inspection of what he felt to be another engorged pimple. By the time Brazzi got back to the kitchen he saw Madam Goulagrossa sealing the envelope and handing it to the two cops.

A quick knock at the door and the medical examiner came in. The two cops made way for him, pointing at the body as if he wouldn't otherwise have been able to find it.

"You two can go," said Detective Horney. "We know where we can reach you if we need to keep in touch."

Brazzi and Madam Goulagrossa waited until they reached her place before speaking. They had been walking softly, as if afraid the cops would change their minds. Brazzi threw himself on the soiled couch as Madam Goulagrossa went to the kitchen and brought back two beers. Brazzi chugged his down and sat back.

"It really got me sick," he said. "We should've taken the money and left. Let somebody else find her."

"It was the right thing to do," Madam Goulagrossa said. "Besides, suppose somebody saw us leave? Suppose we ran into one of the other boarders?"

"I keep thinking of all that dough. And that bull about their instincts. Instincts!"

"They were just trying to scare us."

"It don't matter if they did or they didn't. We're out 900 bucks."

"I wasn't scared. And we're not out 900 bucks. Not quite."

Madam Goulagrossa reached into her pocket, pulling out a few folded bills. Brazzi's eyes widened.

"There's about two hundred dollars here," Madam Goulagrossa said. "Fifty-fifty."

"How did you manage it?" said Brazzi.

"I didn't like their attitude. When you ran into the bathroom you distracted them long enough for me to take some money out of the envelope."

"You took money out?

"There it is!"

"But they'll get wise when they count it and find it short."

"So what? Maybe they counted it and maybe they didn't."

"I know cops," said Brazzi. "They counted it, all right."

"They won't make much of a stink even if they did. They'll just get suspicious of each other. Besides, they'll want to keep everything quiet. I've got instincts, too, my man. My instincts tell me they'll just take the 700 dollars and move on."

Brazzi held up his empty bottle. Madam Goulagrossa smiled and began making her way to the fridge.

"By the way," said Brazzi. "You were so set on turning in the money. You would never rob from the dead. Remember that?"

"You're right. I did say that. But I didn't rob from the dead. I robbed from the cops."

Brazzi threw her an appreciative grin.

"I gotta tell you," he said. "You're a piece of work."

*   *   *

A Walk in the Park
or
Madam G.'s First Case

(fourth in a series)

At 281 pounds, 11 ounces, Madam Goulagrossa decided to sit on a straight back chair, leaving Brazzi free to unwind on her couch. Brazzi was glad. He had always winced in discomfort when anyone, especially Madam G., sat too close to him. Only once had she sat beside him. That was the day they had discovered the body of their landlady and afterwards went back to her place for a couple of beers. Brazzi had chugged his quickly and grew restive, agitated, moving as far as he could toward the end of the seat until the wrinkled pillow and soiled antimacassar on the arm of the couch impeded him. He credited her, now, for remembering that occasion, for recognizing his distress and letting him drink his beer calmly, comfortably, in the placid security of distance.

Madam Goulagrossa smiled as Brazzi wiped his mouth with his sleeve and burped.

"Cold enough?" she asked.

"Nice," said Brazzi. "Perfect."

They sat quietly for a spell. Then Madam Goulagrossa said. "You know, this is the third or fourth time you've had a beer in my place."

Brazzi was too quick for her. "Well," he said. "I'd invite you to mine, but I've got the decorators in there right now and it's a mess. You know how it is."

"Oh sure," Madam Goulagrossa said. "Don't worry about it. I've told you already that I respect your privacy. I meant to say that you've been here a few times and never told me much about yourself."

"Asking questions about my life history. How's that respecting my privacy?"

Madam Goulagrossa laughed. "My beers ought to be worth something. Decent conversation, at least."

Brazzi appeared to think about her remark.

"Maybe you're right. Tell you what. Get me another beer and we'll see where we go, how's that?"

Madame Goulagrossa rose from the chair. Brazzi watched as she pried her wedged flesh from the edge of the seat and made her way to the fridge.

"Running a little low," she said. "Only two left."

"Not to worry," said Brazzi. "Eppy's is still open. You can always run down there for a six pack."

"Here we go," said Madam Goulagrossa, offering Brazzi a bottle. "One for you and one for me. Fifty-fifty."

Madam Goulagrossa now boldly sidled to the couch and sat down, leaving enough space, in her own mind, to stifle panic and kill excuse. After all, it was her couch. And her beer.

Brazzi grimaced. He recalled how together they had gone through the landlady's pockets and how he had insisted they split the money fifty-fifty and how Madam Goulagrossa had refused, deciding instead to call the cops. Fifty-fifty in beer was peanuts compared to what they could have shared if she had listened. But that was all water under the dam, as they say, and now he was obliged to pay for his lousy beer by telling her something about himself.

"Why don't you go first," said Brazzi. "It's kind of hard for me to get started."

"There's nothing to be ashamed about," said Madam Goulagrossa. "You have to learn to trust somebody."

"You start," said Brazzi. "I'm working on it."

"Well", Madam Goulagrossa began. "I wasn't always reading palms. Hard to make a decent living that way."

"I kind of guessed that."

"Although I got to be pretty good at it."

"You were right-on with me," said Brazzi. "I did come into some money. I remember you told me I had a big Jupiter."

"Yes, I do remember. I was impressed with your Mound of Apollo, too. Extraordinary to see both in one palm."

"I guess that makes me an extraordinary guy." Brazzi pretended to laugh.

Madam Goulagrossa saw through to his conceit and simply smiled.

"I'm glad you take my craft seriously," she said. "A lot of folks come in just for laughs, as a gag; most think it's a scam. Still, it's a tough way to live."

"What'd you do before?"

"Before palmistry? You probably won't believe me."

"Try me. Why not?"

"Because I don't look the part."

"Don't tell me. You were a ballet dancer, right?"

Madam Goulagrossa threw him a sharp look. "Be nice," she said.

"How about a lady wrestler?"

"You going to stop with the cracks or do I turn things over to you?"

Brazzi got up from the couch, took the chair. Madam Goulagrossa settled in.

"My daddy was a widower. When he died three years ago," she continued, "he left me, as only heir, his entire estate."

Brazzi left the chair and took a seat next to Madam Goulagrossa.

"It consisted of an old tuxedo, one sneaker, a few plaid shirts and the pajamas he died in at the nursing home."

Brazzi left the couch and took the chair.

"It seems he had a life insurance policy which the nursing home somehow missed. It didn't amount to much, about 500 dollars, so I guess they didn't make much fuss about it when it came to me. Anyway, I had 500 dollars and a decision to make. One, I could put the money in the bank and stay with my part-time job waiting on tables at Vito's Clam Bar. But the job paid lousy and my feet hurt at the end of the day. Or two, I could take the money and start fresh."

"You can't start too fresh with five C's," Brazzi observed.

"That's what I figured. But I had an idea. You might not think so looking at me, my man, but I've always had an adventurous soul. Even as a kid, I was pretty cool."

"I pretty much kept to myself as a kid," said Brazzi.

"I can readily believe that. But we're talking about me this trip. I said to myself, it's now or never. If I'm going to put the money to good use—justify my daddy's estate, so to speak—then I had to fulfill my nagging, frustrated sense of adventure."

"You can't open a bar with 500 bucks," said Brazzi.

Madam Goulagrossa ignored him. "I took that insurance money and used part of it to run an ad for a week in the local paper. I still have it here. Look."

With straining deliberation she rose from the couch and went into the kitchen. From an empty flower pot designed like a monkey's head she took out a yellowed column of print and handed it to Brazzi. Even while he read the ad Madam Goulagrossa recited it to him:

> "Lost? Missing? Wanted?
> Confidential Surveillance.
> We Operate in the Dark"
> Goulagrossa Investigations   Telephone
> 123 456 7890"

"You're kidding me," said Brazzi. "That's you? A private dick? Jeez, you're a piece of work".

"You could laugh all you want," Madam Goulagrossa said. "But the ad left me with enough money to buy an outfit and get a phone and answering machine installed; that's all I needed to start. I didn't want anybody coming into this place as if it was my office. Hell, one look around and nobody'd believe I was serious."

"It's not so bad," said Brazzi. "Your fridge keeps the beer nice and cold."

"Anyway, it was easy for me to make house calls. Why not? For a while I just sat around waiting for the phone to ring. That was a Monday. I went out a few times during the next few days, but when I came back expecting a caller I was always disappointed to find the machine blank. After a while, with never so much as a wrong number, I began to get anxious, real nervous. The 500 dollars wouldn't last much longer. Next Monday came and nothing happened so I tallied how much I had left and talked myself into holding on for another week."

"What'd you do in between?" Brazzi asked. "To pass the time, I mean."

"I ate," said Madam Goulagrossa sadly.

Brazzi was about to make a crack but let it pass.

"And then it happened. Right in the middle of a peanut butter snack the phone rang.

"'Goulagrossa Investigations?' the voice asks.

"'You got it,' I says.

"'I'm calling for Mr. Reuben Sandwich. Can you get over here right away? It's rather urgent.'

"'Who are you?' I says.

"'That's of no significance at the moment. Mr. Sandwich wishes to discuss a possible commission. You have nothing imminent, no pending engagements, I presume?'"

"'You presume right,' I says.

"What's with this clown?" said Brazzi. "I wouldn't trust him right off the bat."

"The guy gives me the address and I hang up. An hour bus ride, including a free transfer, and a short hitch by thumb finally gets me to the Sandwich place. The house is out in the suburbs, one of those stately old piles once owned by long-forgotten movie queens or some latter—day plumbing contractor. I was let in by a grotesque little man with pop eyes and a runny nose who just stood there scratching his crotch, smiling up at me. He throws me a sly wink and I'm about to haul off and slug him.

"I was beginning to think I had the wrong address when a tall, dignified fellow relieved my doubt by coming between us and putting his hand on the smart aleck's shoulder.

"'It's all right, Walter,' he says. 'I'll handle it.'

"The crotch guy crawls off into a hole somewhere and my dignified guy turns to me and shakes my hand.

"'Goulagrossa Investigations?' he says, and I recognize his voice as that of the guy on the phone. "'So good of you to come', he says with a crooked smile. ' Mr. Sandwich is in the library.'

"He escorts me into a large, wood-paneled room. Why it was called the library I couldn't guess: there wasn't a single book anywhere except for a back issue of Playboy lying on a coffee table against a wall on which hung a stunning portrait of a group of dogs playing poker. I've always liked dogs. The picture was O.K., I guess, as pictures go.

On the wall opposite was a painting of a weeping Elvis, done on a dark blue velvet background. It was impressive. It looked expensive. Scattered among tables and shelves was an assortment of odds and ends, junk of all sorts, urns and vases and bronze statuettes, one of a funny-looking black bird. In a far corner sat a pinball machine featuring naked women whose breasts and private parts were assigned certain numerical values. But I wasn't there to look at Sandwich's pictures or admire his taste in art.

"Besides, there was hardly time for that. I kind of got the feeling that I was being watched, as if a set of unseen eyes were studying me, sounding me out, as if waiting for me somehow to prove myself. Or make a mistake.

"My dignified guy smiles. 'This is Mr. Sandwich', he says.

"I looked around but saw only a massive desk sitting squarely on an oriental rug in the middle of the room.

"'Where?' I says.

'Here,' says the dignified guy, walking behind the desk and coming out pushing a little wheelchair on which sat a dwarf. The dwarf is wearing a plaid cap which matched the blanket tucked snugly about him. Misshapen legs dangled a few inches from the foot-rest.

'This is Reuben Sandwich.'

'The dwarf nods but doesn't smile. Instead, he begins to gesture with his fingers, flailing them in the air, as if trying to catch wild birds. With each gesture the dwarf squinches up his face, like he's smelling shit. It doesn't take long for me to realize that Reuben Sandwich is using sign language.

"'Mr. Sandwich reads lips very well,' says my dignified guy. 'We need not feel uncomfortable.'

"'What's he saying?' I ask.

"'He says he didn't expect a woman.'

"I guess I should have been insulted. In fact, I was insulted. I thought of telling him, 'Well, I didn't expect a dwarf!', but this was my first case and I needed the money, so I thought better of it and kept my mouth shut."

"I still don't believe it," said Brazzi."

"You wanted me to go first, so just shut up and listen. Where was I? Oh, yeah. 'You said on the phone it was urgent,' I says to my guy but looking at Reuben Sandwich. Sandwich makes a few more squinches and flexes his fingers at more birds.

"'Mr Sandwich is relying on me to convey the information and to make the ultimate decision on whether to offer you a commission. You will, of course, deduce from the surroundings that monetary considerations are of no concern to Mr. Sandwich.'

"' They are to me,' I says. 'We all have to eat'.

"' Yes,' he says, coldly looking me up and down. 'I quite understand.'

"I would've punched out the sucker," Brazzi observed.

"'I have been instructed to offer you a most equitable emolument,' he says.

"You should've walked out right then and there," said Brazzi. "Guys who talk like that always try to screw you."

"'O.K.,' I says. 'What's so important?' I wanted to impress my guy with my experience. Act sort of impatient to get on with it. Tough, you know what I mean?"

"'Look around and you might be able to guess,' says the guy. 'Mr. Sandwich is an avid collector, a fact that may be gleaned from even a cursory glance at the rich display before you. I might add that these are only a small sample of his incredible collection. Most of the prized acquisitions are housed in the Rosebud room above us. Naturally, its precincts are strictly guarded, rigorously secured, visited only by Mr. Sandwich and, of course, myself.'

"'You still haven't answered my question. Where do I fit in?'

'Mr. Sandwich has recently learned through his extensive network of informants that a certain artifact has just surfaced and has, shall we say, become eminently obtainable to the right people for the right price.'

"'And Mr. Sandwich, of course, is one of those right people,' I says.

"' Allow me to correct you,' my guy says. 'Mr. Sandwich is the only right people. The only one wise enough and rich enough to deserve it.'

"' I see. But just what are we talking about here?'

'Something whose uniqueness puts it on a level beyond the priceless. Something whose historical and cultural values are incalculable.'

"That means you should hold out for more money," said Brazzi. "Don't be a sap."

"'You're making it hard for me to work cheap', I says to the guy. 'But so far you're all talk.'

"Suddenly the dwarf gets real upset, squinching and pouting and flailing, tossing about in his chair as if suffering a powerful itch.

"'All right. All right', says my dignified guy to Sandwich. Then he turns to me. 'Let me tell you specifically what service you will render, though I doubt you will appreciate its immense significance. What we seek—what you will secure for us—what Mr. Sandwich must have above all other things, compared to which everything else in his collection will dissolve into mere dross,—is none other than the authentic remaining piece of wood from the box that housed the Holy Grail'

"I put my hand to my mouth to disguise what I recall was a smile, but my dignified guy recognized my cover.

"'You may very well smile,' he says. 'If I were unfortunate enough to be in your place I expect I should laugh like a madman. Under these circumstances I could well appreciate your incredulity. But I assure you this is not a delusion. People in your line of work are predisposed to a certain kind of myopia. Call it cynicism, if you like, a lack of vision. You are constitutionally inclined to regard every enterprise as mere folly, or some worthless scam. That is why visionary people like Mr. Sandwich are wealthy and have inherited the earth, whereas people like you . . . '

"Once again the dwarf goes nuts; my dignified guy gets the better of himself at this point and swallowed his words. He was stalling, bending over Sandwich and making sure his blanket was secure, even tucking it about his ankles. He comes back up for air and looks me right in the eye.

"'Let us, as you people say, cut to the chase. This artifact, as sufficiently attested to by scholars intimate with the history of the Knights of Malta, found its way to America by a series of events needless to enumerate. Owing largely to the remorseless workings of human greed and ambition, it disappeared for a number of years only to have turned up last month on a farm on the outskirts of Shelbyville, Indiana. The farmer, a prehistorically dim-witted creature with a hair-lip, was ignorant of its significance and sold it for a carton of Camels to an antique dealer who happened to be in the neighborhood. That dealer was well-aware of what he had stumbled upon. But the poor man was found dead in his shop soon after and the wood once again went missing. Now, however, it has re-surfaced and is presently in the possession of Big Jack Lumbago.'

"'And you want me to find him, is that it?'

"'Not exactly, no. Big Jack would gleefully cut out your heart with a can opener, but that was in the old days. He leads a quiet, respectable life now, investing in securities and disposable goods.'

"Disposable goods. You mean like television sets, or fur coats. Or the wood.'

"My dignified guy smiles.

"Something wasn't right here. When you put two and two together you ought to get four, but in this case the figures didn't add up.

"'Tell me something,' I says. 'If Big Jack is leading a respectable life, if he has the wood and is willing to dispose of it, why not buy it outright from him? One of your people could easily do it. Why do you need me?'

"'Big Jack is capricious, call him whimsical, if you like. He's also a shrewd business man. He knows how badly Reuben Sandwich wants that piece of wood and in all likelihood would raise the stakes to a level I should define as grossly obscene.'

"'Who wouldn't? Besides, you said yourself that for Sandwich money was not an issue.'

'Principle, my dear lady. Principle. Reuben Sandwich will not be gouged. That having been said, we need to send an unknown agent to act on our behalf. Let me add, of course, that we've done our homework. We know this is your first assignment, your silly attempts at bravado not withstanding. You've been selected precisely for your anonymity. Believe me; what we want you to do will require no especial wit or dexterity. To be sure, Mr. Sandwich is extremely anxious to secure the artifact under discussion. He has decided, thus, to forego the process of negotiation.'

"While speaking, he reaches down to Sandwich's feet, turns aside the blanket, and from the footrest takes up a doctor's black bag.

"'Listen carefully,' he says. 'Everything is in place to strike a deal. I am not at liberty to tell you all the details. You do not need to know anything beyond the instructions I shall now dictate. Take this bag and upon immediately leaving the premises engage a cab to the nearest bus stop. Take the number 9 bus. Change at Archer Street to the number 14. Proceed six stops to Spade Avenue. Get off and walk three blocks to Gutman Plaza. Board the number 27 for Cairo Boulevard. Disembark at the last stop. Walk two blocks east. You will come to a park. The Thursby Gardens. Look for a bench immediately adjoining the statue of Calvin Coolidge. Be seated and wait.'

"'You expect me to remember all that?' I says.

'You're a detective, are you not? God and detectives are in the details.'

'What next?' I ask.

"'You should arrive at the Coolidge statue at noon. Someone from Lumbago's people will approach. He will ask if you know of any good tattoo parlors in the neighborhood. You will answer, "Buzz off, Asshole". You will then give him the bag. Expect him to count the money. You won't negotiate. It's all there, you tell him. No questions asked. He will hand over the wood. You get up, retrace your steps, arrive back here at about 4 p.m. Give us the wood. We give you a handsome remuneration. Simple. Transaction complete. You leave with Mr. Sandwich's best wishes for a long and happy life.'

"It all seemed so simple. Too simple. Something about the whole affair just didn't jibe."

"You mean they were taking a chance you'd play it straight." said Brazzi. "I don't know as I'd trust anybody with all that money."

"I wasn't so much concerned about their trust. I figured they'd have somebody watching me all along the route. Besides, the bag was locked on the outside and Lumbago's people would see that it was tampered with. No, that wasn't it. The whole thing just smelled bad."

"Like what?" said Brazzi.

"All that hullabaloo for such a simple transaction. It all seemed so much double-talk. But I was already out almost 500 bucks and already in this screwy situation. This was my first P.I. job, so what the hell, I might as well play it out.

"I followed instructions and got to Thursby Gardens a little before noon. I sat by the Calvin Coolidge statue, looked around, saw no one. I must've been sitting there for half an hour, the bag on my lap. A couple of kids come by on skateboards. I smile and ask how come they're not in school. One of them gives me the finger. Serves me right, I says to myself. The little punks. When I look at my watch I see that it's almost a quarter to one. My contact wasn't going to show up. I'd give it another ten, fifteen minutes, then get the hell out of there. It struck me suddenly that I'd been set up. Maybe some guy with a rifle was scoping me out right now. I could easily have been whacked from anywhere in that park, the bag snatched, the killer later bragging to his pals how much of a cinch it was. Somehow my being out almost 500 bucks didn't matter any more.

"'Any good tattoo parlors in this neighborhood, friend?' It was a raspy, guttural voice, its tone not so much a question as a kind of sneering comment. I look up, fitting a face to the voice. It was that of an old lady. Raw, brown teeth give off a stale odor as she gums a smile. Her gray hair is tucked beneath a red beret and she's carrying a plastic grocery bag. I could see a head of celery sticking out. Her eyes are hard.

"'Buzz off, Asshole' I says.

"The old lady says nothing, drops the grocery sack into my lap and almost simultaneously makes off with my black bag. In a second she's gone, sprinting up the hill behind me like a twenty-year-old."

"I've seen a few old hens like that in my own business," said Brazzi. "Someday I'll tell you about it. But go on."

"To make a long story short, I get back to the Sandwich place about four-thirty. I knock, the door opens and there's my crotch man, Walter, again. He looks different this time. He's not smiling and he's not scratching his crotch. And he's holding a gun.

"'Come on in,' he says. 'Join us in the library.'

There's something about Walter now that puzzles me. He's walking with a swagger, a confidence I didn't observe that first time. I couldn't have known then that in less than five minutes my confusion would be cleared up.

We walk into the library and I see my dignified guy standing beside Reuben Sandwich. Only Reuben Sandwich is not in his wheelchair. And both are in handcuffs.

"'You stupid bastard', Sandwich says, holding on to the dignified guy's leg. 'I told you it wouldn't work.'

Just then another fellow walks in. Attached to his wrist, in cuffs, is the old lady. In his other hand is the black bag

"'Here she is, Lieutenant. Caught her with the goods, just like you figured. Runs pretty fast for an old dame.'

"Except,' says the Lieutenant, alias Walter. 'Except she's not a dame. And she's not an old lady'

"He walks over and pulls off the red beret. With it comes the gray wig. The other cuffed guy gasps. 'Why, it's big Jack Lumbago!'

"'You fools!' says Big Jack.

"'What about the fat one?' asks the officer cuffed to Big Jack.

"'Just an innocent schlep," says Walter, taking the grocery bag from my hand.

'They were playing you for a sucker, missus.'

"'Madam Goulagrossa, if you please,' I says.

"'It was all an act to throw all of us off. You especially. Kind of neat counterfeit scheme when you come right down to it. Big Jack here had the plates, Sandwich the real dough. Sandwich was buying the plates and Jack was retiring. You'll be retired a long time, Jack, but not in Palm Springs. They needed a shill, an unknowing one if they could get it. Just a dumb go-between who'd believe that cockamamie story about the Knights of Malta and the Holy Grail.'

"'I didn't really fall for it,'I says. 'Not entirely.'

"'Doesn 't matter. You ran interference for them anyway. They probably would have paid you with a bullet. You were safe, though. We had you and them staked out all the time. I got this job six months ago and they never caught on. Some piece of acting on my part, too, don't you think?'

"'Academy Award stuff, lieutenant', says the other officer.

"'Fools,' says Big Jack.

"'Vile caitiffs,' says my dignified guy.

"'Stupid bastards,' says Sandwich. And that's the end of my career as private investigator."

Brazzi said nothing at first, sitting there on the couch lamenting the empty bottle.

"I don't believe a word of it," he murmured.

"You could believe it or not," said Madam Goulagrossa.

"That's what you get for being so trusting. I would've been suspicious right from the get-go. By the way, how much did you say they gave you for that job.?"

"I never mentioned it. But they gave me a thousand dollars for that walk in the park. And they told me it was only an advance, "retainer" the guy called it.

"So you wound up making money on your first case. It wasn't a total loss. And you didn't get paid in bullets like that cop said you would."

"I made nothing, my man. They paid me in counterfeit money. I had to give it all back to the cops. It was a total loss."

"Oh well," said Brazzi. "At least your beer is cold."

*   *   *

The Catered Caper

(fifth in a series)

"Hey. How about going out to breakfast?"

Brazzi was standing in the doorway, hands in pockets, smiling blandly.

"And good morning to you, too," Madam Goulagrossa said, wrapping her bathrobe tighter. "I didn't think you got up this early."

"How about it?" Brazzi asked, following her into the kitchen. "I got a good place picked out."

"I'm short right now. Can't even offer you anything."

"You got me all wrong," said Brazzi. "Breakfast's on me. Honest."

Madam Goulagrossa took a sip of her tea.

"What's come over you, my man?"

"What do you mean?" said Brazzi, sensing that he was peering beyond the sarcasm into the heart of a genuine solicitude. Such insight made him downright uncomfortable. Maybe he shouldn't have asked. Maybe he should have stayed in bed or had breakfast alone. But it was too late now to withdraw.

"It's a real good breakfast," he said. "Eggs and bacon and rolls and all the coffee and juice you can drink."

Madam Goulagrossa sat at the card table, slowly sipping her tea.

"Look," said Brazzi. "You do what you want. But I'm taking care of breakfast. No strings. Besides, it's not costing me anything."

"That sounds more like you," Madam Goulagrossa said.

"You want to eat or not?"

"I've already told you I can't afford it."

"And I'm telling you not to worry. Just trust me."

"I can give you a cup of tea." Madam Goulagrossa said, unconvinced. "I'll even throw in a fresh tea bag."

Brazzi gave up. "Have it your way. You're the loser, not me. I'm just trying to be nice."

"I'm sorry," Madam Goulagrossa said. "It's just that I know you too well."

"Forget about it. It's not like you're my girlfriend or anything like that."

"No", said Madam Goulagrossa.

"I mean, so what if people see us eating together? What does that mean?"

"We're just two people having breakfast."

"Right," Brazzi said. "Can't two people just lead their own lives? Hang on their own hooks without being boyfriend or girlfriend? Nothing too involved."

"Nothing personal, right," Madam G. said. "You're sure about this?"

Brazzi couldn't tell if she was referring to the breakfast or the relationship but he made the safe leap:

"Eggs and bacon and rolls. Plenty of juice and real hot coffee."

"O.K. I can be ready in a few minutes. Sit down while I get dressed."

Madam Goulagrossa walked into the adjoining space, separated from the kitchen by a curtain. Brazzi could see the curtain rippling and bulging as Madam G. readied herself. Meanwhile he sauntered over to the refrigerator and checked it out, selecting a half-empty quart container and scooping up with his fingers a darkened wad of Wong-Fu's specialty of the house. He quickly downed it, then put back the carton and sat at the table just in time to see Madam Goulagrossa emerge, brushing her hair.

"I'm ready," she said. "Where we going?"

"You'll know when we get there. We'll take your car."

Madam G. looked at him sharply.

Brazzi threw her a weak smile. "Mine's low on gas. By the way, bring an empty suitcase if you got one."

2.

"What's the problem? Why are we sitting in the parking lot?" Madam G. had turned off the engine and was adjusting the cushion under her rump.

"Research," said Brazzi.

"What research? You got me going on this breakfast thing. Now I'm hungry. And all you want to do is sit in front of the Holiday Inn Express."

"I'm studying," Brazzi said.

"Studying?"

"Not from books, if that's what you're thinking."

"As a matter of fact, that's the very last thing."

"Yeah, well you could mock all you want, but right now I'm studying the right time to get breakfast."

"I knew it was too good to be true. You buying breakfast."

"I never said 'buy'. I said it wouldn't cost me nothing."

Madam Goulagrossa dropped her head onto the steering wheel.

"That's where the research comes in. It's all brain power." Brazzi pointed to his temple. "There's a lot about me you don't know. I'm patient. I observe. I get ideas."

Madam G. rolled her eyes.

"I study things out and then move. About breakfast here, for instance. Did you know it's free?"

As he spoke he reached into his pocket and pulled out the rough, brown paper towel he had commandeered the night before from the dispenser in the hotel washroom. Laying it on his lap, he began smoothing out the wrinkles.

"Only for people who spend the night," said Madam G., already having guessed Brazzi's scheme.

"But who knows if you spend the night? They don't really check. Anyhow, that's only part of it. Work with me on this and I'll show you what a genius I really am. I got it all figured out. Look here"—pointing now to the crude pencil rendering of the lobby floor plan on the towel. "You'll notice that besides the lobby entrance there's a side door always locked at night but which can be opened from the inside. Over here, just beside the reception desk, is the elevator."

"You spelt 'elevator' wrong," said Madam G. "There's no 'i'."

"Here's the gig," continued Brazzi. "In about five, ten minutes the night clerks get off. The day people come in and that's when we pretend to arrive. We don't do nothing, see, just sit in the lobby like we're waiting for somebody. This here's where the lounge chairs are. Pretty soon some schnook'll come to the desk wanting to check in or check out. It don't matter which. That's the time we move. But not together, no. You go first. Leave your suitcase

with me. You go to the desk while the clerks are taking care of the
schnook and you say, 'Excuse me, please. Where's the restroom?'
They'll direct you to it, right off the dining room, out of sight of
the front desk. which is here. I checked it all out last night when
the idea first come. They'll be too busy to notice anyway. Then I
get up, pass the desk, suitcase in hand, like I'm ready to leave or
whatever. That's the tricky part. But they won't ask questions. I
meet you in the dining room. Here. Breakfast is all laid out, boofay
style. That's here. Fill our plates and bone appetite. If our timing's
right we can even fill the suitcase with rolls and pastries and some
fruit. A quick exit down the corridor through the night door here
and we're home free. All compliments of yours truly. Thank you
very much."

Brazzi looked at Madam G. and smiled.

"Compliments of Holiday Inn Express you mean," said Madam
Goulagrossa. "That's really disgusting."

Brazzi glared at her. "I don't know why I bother talking to you
and trying to be nice. You're always so quick to put the kybosh on
everything. You want breakfast or not?"

Madam G. was silent.

"If not . . . " said Brazzi.

"You got my hopes up. I'm good and hungry now."

Brazzi smiled. "O.K., then," he said. "Let's roll."

3.

"Didn't I tell you? Look at all this stuff. Here, have some more
bacon."

Madam G. was sitting at the table before her emptied plate.
"I'm full," she said. "For God's sake, haven't you had enough?"

"This is it," said Brazzi. "Let's start filling the suitcase you brung.
I'll get the rolls and pastries."

Brazzi had chosen a table out of sight of the lobby and reception
desk, a perfect place to eat in peace, unnoticed, unfazed, where
one could properly stuff a suitcase and effect a hasty retreat.

Madam G. was munching contentedly on an apple. It had been a
while since she had been to a decent restaurant, one with carpeting
and napkins and a garden view.

At the same time, she could appreciate Brazzi's caution, especially
now when she could comfortably overhear a conversation from
several tables away.

An older man in running shoes, shorts and tee shirt was leaning into the face of a young woman with short red hair, dressed in jeans and crisply tailored white blouse. He had almost touched her nose with his lips.

"I'm telling you, Babe. It all comes down to detoxifying your colon. There's so much poison in the system, so many free radicals destroying the temple of the body. Even yours. I take the stuff twice a day. Cleans me out. Keeps me trim and strong. You ought to try it." Here he reached into his pocket and brought out a plastic bag from which he poured three green pills onto his plate. "Stay away from red meat, too. The system works overtime trying to rid itself of all those toxins. And the fat clogs up your arteries."

Madam Goulagrossa watched as he picked up each pill, carefully placed it on his tongue and washed it down with a swig of water.

The young woman sat quietly, biting her lower lip. Then she opened her bag and began daubing her face with make-up.

"Well, shall we go?" the man said, rising and drawing out her chair. Madam G. noticed how he reached out to her, as if to take her arm, but the young woman had already gotten up abruptly and quickly strode ahead of him. He left her chair askew, scrambling to keep up with her.

"I've got some pastries nicely tucked away," said Brazzi. "I'm not much for yogurt, but if you like it I can shove some in the suitcase. There's still some room."

"You're embarrassing," Madam G. remarked.

"You're such a ball breaker," Brazzi said. "Nobody saw anything."

"I was just watching that couple."

"That older guy with the young chick? I noticed too, so what? I guess he got what he wanted."

"I guess you got what you wanted, right?"

Brazzi hefted the suitcase. "Hey," he said. "Live and let live. Let's get some of this stuff into your fridge before it spoils."

He began making his way to the side door when Madam G. called out to him:

"I'm not sneaking out like some cheap crook. We'll leave by the lobby like regular people. And we'll go out together. Both of us."

"Don't be a ball buster," said Brazzi. "You'll ruin everything."

"Right out into the lobby. Dignified. Like two people who've just eaten their breakfast. Remember?"

4.

As they passed the desk Brazzi put into effect his contingency plan. He now assumed a limp, enlarging its effect by turning down his mouth, pouting his lips into a scowl, just as he had practiced the routine for three days in his bedroom mirror. At every third limp he winced and subtly groaned, making sure his left foot turned inwards while he hobbled.

A well-dressed fellow in horn-rimmed glasses sat in one of the lobby chairs, reading a newspaper. Only a few yards from the front doors now and they'd be home free. Madam Goulagrossa was just behind him. He could sense her stony expression. He was beginning to sweat, resenting her defiant attitude, her attempt to face down the clerks. She would spoil everything with her bravado. It was so much safer, so much smarter, to go out the side door, through the garden. Never mind all that food in the suitcase. He envisioned the clerks calling over the security people, maybe even the house dick who would clamp his grubby hands on Brazzi's shoulder and glare sardonically into his eyes and force him to open the suitcase

In spite of these horrifying visions Brazzi suddenly found himself admiring Madam's courage; he caught himself thinking that of the women he had known this one had balls.

The fellow reading the newspaper looked up briefly and went back to his paper.

Two or three more steps and out; that was all. The preoccupied clerks seemed not to notice, but quickly looked to the front door when two figures stormed in.

"They're here," said the short fat man, glancing down into his note pad. "They checked in last night at exactly 10:42."

"You're sure about this?" the other man said. Brazzi guessed him to be in his early thirties, a yuppie already working on his second million.

"That's what you hired me for. They're here, all right."

The two men were about to approach the desk when the elevator doors opened and the couple at breakfast walked out. The young woman with red hair was carrying an overnight bag; the older man had changed into a suit. The man seemed startled. The woman, merely annoyed, stood her ground.

"Oh, for God's sake, Jimmie," she said. "Let's not make a scene."

"A scene!" the yuppie yelled. "A scene! I'm ready to script the whole goddam play. What's gotten into you? Who's this asshole?"

"Watch who you're calling 'asshole', asshole"

Jimmie lunged, but the man with the detoxified colon parried, and Jimmie found himself stumbling over Brazzi's suitcase. The young woman stomped out.

This would have been a perfect opportunity to scram, a rare stroke of luck by which for the first time in his life Brazzi had found himself the darling of circumstance. He knew it was time to get the hell out. But this raw spectacle of violence allowing him to be an observer out of harm's way had too strong a pull.

Jimmie threw a punch, then charged, lowering his head, butting and flailing wildly into the air. The older man threw out his leg in an aimless kick, sending his shoe somersaulting onto the reception desk. Quickly the short fat man with the note pad pushed his body between the rivals. "Take it outside, boys," he said.

"Watch who you're calling asshole," repeated Jimmy. "And stay the hell away from her. Laurie! Laurie, honey!", running out after her.

The older man offered a middle finger to the retreating Jimmie. "Take that, you asshole," he shouted.

"Your shoe, sir" offered the clerk.

The older man put on his shoe, asked for the restroom and withdrew.

Madam Goulagrossa had come back into the lobby. "What's keeping you?" she said. "Let's go."

"We missed a good fight", said Brazzi. "But at least we've got our stuff." He turned to where he had left the suitcase. It was gone, and so was the well-dressed fellow in the horn-rimmed glasses. On his empty lounge chair sprawled yesterday's newspaper.

*   *   *

Leroy

I hadn't seen Leroy since our college days. Then one rainy night, hailing a cab, I found myself bumping shoulders with a competitor. We looked at each other, aggrieved, but realized instantly that half a cab was better than none.

He got in first, and as we pulled away I recognized him at once. There was no mistaking that natural grace of movement, that elegant, dignified air of his suggesting keen intelligence and personifying class. I recalled the innocent ease with which in college he glided smoothly through one course after another with a cocksureness of a being totally comfortable with his superiority. What certified my recognition was his neatly-trimmed goatee, now gray, that he had nurtured as early as his freshman year. We had taken to calling him "Professor" in honor of the thing. When he took off his soaked hat and wiped his brow I noticed his class ring—I couldn't afford one then—and the Phi Beta Kappa pin on his lapel.

"You don't remember me, do you?" I said.

His steady gaze ignited no flame of recognition.

"We were in Economics class."

"If you say so," he said, a drop of rain dripping from his nose.

"You helped me with that paper on Keynes."

"I know I should remember, but it's been so long."

"I recollect you got the only A. You used to sit against the wall in the lounge surrounded by the rest of us normal students all struggling to pull a C.

"Oh, yes", he said.

I could tell from his quizzical expression and the indecision in his voice that he still didn't recognize me. He was a poor liar, but was trying to be agreeable. In any case his failure to place me did nothing to dent my self-esteem. I could easily afford a class ring now.

"I haven't been back to the school since graduation," he said.

"I know. Life intervenes."

"Incidentally," he said, looking at his watch. "Where can I drop you?"

This was Leroy, all right. If possession is nine-tenths of the law, Leroy was the supreme landlord. He was the Grand Poobah, wearing the finest clothes, driving the fastest cars, dating the prettiest girls—mine included.

"No, no," I said, offering my first challenge to his authority since college. "Where can I drop *you?*"

He smiled. "I feel rather awkward about not remembering you. Let me buy you dinner. Call it a peace offering. I know a wonderful place. I was heading there myself."

"Peace offering." That was the best Leroy could do. Apologies were never part of his life-style.

The restaurant was, of course, in the best part of town. I insisted on taking care of the cab fare and, to be honest, was ashamed for feeling privileged to pay, carefully giving the driver the sort of tip a man of Leroy's tastes would approve. This was just the sort of behavior Leroy provoked, a kind of perverse emulation that made one feel oddly embarrassed, even inferior. For years I'd never thought of Leroy as anything but a fleet, nostalgic moment in the long, busy hour of my own personal success. Yet here I was, paying his fare and licking his boots.

Inside we were greeted by the maitre d' who evidently knew Leroy and escorted us to a quiet table by a window that overlooked the city. Leroy asked for the wine list.

"The Pinot-Noir is exceptional here," he told me. He ordered a bottle and two glasses. I kept mum, embarrassed to admit I didn't drink.

In another instant he took possession of the conversation. No; "conversation" is the wrong word. Conversation implies dialogue. But Leroy gave me no opening, left me no chance of saying anything about myself, what I did for a living, what my politics were, whether I ever married the girl he stole from me that one night.

"I'm glad to see one of my disciples has done well for himself." This was his only concession to my presence. He had already scanned me, shaped his opinion of me and saw that it was good.

"I've no regrets," he said. "I'm happy to say I've done it all, and pretty much by myself. My first wife was helpful, of course, in a general sort of way. Provided the standard love and encouragement, that sort of thing. I haven't seen her in years. Did a bit of speculating, made some sound investments. Jennifer, my second wife, loved to travel and we've been all over the world, twice to China. Trust me, you'd better brush up on your Mandarin. The country's going east, young man, not west. I'm taking up Chinese. It's not all that difficult, largely a matter of inflection and tone. I'm presently dating a Chinese girl and this time it's really love. Don't think I'll marry again, but as I say, I've no regrets and wouldn't change a thing."

Savoring his wine, he ordered the most expensive entrée. Once again I was that normal kid with a C average sitting in the college lounge before the feet of the master. I, too, ordered, the most expensive entrée, asserting my independence by choosing mashed rather than baked potato.

He ate with gusto, only my presence across the table keeping in check his open display of delight. Still, he cut his meat into thick slabs, drank his wine in deep, luxurious gulps, took fulsome joy in his opulent dessert. During the meal he talked of his successes, his fiscal theories, his philosophy on the art of living. When he paused to stare out the window I imagined he was waiting for me to express my wonder, expecting me, maybe, to ask how he managed his life so well, as if importuning him, even, to divulge the open-sesame to his wealth.

Instead, he turned from the window and smiled.

"It was great seeing you," he said. He asked the waiter for the check. When it came he reached inside his jacket for his wallet and I noticed his Rolex. He gave the waiter his credit card.

"How about an aperitif?"

"Not for me, thank you," I said.

"I usually have a nice glass of Port".

"No," I said. "I'm done. Thanks again."

He swirled the last drops of wine in his glass. "You know, I can't help thinking that if there really is a parallel universe, as some scientists think, there must be some poor bastard out there with not a penny to his name and drinking supermarket beer."

The waiter came back with the credit card on a little silver tray.

"I'm sorry, sir, we cannot process this."

"My mistake," Leroy said. "Try this one."

He put another card on the tray.

"A minor hazard of the system is keeping one's cards in order," he said, reaching into his other pocket and taking out a thick billfold, secured with a rubber band.

"Keynes has always been my mentor", he continued. "Debt is, indeed, the American way. But as an economist he's never found a means for me, personally, to keep my ducks in a row."

The waiter returned with his little silver tray and a sour expression.

"Please forgive me," Leroy said, without a trace of contrition "Try this one," depositing another card. The waiter tucked the tray under his arm, took the card, looked at it, and carried it away in his clutched palm.

"Look here," Leroy said, showing me his deck of credit cards. "I collect them, sometimes by color. There are sixteen here. I use each one until I'm maxed out. I pay only the minimum each month on all the ones I use. Naturally, I could never come out from under, and I'll die owing, but who cares? They can't collect when I'm dead. In the meantime it's a great life. I'm using their money while contributing to the American economy. It's almost patriotic."

Once again the waiter showed up with his little silver tray. This time he brought along a second waiter. Leroy put a third card, an electric blue one, on the tray. The waiter paused, then turned, looked at his companion and walked moodily off with him.

"As I was saying. The problem is remembering which card is which." He had already slipped out a yellow one just in case. "It's getting a little complicated. I'm now starting a new collection, working my way west of the Mississippi."

Again he gazed at the city lights beyond the window. I wondered what was going through his mind. Going through mine was the vision of Leroy shuffling the rest of the deck until he hit the one not maxed out. How many waiters would come to the table? Maybe even the chef would appear, like in the old films, with a cleaver in his hand.

In the end I felt like an accomplice and didn't wait for Leroy to play all his cards. I excused myself, silently gave the waiter my own card—I had just paid it off—and turned to see Leroy still staring into the night. When I came back from the restroom he was gone. On the table, next to his napkin, he had left a note:

"I really did remember you, that dull, quiet kid with vague ambition.

Leah was a sweet girl, talked about you incessantly. I've envied you for years.

Give her my best."

*   *   *

The Fourth Wife

To look at Uncle Enzo you'd be hard pressed to believe that this short mild-mannered fellow who liked to make pasta sauce in the middle of the night dressed only in his underwear had already killed three wives. That's what some family members believed.

Kith and kin were sympathetic enough at the first wife's demise, fittingly surprised and shocked with the passing of the second. But they grew suspicious and gossipy after the third so obligingly croaked, leaving Enzo the sole beneficiary of her estate: a run-down house by the lake and a secret recipe for shredded sweetbreads. The police, for their part, were convinced that Aunts Carmella and Philomena had shuffled off in ways that allayed suspicion.

Carmella, Number 1, had slipped in the bathtub and smashed her skull—the coroner reported no water in her lungs and noted that the skull was correctly crushed according to the physical laws of gravity regarding immovable objects like the hot and cold faucets; observing also that the science of forensics offered indubitable proof that the skull and faucets were a perfect match.

She had been his wife for a mere 67 days.

As for Philomena, she was run over by a grocery truck driven by an illegal alien from Korea who spoke no English and whined hysterically at the thought that his cargo of tofu, bean curd and bok choi would spoil, bringing disgrace upon him, along with the wrath of Wong Fu, his esteemed employer.

She left Enzo a bereaved widower after only 105 days, thirteen hours.

Number 3, even by the reckoning of the police, was an unusual case. Sadie perished at the circus when Flying Buster Snood miscalculated his trajectory and came aground, cannon ball and all, squarely atop of her.

She and Enzo were on their honeymoon.

A select and influential segment of the family insisted privately that Uncle Enzo, if not a murderer, was certainly unlucky in his choice of partners. Such bad luck made him partly responsible;

he should have known better, they said, after the second try at matrimony.

Still another contingent, headed by Rose, a spinster godmother to a distant cousin, was convinced that Enzo's surname was the real cause of his misfortunes. "La Morte", after all, was an accursed name which could harvest only grief. The name itself bred disaster, a malevolent force waiting to pounce on some poor bimbo foolish enough to defy the gods of destiny and become another Mrs. La Morte. Rose had even written to him suggesting he change his name, to "Mortimer", perhaps, a classy wasp monicker that was as harmless as it was dull. But Uncle Enzo would have none of it. He insisted that "La Morte" was a perfectly good name; in his hometown back in the old country there were dozens of La Morte's—all happy, hardy and hale, some living well into their nineties. And besides, his three wives were not born "La Morte". They had no "La Morte" blood; whereas he was 100% La Morte and hadn't died yet, and didn't intend to die for many years.

You can imagine the chagrin, not to say despair, when Uncle Enzo announced he was getting married again. Number 4 was a thrifty, blue-haired widow who openly admitted to marrying Enzo for his money. She had first met Enzo at his place of business: impudently strolling into his junk yard in quest of a side view mirror for a '61 Ford Falcon. Ordinarily Enzo would have consigned the oddball customer into the incapable hands of cousin Cosmo, an addled young man whose hobby was collecting paper cups. In this instance he urged Cosmo to escort the little lady to the "Ford Falcon Aisle"—part of Uncle Enzo's charm was his sense of humor.

His charm, now, had little effect.

"Cut the crap," she said. "Do you have it or not?"

Enzo was taken aback by her brusque attitude, fascinated by her verve, her confidence, her slick vulgarity which he found so homey.

"This is a junk yard, ain't it?"

"I call it a salvage emporium," Uncle Enzo said.

"Junk. Salvage. What's the diff?"

"Let me show you, Sweetie."

Enzo went over to a wooden crate, marked "California Oranges", against the far wall. From under a pile of rusted gear he pulled out a car door handle.

"Take this, for instance," he said. "In a junkyard this is ten bucks. In a salvage emporium it's a hundred. I deal in salvage, not junk."

"Hey, hey, hey!" she smiled. "You're my kind of guy."

This was the spark that set him afire.

"If you mean dedicated, you bet," said Enzo, waxing poetic. "I even keep my salvage in a salvaged box. Everything in my emporium is of salvage, by salvage, for salvage. I eat, sleep, think salvage. Salvage keeps the world clean."

"Sort of like buzzards," she observed.

"I feel I perform a real service to humanity. Suppose everybody just threw everything away? 'Drop your load at the end of the road'. That sort of thing."

"You have a way with words," she said. "I like that."

"Look at it this way. I'm really in public service. The environment people love me. Average people who want to save money love me. I've furnished my whole house from salvage. I've had three wives and they all loved me."

"I can see that you're a lovable guy. You do public service while making lots of money. You can't beat that. My name's Mona. What's yours?"

"La Morte," said Uncle Enzo, narrowing his eyes. "My name's La Morte. Does that scare you?"

"Why should it?"

"It means 'death'."

"Bull!" she said.

Uncle Enzo was no fool. He realized that this fabulous woman was playing with him, disarming the bomb of opinion, dismissing as nonsense the notion of his fatal name.

He respected her tremendously for her wisdom.

"My first name's 'Enzo'."

"'Enzo La Morte'. It doesn't scare me one bit. It's a real good name."

"I think so," said Uncle Enzo. "It's better than 'Capostrunzo'."

"A man in the salvage trade shouldn't have to worry about what name he carries. It would certainly suit me, I can tell you. Mind you, I'm not proposing or nothing like that. You certainly look harmless enough to me. Besides, I'm naturally immune to curses. So-called evil names, that's a bunch of crap." She laughed. "So don't worry about it."

And that, as they say, was the beginning of a beautiful friendship. Enzo did his best to acquire Mona's mirror, even paying what he regarded as an obscene sum for it from a competitor whom he despised. This rival entrepreneur operated not out of a second-hand trailer, as did Uncle Enzo, but from a temperature-controlled steel building in which his secretary, seated at a computer, was able to locate in seconds even something like a side view mirror for a 1961 Ford Falcon.

"You ought to get one of those for the business," Mona observed one day.

"Why should I?" Enzo said. "Too complicated."

Here he took Mona's hand.

"What I really need is an assistant, a helper. Someone with brains as well as beauty."

Now he looked into her eyes.

"Someone to walk beside me in a life-long search for the ideal salvage."

"You're so romantic," Mona cooed. "Such a way with words. But I don't love you, you know that, right?"

"So what? I'm asking you to help me run the business."

"There'd have to be some changes," she warned.

"Name them." It was now Uncle Enzo's turn to coo.

"Only two," she said. "If you can get a hundred bucks for something today you could easily get a hundred-twenty tomorrow. Things are tough all over these days. Raise your prices twenty percent."

"Yes, dear," said Uncle Enzo.

"Also," she said. "I want full partnership. None of that 'dutiful wife' or 'the little missus' crap."

"Anything you say, dear."

Aside from those demands, Mona was an obliging, generally tolerant spouse. Enzo couldn't have been happier, euphorically remarking to her on the morning after their wedding that his life-long search had truly come to an end, for she, indeed, was the ideal Salvage. Mona smiled indulgently and patted her new husband on the head while she tallied the day's receipts. Never did she complain when Enzo rose at 3A.M. to make his "gravy", as he called it. Once she even got up with him to chop the onions, mushrooms and garlic. As for the relatives, their shock soon wore off, watching with jealousy and awe as Enzo's business became the envy of every scrap dealer in the land.

Meanwhile, Godmother Rose had been ticking off the days after their marriage, estimating that it would be only a matter of weeks now before Number 4 would fall victim to the La Morte curse.

Things were going so well that one day, four years and eight months into their marriage, Enzo spoke to Mona about closing the emporium for a week and taking at last that long deferred honeymoon.

"Where do you want to go?" said Mona.

Enzo was emboldened by her reticence.

"How about Muncie?" he said.

"Where Muncie?"

"Muncie, Indiana," said Enzo. "The Salvage Dealers of America are having their convention there. We could check out the new power equipment and magnets. There's a real classy compactor I want to see."

"You go," said Mona. "I'll stay at the yard. I don't like the way that moron Cosmo is screwing things up."

"He's family, Mona."

"Listen, Enzo. Anybody ever warn you about never doing business with family? I don't care if he's the Pope. I don't want that idiot ruining my business."

"Yes, dear," said Enzo.

In the end they compromised. They would close the emporium for a few days and spend a weekend at the lake, staying in the run-down house left to Enzo by his third wife. While Mona sunned herself, Enzo thumbed through back issues of Scrap Metal Quarterly and drank neat whiskey. In the evenings he took Mona to the local Bocce festival.

On the last day of their honeymoon trip—a Sunday—the subject of Enzo's family name came up. All this time Godmother Rose had been burning with curiosity. She was aggrieved at having lost the family pool in which all the relatives paid a ten spot to guess the time-span between the marriage and anticipated demise of number 4. Only Cosmo was left, but by mere technicality. He had predicted the marriage would last 113 years, five months. In the meantime, Mona had already outlasted all previous wives combined and Rose suspected that something was rotten in the state of Sicily.

On this Sunday morning Mona was getting the last of the sun when she noticed a green 1979 Volvo pulling up to the house. She watched as a frail-looking bespectacled woman came out from behind the wheel and walked carefully across the outcropping rocks. As she walked she waved her arm, half in greeting, half as in alarm.

"My God, if it isn't Mona La Morte. How are you?"

"Do I know you?" said Mona.

"I'm Godmother Rose. I'm sorry, by the way, that I never came to your wedding."

"I don't remember inviting you."

"That's all right. I know you two had a million things to do. I never sent a present, anyway. What a small world, running into you this way."

"Cut the crap, Rose. What brings you here? We're on our way back to the yard."

"Cosmo told me you were on vacation, and I really didn't want to bother you."

"So, bother," said Mona, fetching up a modicum of civility. "As long as you're here, come in." She had already risen and was shaking out the blanket. Now she made for the house, Godmother Rose following.

Sitting at the table watching Mona pack—Enzo had taken the truck for gas—Godmother Rose decided to take Mona's advice to cut the crap and come to the point.

"Something's been bothering me," she began.

Mona continued packing.

"I won't pretend that we're not surprised."

"Who is not surprised and about what?"

"You must've heard the talk. You know about Enzo's other wives."

"What about them?"

"How they, . . . how do I put it?"

"Kicked off? What of it?"

"Didn't Enzo tell you what his last name means?"

"So what's the big deal?"

"'La Morte'. The name's a curse. Anyone connected with him takes his name and dies suddenly. Poor Philomena! Poor Carmella! Poor What's-her-name. The family has urged him to get rid of 'La Morte', but he won't listen. Don't you realize the danger?"

"Bull!" said Mona.

Just then a truck pulled up. The women heard the door slam and Enzo call.

"Whose car is that?"

He was rushing into the room. His shoulders drooped when he saw Rose.

"Don't tell me," he said

"Yes, you poor man, it's Godmother Rose."

She kissed him, weeping openly.

"She thinks I'm going to die," said Mona.

Godmother Rose began to sob.

"It's not happening," said Mona. "Your theory's all wet, Rose. I've told Enzo a million times that I'm immune from such crap."

Rose looked up. "So you're not going to die?"

"Mona is safe," said Enzo. "Her maiden name cancels out the curse."

"What is her maiden name?" said Godmother Rose.

Enzo held Mona's hand. "It's 'Della Vita." he said. "'Mona Della Vita'".

"That's it in a nutshell," said Mona. "I'm going to outlive all of you bastards. As I keep telling Enzo, life is always stronger than death. Always. Isn't that right, Enzo?"

"Yes, dear."

*   *   *

Clarissa

Sitting here waiting for the guard to check in the last of the visitors, I am watching Clarissa nurse the infant. It seems nothing but mouth, sucking voraciously at the breast, mindless of the pain it inflicts. Though Clarissa says he is my son and I want to believe her, the puling little thing is not very cute, not even human, all wrinkled and red, like a log of spoiled cold cut. Clarissa looks fine, as always, Madonna-like, one of those rare "alabaster" maidens so beloved of the poets. Clarissa doesn't like poetry, claims not to understand it. Yet it was my own poetry that first brought us together, and even now as she nurses I'm already thinking of my next poem. I haven't come up with a title yet, but my original tone of sardonic humor has already shifted to one of cold, subdued malice. The trick is going to be to evoke that malice in the sprung rhythm of Hopkins, my idol.

Clarissa glances up from the infant to look at me. She smiles weakly and says nothing. I have long ceased to discuss my poetry with her. There's very little, in fact, which I care to talk to her about. Early on she had wanted to know everything about my work, my real, creative work, not those contracts—"disposal errands" I called them—that I carried out for my daily bread. From the very first she was convinced of my genius, regarding me as a mysterious purveyor of wisdom, a kind of magi bearing gifts of sound.

Now she could not care less about my poetry and even less, it would seem, about me. Her infrequent visitations are brief and begrudging and I get a sense that today is the last time I'm going to see her and that vapid smile of hers and that rotten little sucking squinch at her breast. Considering all that's happened, I guess that's all right by me.

"How old is he?" I ask.

"Isn't he cute?" she says.

"What are you telling me? I've been in here two years."

"He's yours, I swear it," she says.

I want to believe her, just as she once believed in my genius. But it's getting difficult to concentrate in here, so many distractions, so many stupid routines in the cause of my so-called rehabilitation, which will never happen because I'll be 125 when I get out. It's getting hard even to feel anything for Clarissa. I wonder what it was about her then that so attracted me. It's true, I've always had a weakness for big, heavy women. Clarissa's huge softness, her unwrinkled massiveness used to drive me wild with excitement as she came over to my booth in Gimpy's Finesse Diner, and took down my breakfast order, her stubby little fingers smothering the pen as it made its way across the pad: "too eggs, crisp bakin. Side toste."

Gimpy's had been an afterthought, a quick coffee-stop on the way to my last stake-out on one of my contracts. But from that day she first waited on me the diner became an habitual rendezvous and every morning for weeks I'd sit in the same booth waiting for Clarissa to ring my chimes. So far as I was concerned, the contract could wait. He wasn't going anywhere in that wheelchair; and that phony name the Feds had given him wouldn't keep him safe. I had done my homework, for weeks had scouted his activities, could name his bodyguards and the time of day he went to the bathroom—unassisted it turns out—or publicly rolled into the garden to smell his roses. He wouldn't be smelling them for very long now; he simply awaited my own convenience.

Meanwhile, Clarissa was worth the delay, worth every inconvenience. At first she didn't believe I wrote poetry. I didn't look the type, she said. To her mind poets were weird, quiet guys who smoked pipes and spoke in English accents and anyway she didn't like poetry, though she kind of liked me, she said, even if I was a poet. I remember that I had been working on a poem called "Wheelchair Blues"—the subject of my contract—and was stuck for a final line. She had just finished her shift and we were sitting in a booth in a closed section of Gimpy's. Her beautiful body had consumed the entire banquette and I was sitting opposite, mooning over her like some schoolboy.

"You wrote another poem?' she said, as if writing one poem were miracle enough, but two, a very act from Genesis.

"Never mind me," I lied. "You're exquisite."

Clarissa smiled. Of course she knew she was beautiful; I was sure she had heard her beauty praised by all the other men blessed enough to know her.

"You must be very smart," she said. "What kind of poems do you write? Do they rhyme?

"Sometimes," I said. "But close rhyme is fit mostly for social verse—couplets and epigrams and poet laureate stuff. Real poetic discourse demands sincerity. For the deepest personal expression, free verse is best, where the words form an organic rhythm and logic all their own."

Admittedly I was showing off, but I sensed that this enormous beautiful babe was the only person who really appreciated my poetry and I was prepared to make a fool of myself for this paragon of all women. When she put one pudgy mitt on her cheek, the flesh seductively folding over one eye, it was all I could bear. I had to have her.

"You must be awful smart," she said again.

"Smart enough, my love, to adore you above all creatures who walk this sterile promontory called Earth."

Clarissa giggled, her eyes now almost closed by the fleshy cheeks that enveloped them.

"I wish I was smart. When I was a little girl I could do jigsaw puzzles faster than anybody. Nobody could beat me. Not even my uncle who lived with Mommy and me after Daddy left to buy some Juicyfruit gum and never came back. Every week Uncle Mack used to bring me a jigsaw puzzle and by the end of the day I'd have it finished."

"You are a luscious juicy fruit, my dear. A perfect poem."

"I'm hungry," she said.

"'If music be the food of love, play on'", I said.

Suddenly Clarissa put her hands on the table and began hoisting herself out of the booth, advancing layer by layer along the seat, like a flow of lava. I myself was getting hot watching as she came to her feet, pulling down her skirt over jurassic thighs. I grew ecstatic when she reached across the counter to the tiered rows of candy and selected a Pay Day chocolate bar. Her choice was fraught with almost oracular significance, for I was confident that my pay day with Clarissa drew near.

"So," I said. "Would you like to hear my new poem?"

"Right here?" she said. "Right here in Gimpy's?"

"Well," I said. "We could go to my place."

Clarissa giggled. "Oh, no, silly! Well, go ahead and read it, then."

While she began unwrapping the Pay Day I began unwrapping my verse. First I cleared my throat. Then I put on my glasses. Then I dressed myself in my best voice:

Wheelchair Blues
A lonely, sated, fated man is he
Who rolls about his garden publicly.
A man whose money cannot pay his debt,
Who cannot cleanse his deeds, his past forget.
Yet, I bet
He will not stay for long among his blooms—
Though they impart their smell through all his
rooms,
Unknowing of their fate, they bow and die.
And so shall he . . .

Here I ceased, for as I said, I was stuck for a clinching line. Clarissa didn't appear to be aware of any technical problem.

"Gee, that's nice," she said. "It rhymes. I thought you said it didn't rhyme."

"This one does," I said. "It's a kind of ode, commemorating a formal, social occasion. Nothing personal. Just business."

It was at this moment that I became convinced of my own genius and of Clarissa's powerful influence on my creative life. For as I spoke, watching her devour the last of the Pay Day, the final line came to me in a flash:

"And so shall he, but know the reason why!"

That night, Clarissa and I made love for the first time, and for days afterward my pen had difficulty keeping up with the demands of my inspiration. Poem after poem flowed from my teeming brain, sonnets, lyrics of all kinds, epigrams, dramatic monologues, odes. Meanwhile Clarissa continued working at Gimpy's. I was often sick with jealousy when I wasn't with her. Any man could stray in for a cup of coffee and become bewitched, just as I had become; bewitched, bedazzled by her monumental flesh.

But sooner or later the contract on Mr. Wheelchair—the phony—had to be concluded. I was forced to think about concluding it when Clarissa one day didn't come to work. I had not seen her for almost a week, having flown to Chicago for an important meeting with "The Man". My first day back I went to Gimpy's, sitting in the same booth where we had first met. But she never showed up. Gimpy, the Greek manager, said he hadn't seen or heard from her, that she had not even come in for her pay. Naturally, I was worried. A beautiful thing like Clarissa was a lamb in the slaughterhouse of this world. Beyond worry, almost desperate, I turned, not to poetry, but to the business of my contract, anything to get my mind off the intimations of the horrible things that could befall my lovely beauty.

The contract for disposal was an informer, a snitch. Like most snitches he was only interested in old number one, taking such pains in saving his skin that he changed his name, address, everything that could be traced. But none of that worked out. The Feds did the best they could to make him invisible but if you exist anywhere in the world as flesh and blood, sooner or later you're going to be found. As the poets say, there is no such thing as perfection below the moon. The Feds aren't poets. They take a practical, earthly view of things, like protecting this snitch. But "The Man" hired me precisely because I'm not practical. I'm a genius, a poet.

Some disposal men like to get fancy, practical: rifles and scopes and deadly accuracy within a thousand yards. That's playing it safe, and as a professional I have no problem with that method. But the poet in me wants to get up close, to dot the "I's" and cross the "T's", so to speak, with a pistol. It's a lot riskier, but all poetry is a risk, as every poet knows. I look at my job as a kind of poetic process—taking a risk but creating a masterpiece. The rest is just hack work.

Besides, at a thousand yards the mark doesn't know he's the mark. He doesn't have time to be afraid or to realize the quality of the vengeance being taken. But up close, as he's looking down at the barrel of a good old Smith and Wesson from, say, twenty-five or thirty feet, he has time—a few seconds, but enough—to realize what's happening, to know the how and the when, and more importantly, the why.

"I want you should make sure Al knows why he's being whacked," The Man had told me. "I want you should make sure he knows who sent you."

And so, as I've said, heartsick over Clarissa's absence, I threw myself into my work. The job wasn't going to be easy, but writing an ode is a lot harder, and I was bolstered by the conviction that the job itself would provide material for a future poem, perhaps even my next one on how Al got whacked, "staining the floor with filthy gore", or something like that. I'd have to work on it.

Besides, as I've said, I had done my homework. Al was living in a sprawling ranch-style house just outside Vegas. That section of the country was booming. Skeletons of houses-to-be and embryos of cloned communities grew amid the red dust and clay of the desert. Al's house was at the edge of a development called "Regal Promenade." I recall laughing to myself as I pictured this king-turned-snitch taking a wheeled promenade about his grounds, guarded by two Feds, muscular young men who looked like graduate students. Apparently Al wasn't important enough to the government to merit more experienced watchdogs.

I myself was a watchdog of a more aggressive breed, assessing the opportunities and the occasions and the environment. It was easy enough to acquire a hardhat and wander about the adjacent building sites, a clipboard under my arm, as if I were a contractor—which, come to think of it, I was, in a way. Another day I posed as a potential buyer and surveyed a model house laid out almost exactly like the one Al was occupying. With a stiff smile and a clipboard of her own, the agent showed me room by room, closet by closet. By the end of the tour I was sure I knew the house better than Al did.

"It's a great opportunity," the agent said. "This is going to be a big hit."

"Yes, indeed," I said. "I'm sure it will be."

I would whack Al at night. For four days, I had parked a binocular's distance from the house, noting every move of the graduate students and the man they were supposed to protect. Knowing how the Feds operated, how they thought in practical, earthly terms, knowing how they, too, would be keeping a binocular view of the grounds, I rented a different car every time and parked in a different spot, but always where I could get a full prospect.

Now I was ready. Yet in the midst of my preparations, while dressing in what I call my "blacks"—sleek and skin-tight— I suddenly thought of Clarissa. Why had she quit Gimpy's? She had never told me where she lived. She would not let me take her home after our night of love-making in Gimpy's Motel Elite, across the road from Gimpy's Finesse Diner.

In any case, thinking of her would blunt my purpose. And so forcing her out of my mind, even as I passed Gimpy's on the way to Regal Promenade, I outlined once again how I would proceed.

At two in the morning I parked the car a block from Al's house. The development where I had posed as buyer was next door, glaring with spot lights, so I made my way behind it where the backyard was still covered by brush and littered with piles of construction debris. Twenty yards from the house I began to crawl, keeping toward the back, picturing in my head the layout: master bedroom at the end, separated from the living quarters by a bath and a short hall corridor. I knew how the Feds worked. Al wouldn't be in the master bedroom. No one would be. He'd be installed in the smaller room in the middle of the house, behind the living room. It would have just one small window at an awkward angle to the bed, making it difficult to get a clear shot. I would have only a few seconds to awaken Al by shouting, announcing his official whacking and the reason for it, as per contract. But before that I would have to take care of the graduate students, though with luck only one would be awake. I would wait in the brush until I saw a light go on in the bathroom. The odds were it would be one of the graduate students, because I knew Al was a sound sleeper. A man without a conscience usually is.

I was now a mere ten yards from the house. As I crawled I noticed a light in what would be the kitchen. It may have just come on, or I might not have seen it from my position in the back. In any case I would have to check it out. Slowly, quietly, I made my way, coming up to the back wall, inching along, my body pressed against the siding. I heard a laugh and then a squeal which sounded oddly familiar. Arriving at the window, I pulled out my gun and squatted below the sill. I heard another laugh and then another squeal, a half shout, as if in celebration. Carefully, cautiously, I started to rise from my crouch. My eyes caught first the rich wood finish of the wall cabinets and then the glint of the stainless steel refrigerator, then a wheelchair, folded and abandoned in the corner. Another laugh, another squeal and my eyes saw what my brain reeled against. At the kitchen table, in his underwear, sat Al. He was drinking a beer and smiling. On the table, set at his elbows, lay a jigsaw puzzle. Only one piece was left to complete it and I saw with shock the pudgy fingers of my Clarissa taking up that piece and fitting it into place. She laughed. He laughed. They slammed palms together. He drank the rest of his beer. She ate the rest of her mammoth sandwich. I stood there, almost ready to cry. Then I heard a shout from the graduate student and felt a blow to my head . . .

"Sorry, Mrs.", the guard is saying to Clarissa. "You can't do that here. You know better than that."

I watch as Clarissa pulls the breast abruptly from the runty cold cut and closes her blouse.

"This is my last visit," she says to me.

"I kind of figured that."

"Al gets mad."

"I don't blame him. You never really told me about Al."

"He come into Gimpy's one morning. Just like that. It was when you was away on business or writing poems or something."

"If my business had worked out," I say, "Al wouldn't be around."

"Well," she says. "He is around and he got mad when I said I was going to visit you. But I told him this was the last, just for old time's sake. You were my first boyfriend".

"I can't believe that," I say. "And now it's Al."

Clarissa giggles in that sexy way of hers.

"I guess you know the baby's not yours. I lied before."

"I kind of figured that, too"

Clarissa sits there, awkward, shifting about, avoiding having to look at me, unable to think of anything else to say. In the old days she would've reached for a candy bar.

"What does Al have that I don't?" I ask.

"He's a riot," she says. "A real sense of humor. He rides around in a wheelchair when he's not home. But you know what? He doesn't really need it. He only does it for show, for laughs. You were always so serious."

"Serious about you, certainly. Serious about my work, yes."

"And you know what else? Al loves to do jigsaw puzzles. He's almost better than me. One night we finished one of them three dimensional jobs. It was the Great Wall of China and we needed the whole living room."

Clarissa wraps the baby tighter and hoists herself up, the chair wedged to her thighs as she rises.

"Well," she says. "I gotta go now. Have a good life."

"Very funny," I say. "Very funny. When I get back to my cell I'll write you a poem. Give me your address and I'll send it to you."

"Don't bother," she says. "You're a nice guy, but your poems suck."

*   *   *

Valentino and the Rooster

Roy had heard the car before he saw it. He was stooped over, coming out of the old man's chicken coop, Cafone squalling into his face, its claws flailing against his forehead and lashing at his eyes. How he hated that goddamned rooster. Someday he would wrench its neck and put an end to its vengeful temper. Meanwhile, the yellow Hispano-Suiza caromed into the front yard, churning up dirt and gravel into a rattling little dance among the spokes of its wheels.

Valentino himself emerged from the driver's seat. He was wearing goggles and a tan cap turned backwards. Pulling off his lemon-colored kid gloves, he began slapping the dust off his brown jodhpurs, all the while unswaddling himself of his yellow silk scarf.

"Look who's here", Roy said to himself, closing the coop. "First the rooster and now the peacock."

"Hello there, my friend," Valentino smiled as he approached.

"You'll excuse me if I don't shake your hand. Mine's full of chicken shit."

Valentino narrowed his eyes into a concentrated glare, a near-sightedness that made him look peevish.

"Isn't this the Ciaravino place?"

"The old man's in the cellar."

"And you are . . . ?" Valentino asked, snapping back his shoulders as if ready to return a salute.

Roy turned toward the house, gesturing for Valentino to follow. As the two made their way across the yard Roy noticed Valentino glancing back at the car where Cafone had already come to roost on the steering wheel, preening his spurs, casting reptilian, proprietary eyes at the newcomer. The least that goddamned bird could do to make amends would be to swoop onto this peacock's hide and scramble his feathers, mess up the greased, neatly-parted hair, the smooth, even skin, the clear, dark wop eyes. Roy had read about fellows like this with their jazzy cars and hermaphroditic

clothes and their imperious manners, who carried canes and
wore lemon-colored gloves and presented calling cards with crests
and names prefaced by "count" or "marquis". How triumphant it
would be for Cafone—whose avian life was one long feud against
intruders, human or otherwise, whose viciousness was ignored,
even excused, in the interest of a daily dozen eggs—finally to do
something nice. Cafone was especially hateful for his inconstancy.
On any given day Roy could go into the coop, snatching a clutch
of eggs while Cafone would quietly perch on a beam above the
door, soberly looking about, as if assessing the weather. On these
occasions Roy would hum a tune, some shapeless diatonic air, a
kind of personal amulet against the bird's attacks. Yet on another
day Roy could be on the way to the mulch pile, merely passing
the coop, paying no attention to chickens or eggs—and so not
humming—and Cafone would squawk and flutter and dive, his
spurs jutting out at Roy's eyes or ears or the tip of his nose. Even the
old man who loved Cafone, once threw an axe at him, exasperated
at the bird's unpredictable malevolence.

Perhaps his own malevolence against this Valentino fellow
was uncalled for, Roy thought, but the sound of the wop's car
had distracted him, making him ignore his talismanic tune and
doubtless riling Cafone. On the other hand, this peacock's looks
and his unexpected appearance on Immaculata's birthday was
cause enough for un-ease.

Valentino's next question curdled un-ease into thick suspicion.

"Is Immaculata here?"

"The old man's in the cellar," Roy repeated and led the man
with the lemon-colored gloves into the back door and below, down
the narrow, concrete steps. A single bulb burned dimly; the reek of
fermenting wine mixed with the sharp, acrid odor of coal heaped
in a bin beneath the only window that looked out onto a sickly
peach tree. It was under this coal pile that the old man hid the
gallons of wine he had made to sell to the locals and which revenue
agents could never find.

He was sitting on an overturned tub, sipping wine from a
cracked, handleless cup, when he saw the two men descend. He
squinted in the gloom.

"Is that you, Roy?"

"I've finished with the chickens, signore." Roy knew that the
old man liked to be called "signore" even though he was an
illiterate peasant when he came to America and after ten years was
still illiterate and deeply profane, as only a peasant could be. But

Signor Ciaravino had managed to save his money, penny by penny, and was able to do in America what he was unable to do in Italy: buy the land on which he built, stone for stone, his house and all the outbuildings, especially the chicken coop over which Cafone now presided. Land, for the old man, made him a padrone and earned him the title of "signore". As for educated men, they could go to hell.

He finished the wine, rose from the tub and hitched up his pants. His eyes brightened.

"Rudolfo!" he cried. "Rudolfo Guglielmi."

He put out his hand, in the American way. Roy noticed that the old man was bigger than Valentino and that for the first time Valentino seemed less self-assured, more fragile.

The signore led the way upstairs and the three of them found themselves outside where the old man bid Valentino sit under the peach tree. Roy took a seat in the sun.

"I heard you left Castellaneta and came to America," the old man began. "But that was two, three years ago. What took you so long to visit your old friends?"

Valentino sat back, crossing his legs, smiling. It didn't take him long, Roy noted, to regain his sense of superiority. For several minutes he talked of the old country and his long pursuit there of an occupation befitting his status as a gentleman. And when the peacock reached into his coat pocket and pulled out a silver cigarette case, Roy observed that he was sporting a wristwatch, another unmistakable sign of this parvenu's decadence. Where was Cafone when you needed him?

Valentino offered them a cigarette but the old man had already lit his black stogie and Roy ignored the offer. The man with the lemon-colored gloves took a luxuriating puff, then blew smoke toward Roy. Their eyes met, and for a moment Roy sensed a smirk.

"I've been quite busy. I know it's a poor excuse, but my delay in coming was the result of a big lie. The streets in America are not paved with gold, after all. Life is a lot harder here than I thought it would be."

The old man chuckled.

"Yes, that's true, Rudolfo, but you were never much interested in hard work even on the other side."

Valentino shrugged.

"Well, I'm certainly working hard now, much harder than in Castellaneta."

"There was nothing in Castellaneta. That's why we left. That's why you left. What are you doing now? You look as if you've found your street of gold. That's a pretty fancy car I see. What do you think of it, Roy?"

"Looks like a pimp's machine," Roy said.

"You must be doing well, Rudolfo. Not like back home when you drifted along like the dust, some lazy sirocco. Tell me. What do you do?"

"I really came to see Immaculata," Valentino said.

Roy sensed Valentino's evasion. He resented the way the peacock had shut him out and the way the fellow glared at him when mentioning her, Roy's own girl. Why else, after all, would Roy himself put up with spending two or three hours a day helping the old man keep the place going, wasting more profitable opportunities while getting his hands full of chicken shit and parrying with that goddam rooster, if he wasn't to be able to see Immaculata every day and secretly moon over her? To Roy, Immaculta was worth catering to the old man's whims, worth the silly labor of cleaning out chicken coops or shoveling coal onto the still and the wine jugs when the government agents drove up loud and obvious, as if announcing themselves. Yes, Immaculata was worth all the kowtowing. It wasn't just the dark fierceness of her eyes or the peasant solidity of her body, or even the faint suggestion, a mere smudge, of a mustache at the corners of her mouth, that so battered Roy's heart. He was smitten most of all by her sense of command, of being in charge, her self-confidence that made his own advances seemingly ridiculous, that reduced even the ruthless sallies of Cafone to nothing more than the dumb clucking of a diffident chicken. Roy recalled the first time he had seen her, walking up the gravel road, basket in hand, a flat carpenter's pencil in her ear, a sheet of yellow paper fluttering languidly in her hip pocket. He remembered how his heart pulsed and his mouth went dry when she asked him if he wanted some nice fresh eggs or some cheese. He would have bought the whole goddam basket if he had had any money instead of just two bits and a part-time job as dishwasher in a Chink's restaurant. And now here was this greaseball, this pimp and his machine . . .

If the old man, though illiterate, had also read the evasion; if he understood the glint of rivalry between the two, he gave no sign.

"My daughter should be back by now. Roy, did you see her?"

Roy was spared an evasion of his own when a distant shout floated across the road, drifted over the front yard and came to rest among the three men as they sat beneath the stunted peaches.

A dark-haired woman with eyes the color of slate came running through the house and stood before them. She quickly brought one hand up to her hair. In her other she held a paper with names and numbers on it. From where he sat in the sun Roy could see that she was breathing hard and his own heart beat faster.

"Whose car is that out front?" Immaculata said, and before any of the men could speak, her eyes widened, her face reddened and her own heart beat faster, though Roy understood that her quickened pulse was not on his account.

"You!" she said. "My God."

Valentino smiled awkwardly and for a few moments seemed too stunned to stand.

Seeing his chance Roy quickly got up, brushing his chicken-shit hands onto the legs of his pants. Then Valentino rose, his face more darkly cast amid the shadows of the leaves. The old man kept his seat.

"Rudolfo's finally paying his respects," he said. "Did you get the orders?"

Immaculata took up the paper and began to read off the names of tailors, carpenters, tradesmen, and Roy vaguely wondered how much money the old man really made selling the gut-swill wine, the Cafone-engendered eggs and the nauseating goat cheese churned by Immaculata's lovely muscular arms. It occurred to him as a wild species of injustice that his girl, his own One, should toil so ingloriously while this peacock sat preening under the shade of a tree, combing his self-admiration.

"Rudolfo's been telling me how hard he's been working," the old man said.

"Yeah," Roy said. "That big car must be real tough to steer."

Immaculata shot a glance at Roy, then looked away, avoiding Valentino's eyes.

"I'll take you for a ride if you like," Valentino said. "After all, it's your birthday."

"Happy birthday, Immaculata!" Roy said, wishing not to be trumped.

The girl seemed not to hear him. For a moment no one spoke and Roy felt the heavy burden of the silence.

The old man pulled out a handkerchief and blew his nose.

"Roy," he said. "Before you leave, do me a favor and check the rabbit hutch. Cacciacavallo's mutt is loose again."

"I don't have to go yet," Roy said. "It's Immaculata's birthday."

"I'll check the hutch," Immaculata said. "Rudolfo can come with me."

Valentino looked at Roy, the corners of his mouth subverting a smile.

"Afterwards I'll take you for a ride," he said, bowing to Immaculata.

"I'll come along," Roy said. "Cacciacavallo's dog is vicious. I can deal with him."

"There are all kinds of vicious dogs," Valentino said, looking at Roy. "They don't frighten me. I can protect her. Just like in the old days back home."

Roy hated the way Valentino smiled at his girl, the way he neatly insinuated his arm around her and looked into her eyes. Roy had been doing odd jobs at the old man's place all summer and had never once touched her, and here was this dago from the other side stealing her from right under his nose. Roy looked at his hands and then smelled them.

He had been asked to leave, but knew that he could not. As the old man went into the house and Roy watched his girl slip off with the peacock, he determined to stay, to watch, to listen, to do something. If they were going to the rabbit hutch and then perhaps back to the chairs under the peach tree, the best place to hide and to get the dope on this pimp and his intentions would be the chicken coop. From there he could lie unseen on the straw and look over the whole back yard, overhearing everything.

As he lay on the rough-hewn boards of the chicken coop Roy was almost overwhelmed by the smell. Worse than chicken-shit, he thought, was the ammoniac stench of rot and decay. Besides, the straw scratched his arms and legs, and he recalled now why the idea of a romp in the hay had always seemed so dismally unromantic. But none of this discomfort mattered, not even the humiliation of having to spy on his Beloved or the real danger of having his ass hacked and spurred by Cafone.

He had just plucked a spear of straw from inside his sock when the peacock and his own Immaculta emerged from the rabbit hutch. They were holding hands and smiling.

That bastard, he thought. He watched as the two of them sat under the peach tree, knowing that the old man had discreetly gone back into the cellar to work on another cru of Ciaravino Red. Their voices carried as clearly as if he were still sitting among them.

"You could have written," she was saying. "I can read, you know."

"What can I say? I was embarrassed with my English. Who could I have gotten to write such personal things as I wanted to tell you? And besides, I didn't forget your birthday, did I?"

That dirty bastard, Roy thought. Maybe he's already slipped her his present in the rabbit hutch.

"I've even brought you a present."

Immaculta looked at the ground, calm, controlled, still in command, everything Roy loved about her. She had not seem surprised, or delighted, but as composed as if perusing her list of customers.

"It's out front," the peacock cooed. "I'll take you for a drive."

"That can't be yours, Rudolfo."

As if to make up for a personal failure Valentino took out his cigarette case and, flaunting it, lit a cigarette. "No," he said. "Not yet, but someday."

They sat there for a while in silence. Roy heard a noise and quickly glanced behind him, expecting Cafone to attack, but he saw only one of the hens slip from the perch and peck randomly amid the straw. He saw Immaculata put her hand gently on the peacock's thigh. That bastard, he thought.

"You haven't changed, Rudolpho. Still dreaming of a life of luxury."

"And why not? I've always felt that labor was not my destiny."

"Well," Immaculata said. "What is your destiny? You were going to make me your princess, I remember."

Valentino laughed. "To make you my princess I have first to become a prince."

"You're going to be disappointed. There are no princes in America."

"Ah, but there are," he said. "There are."

"And they all drive rented cars!"

Roy watched as the peacock took out another cigarette from his glistening silver case and offered it to Immaculata. He was shocked to see her take it and put it in her mouth as if the gesture were the most inveterate of habits. He noticed that Immaculata glanced quickly about her, as if making sure the old man was gone. He seethed as Valentino lit it for her with a fancy lighter. He felt a vague sense of betrayal as she sat back and nonchalantly puffed out smoke rings.

"Well, I didn't exactly rent it. I borrowed it."

"From a prince?"

"Sort of," he said. "A gangster. He dropped it off this morning at the garage. He'll pick it up tomorrow."

"Is that the kind of prince you want to be?"

"I would be embarrassed to tell anybody else, but not with you, Immaculata. No, I'm not a gangster. I used to wash cars at this garage and sometimes the fellow I worked with there lets me know when a car comes in overnight. I give him four bits for his trouble and I get to drive the car for a few hours."

"Washing cars is not for a man whose destiny is to be a prince."

"No," said Valentino. "I don't do that anymore."

"Well then," said Immaculata, pulling away her hand. "What do you do?"

"Yeah, thought Roy, tell her you're a pimp.

"I am what they call a taxi dancer," said Valentino.

Just as I thought, Roy said to himself, a pimp and a peacock.

"You drive a cab?"

Valentino laughed, then crossed his legs and put his arm around the back of Immaculata's chair. Roy felt the straw now tickling his ankle.

"How shall I say it?" Valentino said. "I work at a sort of club, a classy place for ladies and gentlemen. But mostly for ladies."

He paused. With his other hand he picked off a grain of tobacco from his tongue.

"I'm still waiting," said Immaculata.

"Where was I?" said Valentino.

"Don't try to fool me, Rudolfo. These are not the old days and this is not the old country. 'Ladies', you said. A classy place for 'ladies.'"

"Yes," Valentino continued. "Mostly ladies."

"Princesses, no doubt," said Immaculata. Roy couldn't tell if she was smiling.

"Perhaps, yes," said Valentino. "Some are quite rich. Some are lonely, Most just want to have a good time."

"And you give it to them?"

Roy smirked triumphantly, the greaseball's finished now.

Valentino cocked his head, cupped his palm under Immaculata's chin and smiled.

"Oh, my dearest," he said. "What do you think of me? I dance with them. I merely dance, that's all. They pay me a small fee to dance with them."

"It seems a strange way to make a living."

"It is very modern and very proper,"

"I guess it's modern all right, Rudolfo. But I'm not sure it's all that proper."

"It's as you said, dearest. This is not the old country anymore."

Valentino rose from his chair, quickly pushing it some distance from him.

"Here," he said. "Let me show you how proper it really is. Then I'll take you for a drive."

He bowed and reached out his hand. "Good evening,madam. How charming you look. May I have the honor of this dance?"

Immaculata did not rise, did not smile. She sat unmoved, like a queen, unamused. Oh, how he so loved her, Roy thought.

"You told me they paid you a fee," she said.

The peacock stood erect. "Well, yes," he said. "That is true. Often it was the madam who asked me to dance. But it is all quite proper. As proper, my dear, as smoking."

Roy watched as Immaculata threw down her cigarette. In one quick, agile movement—in less time than it took Roy to scratch an itch from the straw—Valentino had lifted her from her chair, cradling her into his arms.

"This is called the tango," he said. "A graceful dance of great elegance and beauty. A dance of submission."

Before she had time to speak, to object, to scoff, she was tenderly cosseted in his embrace.

"Tango is not about your feet," he said. "Relax. Follow with your spirit, your mind. Let your body remember."

Valentino held her close, guiding her, his voice soothing, crooning things that Roy could not hear. Slowly, smoothly, they wended round the old peach tree, raising gentle wisps of dust, gliding almost in unison, Valentino's leg entwined with hers, Immaculata following almost instinctively. He brought his cheek to hers, turned her, drawing back again. She was cooing things in Valentino's ear, and now he gently bent her back as he leaned in upon her, gazing fiercely into her eyes. Immaculata straightened from the dance-swoon and circled with her partner, brushing against him, returning his gaze with a dark, serious stare.

By the time the pair had made a second circuit of the peach tree Roy realized that they were dancing to music he would never hear;

he knew in his heart that he had lost Immaculata forever. The greaseball had won; plainly and simply had seduced his love while he, Roy, watched helplessly, lying on his belly in the shit-dotted straw.

He gritted his teeth as he watched Immaculata pant and sit back in the chair while the peacock sat easefully beside her. It angered him that for a few minutes they sat quietly, languidly, as if waiting for the music to stop.

"And now, your Highness," said the peacock. "Your coach awaits."

Valentino rose and took Immaculata by the hand. Roy noticed that she was smiling.

She stood and allowed Valentino to take her arm in his. They were about to go off together in the pimp's machine. He would be left to stew, to clean out the chicken coop and maybe get drunk on the old man's wine.

Yet even now he sensed that there must be something he could do. It was clear what he couldn't. He wasn't such a fool as to rush out like a cop and yell, "Halt!" He wasn't about to engage the peacock in a fight. That would only make Immaculata even more disdainful of him. Besides, the little dago was probably carrying a stiletto in his boot. Everybody knew dagos carried knives. He couldn't run out to the car ahead of them and puncture the tires. Didn't the wop tell her the car was owned by a gangster? Did he want an ugly, broken-nosed hit man with a tommy gun storming into the kitchen of Wang Fu's Chop Suey Emporium and riddling him full of holes? That would certainly be a lot worse than fending off the attacks of that hateful bird still perched on the steering wheel of the pimp's machine.

As with the vivid clarity of genius, an idea now began taking shape in Roy's mind. All those months of parrying and coping with the depredations of Cafone, he realized now, were mere preparations for this one act of sweet revenge. What could be more appropriate to breaking his connections, once and for all, with the Ciaravino tribe, father and daughter, than by using that goddam rooster in a final act of terror? If he could incite Cafone to fly into the wop's face, perhaps gouging out an eye or scarifying that sissy-smooth skin; if he could see the pimp choke on that phony dignity, see him sweat in fear, even the pain of losing his girl would be worth it. Besides which, he calculated, he himself would be come off as blameless, Cafone's unpredictable ferocity being a given. It was exactly this unpredictability that offered itself as the heart of the challenge. Roy's mind was working quickly. There was little time left. Already the pimp had taken hold of her arm and was escorting his Immaculata across the yard, through the house and out to the car. Even allowing time for the couple to shout their goodbyes to the old man—by now stuporous in wine—Roy estimated he would have less than two minutes to rile Cafone into attacking. He knew the critter was a jealous fowl, protective of all his hens, but especially enamored of a hair-brained little pullet with only one eye who ran into walls and pecked errantly at the feed that the other hens stole from right under her beak.

Sensing an opportunity, Roy fetched up the pullet, busily scrounging about his ankles, and with the hen clucking contentedly under his arm, ran out of the coop. If he could scoot past the pimp and get to the car before him, he would, at the last second, fling the bird into the driver's seat at the approach of the dago and wait for him to make his fatal plunge into the car and for Cafone to exact retribution. Roy knew Cafone would never attack Immaculata. Like him, the bird seemed to understand her self-sufficiency, to respect her casual affirmation of authority. But there would be no respect for this little pimp who drove gangsters' automobiles and smoked scented cigarettes and wore gloves and a wristwatch.

Somehow—perhaps because the pimp and Immaculata were too distracted with looking and smiling at each other as they walked—Roy reached the car before them. There was Cafone, glaring maliciously, perched on the steering wheel. The pullet still clucked contentedly in Roy's arms as he stood by the car, snickering faintly. He watched as the pimp opened the passenger door and bowed. He sickened as he noticed Immaculata smiling and sliding with wonderful ease into the front seat. His heart quickened as he watched the little peacock amble around to the driver's side and open the door. All the while Cafone regarded him with his usual ferocity, but Valentino took no notice. And then, just as the dago was about to get in, Roy plucked at the pullet, causing it to squawk and flutter and giving him the excuse he needed to fling the bird into Valentino's lap, as if the hen had gotten loose.

But in one, suave, athletic motion Valentino swooped up the pullet and dropped it outside the car, then swiped at Cafone, waving it away as if swatting a fly. Unconcerned, Cafone quietly bobbed over to his pullet. Roy watched as Valentino started his machine.

"Hold tight, My Lady," he yelled and putting the car into gear, drove off, the dust curdling round Roy's legs and raising a little plume which settled into his hair. His last sight of his Immaculata was her broad smile, his last sound of her the squeal of joy as the car scudded up the road, taking her far away from him as if to the other side of the moon.

But he had no time now, even for melancholy, for the next sound he heard was a hoarse croaking, low at first, then a sweeping, guttural rasp, ferocious, threatening, followed by a fluttering of wings. He recognized the sound at once, as Cafone's war-cry.

He had only a second's glance into the red, unblinking eye of the bird and he realized now that he was running into the house, flailing his arms over his head as the rooster made one sortie after another onto the back of head, ears, shoulders. He could not close the door behind him, Cafone diving and clawing, tenaciously atop of him. Roy did not call to the old man, who would not have heard him anyway. His only chance was to make for the chicken coop where he could retrieve the shovel he had left against the wall and which he could use to smash Cafone's skull, finally putting an end to the bird's miserable career.

He had gotten to the back yard, but Cafone had somehow cut off his retreat and was suddenly come aground just ahead of him. The two faced each other. Roy was out of breath, but Cafone stood cocking his head and scraping his claws into the dirt. Slowly, Roy moved amid the chairs under the peach tree, but Cafone followed, unblinking, confident. Keeping his eye on the bird, Roy slowly moved around the tree. Cafone followed, circling, watching. Roy put out his leg, as if ready to run, but Cafone moved with him, advanced a claw as if in defiance. Roy muttered soothing words to Cafone, but the fowl just glared and followed Roy, almost step for step around the deserted wire-backed chairs encircling the peach tree. Roy picked up a chair, flung it at Cafone, but the bird was too quick.

Suddenly Cafone lunged, driving him backwards against the tree in a final charge. Roy could feel the rush of wind, could hear the violent beat of feathers and the guttural squall. A strange, diatonic tune came to him and as the bird made for his eyes Roy inexplicably remembered the words of an old song and began to hum.

*   *   *

The Long and the Short of It

So like I was saying, Dominick, I've had her. I did her. Let me tell you she's even more beautiful in person. Classy, real elegant, not full of herself like so many of them, you know what I mean? It all happened so natural, like it was meant to be. I was just walking down Ninth, last March it was, and still cold. There I was, minding my own business, hands in my pockets, when I see this commotion up the street. All sorts of lights and fancy equipment and cars parked every which way. People standing around. I could see their breaths fogging up the air.

All of a sudden this guy comes up to me; he's young, heavy-set, wearing just a tee-shirt and baggy shorts, this is March, you understand, and he's got headphones and a mike jutting from one ear. He points to me with his clipboard. "How'd you like to make a hundred bucks?" he says. I just stand there, you know, and he says, "Come on, come on, you want to make a hundred bucks or don't you?"

"Sure," I says. I figure what could be wrong, with all these people standing here? Maybe they're all in line for a hundred bucks, am I right?

Turns out they're making a movie, some sci-fi flick, I forget the title, and Mr. S.—that's what the guy with the clipboard called the Director—Mr. S. needs more extras. Me and these twenty or thirty other people just off the street are suddenly given clubs and hammers and things—they gave me a pitchfork—and we're supposed to walk to the end of the block, then come walking back down the street behind a bunch of real actors. I says to the guy with the clipboard—you know me, I can't keep my mouth shut—"This is the city, pal. What am I doing with a pitchfork?"

"Don't worry about it," he says. "Just do as you're told."

We must've done the scene four, five times before Mr S. was happy with it. Believe me it was no skin off my nose when the clipboard guy comes over and says they want to do a shoot tomorrow for another hundred bucks. This was a Saturday and the next day, Sunday, I wouldn't be working so I signed up.

Hold your horses, will you? I'm getting to her.

Anyway, I go back the next day and I'm early. You know how dead the city is on a Sunday. I see a few trailers and think maybe I could peek into one and see a real star. But it's just a couple of actresses I don't recognize fussing with their looks and makeup and stuff. One of them has her hair all messed up and you'd think the world was coming to an end. The other was eating a sandwich and looking bored.

"Excuse me, ladies," I says to the one having a fit. You know me, always ready to snatch any opportunity. "Maybe I could help."

"Who the hell are you?" she says.

I smile and introduce myself. Then I turn on the charm. And before you know it, so help me, I'm in there and I'm doing her, just like that. Then, I swear to God, the other one with the sandwich, she puts one hand on her hip and kind of leans against the wall, standing there with a hurt look—she was really built, this one—and she says "How about me?" So I says, sure, and in a minute I'm doing her, too.

I did both of them in ten minutes and then there's a face at the door and some guy announcing they're ready to shoot and I had to get lost. So I hitched up my pants and walk out, proud and debonair, not like some hundred-dollar-a-day extra.

Will you hold on, please, and let me tell the story my way? I'm getting to the good stuff now.

We finish shooting my part and I'm about to get my hundred bucks and call it a good weekend when I decide to stay around and watch them shoot the scene with her in it. Even with all that make up and those big light reflectors shining on her face she was a real knock-out, though she looked a little shorter than in the movies. She's standing in the middle of the street and here it is, cold as a terrorist's heart, and she's dressed only in these tight black leotards and a white, low-cut blouse that showed everything God gave her—and He didn't skimp on her, believe me. Mr. S. just points and she takes it as a signal to start. Her face suddenly darkens and she curls her mouth into a snarl. Then she says, "You dirty son of a bitch" and Mr. S. yells "Cut" and that was it. It took about three seconds, and I'm figuring how much money she made per second, multiplied per minute. More than a hundred bucks, I can tell you that.

But that's not the best part. Here's the best part.

After the shoot everybody scatters. Somebody wraps a coat around her and begins walking back with her to the trailer, way up the street.

Now get ready. Here it comes. She sees me and waves me over. I tell you I was stunned. I must have stood there like a dummy because in the next minute I see her point to me, smile and mouth the words "Yes, you." The same guy who put a coat on her comes over to me and takes hold of my arm, gentle like, and we go over to her.

I said she was a class act, and so she was. She puts out her hand and I shake it, and I'll admit that I broke into a sweat, as cold as it was. I was almost in a trance.

Go ahead, you could make fun of me if you want. I see you grinning.

Anyhow, the three of us, we get to her trailer and she takes off her coat. And then the guy leaves. He actually leaves! It's just me and her. I'll be honest with you, it was the first time in my life I was uncomfortable with a woman. I guess she noticed that I was staring at her bazooms. She gives out with a little laugh but makes no attempt to cover anything up, you know what I mean? Like she was used to that sort of thing. A lot of actresses are like that.

She sits down. "Donna tells me you did her. She says you're very good."

"I'm glad she's happy," I said.

"You did Julie, too".

"Nobody ever complained about my work," I told her.

"Bruce, my regular guy, is out today. Ricardo is held up. I wonder if you could do me? I'll pay you well."

It took me a little while to catch my breath. But you know me, the cat, always landing on all fours. So I flash her a smile and turn on the old charm again.

"You've been a favorite of mine for a long time," I says. "I'll do you for nothing. It'll be my pleasure."

She smiled back. And then I knew.

"Shall we get started, then?" she says. And then I did her. I did her right there in her own personal trailer. I did the most beautiful woman in Hollywood. You can believe me or not, but that's the whole story, the long and the short of it.

By the way, how do you like this new chair you're sitting in? Comfortable, right? How do you want me to do you? Take some more off the top? Want a straight back or a regular? Razor cuts are on special this week.

*   *   *

Seduction A La Carte

She was one of the most stunning women he had ever seen. From where he stood just beyond the kitchen doors the waiter couldn't help but admire the smoky glimmer of her eyes, the smooth, flawless sheen of her cheeks and sweet, full lips, the almost sacred aura of perfect health sensuously enhanced by the glow of the candle on her table. He was particularly taken by the delicate, up-turned curve of her nose. Being a nose man himself, he was entranced by the easy swirl of her nostrils, the nearly miraculous way in which they defined that erogenous dimple gently kissing her upper lip.

Yeah, she was a beauty, all right. But the guy opposite her, what a geek. What, after all, could she see in him, this lurching, slouching narrow-shouldered boob, his necktie curdling into his salad. A real clown. A total loser. A first-class schnook. But what a lucky son of a bitch!

Still, the waiter was enjoying a bit of luck himself, for she was sitting by the window at table 6, always his lucky number. Big tippers invariably chose that place, but he didn't give a damn about the tip with this gorgeous babe sitting there, offering him a golden opportunity to pitch his long-practiced charm.

His best chance would come when the slob got up to go to the men's room, probably to clean his tie. That would be his cue. Adjusting his black vest, brushing his black, tight-fitting pants, smoothing his hair with his palm, he'd accost her, wearing his most solicitous smile. In the course of a few canny remarks he would let her know that this stint was but a temporary gig while he awaited a call from his agent. "Ah," she would say, "You're in the business, too?"

"I've done some good work, mainly in small parts," he would say. "Working with De Niro is a real blast. But right now I'm more interested in finishing my book."

"Ah," she would say. "So you're a writer also."

"A few earnest stories. I'm waiting now for The New Yorker to get back to me."

"Ah," she would say, her nostrils flaring with excitement. "What a wonderful thing it is to be so thoroughly engaged with life."

'Engaged with life'. He rather liked that. She had a way with words. No bimbo, this.

"You may like to know, my dear"—for by this time she would not object to his being so familiar—"you may like to know that I'm also something of a collector. Not a dedicated one, a mere dabbler, really. I've some remarkable pieces of jade dating from the Tang dynasty. Perhaps you'd like to see them. They are nearly as exquisite as you."

With that last remark he winced to himself for almost overplaying his hand. Admittedly, he had never collected a damn thing, unless you counted the two dozen menus he filched over the thirty years from the restaurants and diners that had let him go. Don Giovanni's was the worst of them, and the last, a snooty place, patronized by the coldest, ugliest women, real bow-wows. Not like this beauty. But he knew for sure that this woman would discover soon enough that his jade collection comprised only a few beads from a broken necklace he had scrounged, though she might not guess that he had fortuitously recalled a Chinese emperor whose name was identical to that of a breakfast beverage. By then, though, she would have taken the bait; the babe would be in his room.

Now as the moments passed he became irked, annoyed when the boob did not get up, did not excuse himself, but merely grinned and placed his napkin on his lap. There was nothing to do but follow procedure, remove the salad plates, ask if they were ready to order. He would not exactly glower at the geek; simply take down his selection. When he turned to her, though, he would smile, displaying his perfect white teeth—5000 smackers in installments, Chet, the maitre'd, having confidentially advised him that diners universally disdained a waiter with green or rotten stumps—and in his most oracular voice would intone the house specials.

Yet even before he moved from his station by the kitchen doors he became aware of something about to go awry. His years as a waiter had alerted his senses to the most subtle occupational tremors. He knew, this waiter, which way the wind blew and his instinct now told him it was working up to a gale. Bingo! A snicker broke onto his face when he observed the boob lean forth and say something to her. The waiter watched as the babe glared at the schnook, threw her napkin into his face and stomped out, almost pulling off the table cloth in her flight.

He congratulated himself on his prescience, but then it occurred to him that her storming out was just as much a crisis for him as for the slob. Both had lost the babe. Quick thinking on his part, though, could salvage what was left of this rare opportunity. He would approach the geek, cast a glance at her empty seat and with a kind of avuncular gesture offer to get the chump a drink, on the house. The boob was shaken, obviously distraught. Two, three drinks would loosen him up. A fourth would get him to talk. "Maybe you should send her flowers," the waiter would say. "I'd be happy to arrange it. Let me have the young lady's address and I'll see to it."

"Good idea," Mr. Bozo would say, a little out of it. "What a great guy! Why didn't I think of that?"

"Because you're a stupid bastard," the waiter would mutter under his breath.

"Here's my credit card and her address. You handle it. I don't feel so good."

How simple it all would be. He'd have the babe's address, deliver the flowers himself and by his role of ambassador reap the physical benefits of such a mission. These young bucks know nothing. With all their fancy cars and fat bank accounts they couldn't measure up to the man of experience. Again he congratulated himself for being in a profession that offered such sweet rewards. But only, as he told himself, to the cleverest, most quick-witted, most experienced. Waiting on table all these years had made him a true man of the world. Not even Chet who often laughed at him but who himself was probably still a virgin could impugn his taste in women. It wouldn't surprise the waiter in the least to learn that the babes came into this place just to be served by him. They could appreciate how he ogled them with such delicate finesse.

How long was it that he was standing by his place near the kitchen? It was time now to make his move. He had actually begun walking to the table where the geek was sitting when suddenly he spotted something that made his stomach churn. The stunning creature was coming back, the babe, not angry now, but sad-eyed, her long-legged stride, slow, hesitant, gentle. The boob caught sight of her but didn't get up. The waiter watched in horror as the babe approached the table, sat down opposite that geek. The waiter could read her lips as she said, distinctly, passionately, "I'm sorry. I love you." She took hold of his hand across the table.

For what seemed a disgustingly long time, they sat holding hands, staring at each other. The waiter shook his head. Now that he had more time to study the pair he decided that the woman wasn't all that attractive. There was something unappealing about her looks, something downright ugly in the way her bony arm stretched across the table. "A bimbo, after all," he thought. "And that geek, that chump, that clown. What a loser."

He would take his time going to their table. The slob would only ask for the check, anyway. Besides, luck was still riding high with the waiter as he scanned the next table, number 7, where a beautiful woman was sitting by herself. Maybe she was waiting for someone. In the meantime he could stand by the kitchen doors and admire the woman's face, set off as it was by a wonderfully hooked nose.

*   *   *

A Question of Priority

a Jamesian ghostly tale

Henry's first thought as he sat at the edge of the bed—if "thought", indeed, it could be called, intervening as it did between the rush of emotions and the stubborn, impetuous protuberance driving its naughty way through the median point of his trousers (a gabardine exquisitely fashioned and having been acquired at what his man, Alistair, had asseverated was a most "discreet thrift shoppe")—had barely rounded into his consciousness when it was quite suddenly dashed by the lurid voice of his companion: "Hurry up, Dearie. Let's get on with it. Time is money."

Ah, time, he thought. There should have been time in the natural order of things to meet his companion under less "arranged" circumstances, but in point of fact the urgency of the assignation was the end result of a desperately needed hiatus, a quotidian halt between the termination of one creative enterprise (a story, lately come to him, of a man upon whom nothing was lost except a laundry ticket, the search for which had led him to some rather bizarre establishments and even more hideous associations) and the commencement of another, still more earnest, as he believed, call of the muse.

The present invocation, indeed, was only slightly less urgent, signaled as it was by the rather disconcerting bulge between his thighs and requiring no less an engagement, though of a decidedly more energetic kind. He had had, to be sure, a sort of pre-vision about it, an idea which emerged "fully blown" at last—his companion would have appreciated the term, so much as it was a part of her provenance as a professional—and Henry, a man, let it be said, who prided himself on his wit which especially now at this delicate juncture was verging on the erotic, chuckled to himself at the aptness of his coinage.

"Come on, Dearie, for Chrissake!"

The voice of his female interlocutor came to him again, a besotted, impertinent cackle which ill-disguised its lurking rancor. Henry marveled at its audacious crudeness, and became all the more frightened at the maddening contradiction by which he found himself increasingly excited by the crudity, this breach of common civility that he perceived at once to be the peculiar hallmark of direct, uncomplicated conversation.

Crudeness was, he reflected, not merely a melancholy proof of his companion's demeanor, so much as a fatal condemnation of her character. That kind of brutality of manner, in the first instance, was tolerable enough if taken, like alcohol, in small doses. Besides, he was luxuriating for the nonce in a generosity of soul, complimenting himself on a plangent benevolence. He was not, when all is said and done, the sort of fellow to hold a grudge or a hasty opinion. In short, so far as his companion's sordid vulgarity was concerned, he was rather inclined to let sleeping dogs lie. But to be assailed, assaulted, as it were, by the sheer physical—one might even say astonishing—ugliness of this personage before him, that was a provocation of such immensity as to call forth, albeit briefly, another turn of the screw. Yet at this very moment it was brought home to him in all the glaring horror of reality that it was, indeed, too late; too late, certainly, for regret, and now, as he felt his member—which in his youth he was wont to call "Master Dildo" and which he had done some very fine things with—swelling with raging inquietude, too late even for physical retrenchment.

Retrenchment, physical or otherwise, was not a consideration to his companion. Behind him, somewhere in the shadows of this ghastly rented room in Cheapside, he could sense her fretting, staring at the back of his head, just where the medulla meets the cerebellum in a kind of competitive alliance; sense, too, her filthy hands thrust onto her bovine hips in truculent impatience, and, perhaps, her foot tapping the carpet—an orgy of swirls and ungainly figures—in barely controlled menace. His thought now—like a light at the beginning of a whole train of reflections that, one by one, would illuminate the track of his experience—was, he realized, suggestive of an act somewhat akin to cowardice. Perhaps, he said to himself, he could close his eyes, shutting from his horrid view the Jurassic torso which had already begun to disencumber itself of its habiliments, first the red wig of multi-hued tresses with its purple bows intertwined among orange locks, then the shoes, size 13 EEE, that lay upended on the floor like a pair of pre-historic mammals, and finally the shedding of the undergarments which slapped, snapped and grunted, sounding to our friend like the giving way of a ship's rigging, the sails unfurling and plummeting to the depths. He would not have been surprised to see her nose, like the false proboscis of a clown he had once observed at a circus in the barbaric hinterlands of New York, to be removed, as well.

"All right, Dearie. I'm ready now. Let's roll!"

Again, the voice of the Provocateur, "as they say in Paris." But provocative or not, the idea of engaging with this troglodyte horrified, repulsed him to the very tips of his hard-bitten nails. Yet even in the light of this repugnance; even in the throes of this potential renunciation, Henry realized the need for decisive action, for a gesture, if you will, which might be understood by those uninitiated in the more subtle aspects of the art of engagement as an act of desperate, albeit specious heroism. He was, in a word, driven by the conviction learned early in his youth that an opportunity lost was a tragic defeat of the spirit, a futile worshiping at the altar of the dead.

The only question looming before him now, then, was not whether he should proceed. The ruthless importunities of his hideous companion—so vulgar an embodiment of the very grossest commercialism—obviated the need for debate and rendered absurd the excuse of delay. No, it was clear what he must do. The appropriate question, the real thing which lurked like a beast in the jungle of his consciousness, casting ominous shadows on the otherwise jolly corner of his self-approbation, the golden bowl, as it were, of his good intentions, was, in fine, not if, but how to proceed. How does one, after all, engage a gorgon? How does a gentleman so acutely aware of even his own breathing—in and out, in and out—how does he commence a physical consummation with something so profoundly paleolithic?

"What's keeping you, Dearie? I haven't got all day."

The creature had snuggled under the bedclothes and Henry could sense her saurian eyes peering greedily just over the rim of the coverlet, waiting to engage him, waiting like some Pleistocene thing to swallow him whole into the immensity of her terrifying embrace. Oddly, he was reminded now of Caesar's animadversions to his wife, so nobly represented in the play of the great Avon bard. Though it had been many years since he read the drama—his ultimate recollection embraced by a pair of cataractic orbs and the rotten, brown grinders of old Larkins, his ancient tutor whose knowledge of Shakespeare grew incandescently as he partook of the Bacchic beverage, all the while pounding away with the rod at Henry's rump, in direct retaliation for certain infractions the nature and gravity of which he could not now after the passage of all these years possibly recall—he did remember the gist of the matter to the effect that cowards die many deaths. In this regard, Henry valiantly resolved to die but once.

The issue, then, devolved on the simple matter of form, a mere question of priority. Should he first remove his shoes, or should he start in the opposite direction and commence by taking off his cravat? Removing first the shoes—boots, really, elegantly fitted, with a sublimely subtle sweep in the heel that elevated his five-foot-one-inch frame to a more compelling height of nearly six feet—would assuredly serve as an effective means of declaring once and for all his avowed commitment "to go through with it." But in contemplating fully the ramifications of such a decision—that is, removing the shoes—he realized that he would fall victim to the necessity of bending over, thereby bringing his body in a direct parallel line with the bed while his hinder parts, the rump that old Larkins loved to throttle, would be thrust into the air, exposing a slight tear in the seat of his trousers. Even more exasperating was the idea, which budded and bloomed like some monstrous shrub, that by assuming such a semi-recumbent posture he would risk sullying his otherwise immaculate sense of decorum, that profound vision of personal dignity which he had spent the better part of his life upholding, even in the privacy of his own room, before his own mirror, standing barefoot and bowlegged in his own shorts.

On the other hand, if he commenced by unlacing his cravat he would likely submit himself to the usual clumsiness of knotting the damnable thing. Thus suddenly he envisioned with horror his lame attempt to pull the cravat from his neck, (such an expensive cravat, of Italian silk, and such a fine neck, of sturdy Irish-English-Dutch ancestry, though somewhat grizzled) with the added peril that he would ruin a perfectly good stick-pin, given to him by his young niece, a Miss Daisy Miller, late of Albany. She it was, in fact, who, more than any other of his acquaintances, not to say relations, had gently scolded him on his retiring habit. "Really, Uncle," she had smiled, pushing the pin through his cravat. "One really ought to get out into the world and see more of life than the confines of one's study. One should enjoy more of society than the matutinal ministrations of one's valet." He recalled that conversation clearly now, as it was the only time he needed to consult a dictionary, the word "matutinal" ringing so mellifluously in his ears, and he so assiduously writing it down in his notebook next to an entry about a woman who eventually learns that her Italian husband was not a count, after all, but a bounder, a cad who had married her not for love nor even money but for the possession of some secret papers once owned by a Danish piano tuner and whose own family had descended from a line of bootblacks. But more to the point at present was the revolting possibility that in the process of tearing off the cravat he would prick or otherwise damage one or two of his digits, even on his writing hand, though for that, he felt that as a dedicated artist, committed only to his work, he could, if called upon, learn to write with his toes.

All of which, as may be imagined, thrust our friend into a most unnatural funk. He thus became besieged by a series of odd, one may say, irrelevant ruminations, the nature of which were frighteningly unconsoling. Where, for example, was Alistair? Could he not solve the dilemma—as he was so wont to do, so valuable a man!—in better, more clarified days? Yet the thought of his valet being here, under the present circumstances, was, he had to admit, rather a vain, even fatuous hypothesis, so singularly at odds with the domestic protocol of master and servant relations. Would it not be more advantageous both to his dignity and to Alistair himself, simply to pick up his walking stick, leave some emolument on the cheap deal bureau and quietly abscond with his hat and gloves? But whence? Perhaps to some great, good place, where the serenity imbued by plashing fountains and plain food served by be-robed communicants would foster in him a sexless placidity and repose . . .

And so our dear friend Henry sat at the edge of the bed, enmeshed in a net of deliberations. Decisions, decisions. Someday they would drive him mad. Meanwhile, the stentorian snorts from his companion gave him to understand that she had long since fallen into the lap of Morpheus. In fine, she had gone to sleep. He glanced over his shoulder and watched for a while the rhythmic rise and fall of the hideous bosom under the blanket. Ah, he thought, putting on his hat, what a dreary compromise is life!

*   *   *

Lunch with the Contessa

Two of us were sitting in the hotel bar in Palermo, nursing a couple of drinks. I was also nursing a couple of sore feet and had slipped off my sneakers, savoring the cool marble beneath my toes.

"Feet hurt, huh?" the fellow sitting next to me asked. "Those walkways at the Valley of the Temples could be tricky. I noticed you lagging behind the rest of us. We had to wait for you a few times yesterday."

I didn't answer him, but he took full measure of my hard glare.

"Hey, that's all right, buddy. I didn't mean anything by it. That's what I do for a living. Name's Rex."

"You get a cut from the tour guide, Rex?" I said. "Rounding up the herd?"

Even while saying it I regretted the sarcasm. I didn't want to be so mean-spirited. I don't think of myself as a humorless hardass, but it's hard to cultivate a joke when your feet hurt, and anyway I didn't believe his name was Rex, anymore than I credited his bonhomie.

"Seriously," he said. "Feet are my business. I could tell the way you're putting pressure on your toes. I'll bet you have a stiff neck, am I right?"

I sipped my wine

"It's okay," he said, as if trying to console me. He reached for his wallet and gave me his business card. "I'm a Reflexologist. Lots of people still don't believe in it. But they're dinosaurs. Trust me, most physical ailments of the human species can be relieved—I won't say cured—by understanding the role feet play in a person's well-being. Your big toe, for instance, can yield valuable diagnostic information on the workings of your pituitary gland. I'd like to examine your feet before this tour's done. What you need, my friend, is a good massage."

"Not today."

"I know from experience that lousy feet can ruin your outlook on life. The whole world sucks. You just don't want to be bothered."

"You're right," I said. "I'd like to finish my wine in peace."

"How about another round? On me."

My answer was to get off the stool and put on my sneakers. Rex looked aggrieved.

"Look," I said. "I'm tired. I just want to relax."

"Sure, absolutely. I get too enthusiastic about my work, I know. This tour can knock you out. All of Sicily in six days. That's pushing it. How do like it so far?"

"Beautiful country," I said "'The burnt land' my father used to call it, but he had no sense of history."

"I'm Sicilian, too. Real name's Renaldo. I had it legally changed. I didn't want to sound too ethnic, know what I mean? 'Rex Peddie' sounds so much more professional. Last name's spelled P e d d i e. Get it? Peddie? Feet?"

"Very clever," I said. Reflexology, after all, was a scam; nothing more than voodoo done up in a tux.

Rex chugged down his Peroni and slid off the stool. "Maybe you're right. Tomorrow's our last full day and I want to be ready for it. You going out with us?"

"I thought I'd look around the old part of town."

"I've seen enough of Palermo. It's a little too seedy for my taste. La Kalsa, isn't that what they call it, the old part? A big flea market."

"Things aren't always what they seem," I said.

"Well, it's your call, naturally. But you might want to think about coming with us. Especially with your feet. Besides, it's not every day you get to have lunch with a countess."

"What countess?"

"Our tour guide's arranged it. The Countess Angelica Bradamante. She's got an estate near Castellamare. Carlo said she offers lunch only to selected groups, to make a little pocket change, I guess. Things are tough all over."

"Especially for countesses," I remarked.

"Carlo says it'll be the highlight of our tour. Not everybody gets to go. The lunch is typically Sicilian country fare."

"And we've been selected."

"Mock if you want to. As I say, it's your call. But I'm going. For a few bucks, what can you lose? When's the last time you sat down to eat with a contessa?" I had to admit that Rex's enthusiasm was contagious, even if only from the vantage of nagging curiosity.

The next morning several of us were greeted in the lobby by Carlo, dapper, dauntless, smiling broadly. He waved a little flag as if it were a battle standard.

"Are we all ready? Everyone here?" He began poking his finger as if each of us were an "i" needing a dot. "Yes, and today we are going to luncheon with Contessa Angelica Bradamante. We will all assemble by the door while I converse with the office. We are one person missing."

"It's Fred," a woman said. "Up all night with the runs. Claims it was the water."

Carlo looked puzzled, but quickly recovered. "What is this 'runs'? Ah, well, that's unfortunate. There is nothing wrong with our water. Be that as it may, we are now in for a treat. This is, indeed, a major highlight of our tour and, if I may say so, a most memorable conclusion. The Contessa has prepared a wonderful meal for us and now I must collect the price. Of course I can also accept your credit cards."

Despite my skepticism—or maybe because of it—I found myself boarding the bus, Rex taking a seat behind me.

"How're your feet this morning?"

I nodded as I stared out the window. Due west of Palermo, the road skirted the sea along a rugged, boulder-pounded coast, simulating a line of fortresses, formidable but reassuring. Over our left shoulders we could see the mountains and feel the road's gradual decent. Then we veered south where the land rose gently with hills bearing groves of olive trees beneath a blazing sun.

In the course of our journey we seemed to have left the main road several times and veered toward the mountains. We turned once more, the paved road now dissolving into hardscrabble. Inexplicably, we saw the sea again, vaguely distant in a blue haze. It was as if we had lost our sense of direction or had arrived at a place where the certainty of fixed latitude was irrelevant.

"We are now entering the estate of Contessa Angelica Bradamonte," Carlo said. "Please debark from the front only and wait for me under the pergola. I will see to it that everything is prepared."

From the pergola I could see a low ranch-style house, open on two sides and forming an "L". Behind the house stood a barn, darkened by wind and a relentless sun. Beyond them, beyond even the shaded pergola, I could see stretches of lemon trees, their fruit strewing the grass, magpies swooping down to peck at the fruit as it rotted in the heat. My attention was caught by a fountain in the middle of the pergola. The stone figure of a beautiful woman carrying a wand from which water spouted dominated the basin. Surrounding the woman, sprawled at her feet, were six stone men in various attitudes of anguish. Or was it rapture? Like the place itself I couldn't be sure exactly. As I drew my eyes around the basin I noticed that the next six figures were not men but men in transition, men in the shapes of wolves or apes or, finally, swine.

"I'm hungry," said Rex. "I wonder what's holding things up."

We couldn't have been under the pergola more than a few minutes when we saw Carlo emerge from the house accompanied by a woman. They were walking side by side, but Carlo was smiling, strutting as if he had just discovered a cure for cancer. The woman was lean, straight-shouldered, dark. She walked easily, her long, formal dress liquefying her movement. I noticed the gold necklace around her well-toned neck and her matching be-jeweled earrings. Sunglasses were perched on her nose, but as she approached she took them off and buried them amid her long fingers. I couldn't make a guess even now as to her age. Her skin was taut, smooth, her cheekbones high.

Carlo was about to say something but the woman smiled and beat him to the punch.

"Welcome, dear friends. It is so very nice to have you here."

"We're honored, Countess," said Rex.

"Please," she smiled. "Let us go in."

She waited for the others to follow Carlo but when she noticed my holding back she paused. "There is some cool wine inside," she said.

"I was just noticing your fountain," I said.

"It is a remarkable piece. It has been part of my family for hundreds of years, maybe longer."

She was waiting, I suppose, for another exclamation of wonder on my part but somehow I wasn't able to respond. I can't say whether she was touched by my rapt silence or disappointed by my inarticulateness. In the end she helped me out.

"The subject of the piece is from the Odyssey. You remember. It is from the story of Circe."

"Yes," I said. "She had a nasty habit of turning men into swine. I suppose we can call her a witch."

"I like to think of her more as, how do you say, an avenger".

There was a gleam in her eyes, a subtle smile on her lips.

"In any case," she continued. "Stories like this abound here in Sicily. The Odyssey is, after all, a Sicilian epic. If you came along the road by the sea you must surely have remarked those large boulders that stretch for many kilometers. Some say they are the rocks the giant Cyclops threw at Odysseus as he made his escape. At any rate, I hope you do not think I am a witch. Come inside, if you please. The wine is cool."

Though she walked beside me there was an awkward silence separating us. I felt a stirring of the air and observed a wisp of her auburn hair blaze in the sun.

"I noticed all your lemon trees," I said, feeling the need to speak.

She nodded.

"Isn't there anyone to pick the lemons?"

"It doesn't matter."

"They must be worth something."

It seemed somehow inappropriate, I may even say, tactless, to talk dollars and cents when both of us were tacitly obliged to pretense. She was royalty, the elegant Contessa with a storied past and I the favored, honored guest.

Her reaction, however, buried pretense. "It is too expensive to pick them. Africa sends us her lemons. They are cheaper. Africa sends us her lemons just as she sends us the sirocco."

We had come not to the house but to the high-vaulted barn. Inside, what used to be several horse stalls now each quartered two or three tables decorated with red linens and bowls of white flowers, enhancing the natural sunlight streaming through long, narrow windows. The others of our group were already seated. Rex waved at me to take a chair next to him. When we were all seated she stood by the door. The sunlight was behind her, her face in shadow.

Her voice was mellow, soothing. "Welcome, all of you. Thank you all very much for coming. I have prepared a lovely lunch. Please enjoy." Then she disappeared out the door.

Rex had already poured himself generous draughts of wine from the elaborately painted jug. Almost immediately the first course was served. The waiters, young black boys, worked quickly and silently. Carlo had told us the meal was to be typical Sicilian fare. Certainly I recognized the cheeses and tomatoes, the pasta with sardines, the eggplant, capers, olives and rich, red sauces. In his exuberance Rex poured me a glass of wine and urged me to drink, drink, and I needed little encouragement. The Contessa was right. The wine was cool, wonderful.

After three glasses I felt giddy, light-headed and for some reason was curious to know where the Contessa had gone. She had not eaten with us and in clearer lights I would have disavowed the curiosity as being none of my business. Surely Rex didn't care; and Carlo was eating and drinking mannerly enough to engage the attention of the blond quiet girl in our group who spent most of her time reading the Michelin guide. But my curiosity—if that's what it was—drove me outside. I thought of the fountain under the pergola, but it seemed too long a distance and under my present condition a likely disappointment. So I made way around the barn. There was the sea again, glimmering in the heat. Around another side I heard the clink of glass and the dull chirps of dishes and crockery. I followed the sounds, came to an opening. I had stumbled upon the kitchen and in my fuzzy apprehension caught sight of the Contessa. She was wearing an apron and was standing over a large basin filled with soapy water. She had taken off her necklace; it lay on the work table next to her.

"Hurry," I heard her say, though my Sicilian was errant. "These have to be ready for the next group tonight."

And then she turned and our eyes met. I don't know what I had expected her to say. I can't remember now my saying anything. I recall only how she dried her hands, took off her apron and looked hard at me as she put on her necklace. She stared at me for what seemed a long while and the remarkable thing was that there was reflected in her face not one trace of embarrassment. Rather, I was the one who felt embarrassed.

Saying not a word she walked quietly to the door and shut it. It was the last time any of us saw her until lunch was over and we returned to the bus. She stood by the door of the bus and shook everyone's hand as we climbed in. Even mine. As we pulled away she smiled and waved to us, but her face was taut, her eyes hard. She kept waving until we had driven beyond the grounds and couldn't see the place anymore. I wondered if her feet were hurting.

*   *   *

A Christmas Carol Revisited

Stave 1: Family and Friends

Scrooge was dead. There could be no doubt about that. Just at the stroke of midnight, Christmas day, it was said, the old man gave up the ghost. He died, much loved and full of years, as the saying goes, his last days a signal contradiction to the course of his earlier life, stained as it was by the toil of getting all and giving nothing. Yes, Scrooge was saved in the end, though I could hardly tell you why. Certainly something must have happened to make a greedy, grasping curmudgeon suddenly view the world from brighter prospects and pursue philanthropy with as much energy in his latter days as he had spent in cornering pounds and crowns and guineas in his prime. For it was bruited far and wide that old Ebenezer Scrooge, good Ebenezer Scrooge, kindly Ebenezer Scrooge, God bless him, had become the beloved benefactor of all of London's Union workhouses and charity wards. Something, I say, must have come between him and his conscience. Whatever it was, old Scrooge and the good old city itself were the better for it.

As for the business, Scrooge's nephew Fred inherited that and gave it a run for a while. But unlike his uncle he had little head for receipts and bills of lading and past-due accounts and turned over the concern lock, stock, and barrel to old Scrooge's clerk before sailing off to Australia with his young wife to see the kangaroos and the bushmen and ultimately to find the peace that passeth all understanding. And loyal Bob Cratchit, the clerk and final heir to the House of Scrooge and Marley, he's gone, too, poor fellow, dead these many years, as is his wife and two of his children. You might say they died of heat prostration. Call it spontaneous combustion, if you like. But it amounts to the same thing: they perished in the conflagration that brought down the whole place when Mrs. Cratchit in her euphoria at being an heiress threw an extra piece of coal on the fire and caused a brand to slip between the floor boards. In twenty minutes nothing remained of Scrooge and Marley, not even the heirs.

Of the two Cratchit boys, son Peter had a better turn for business than his father. It came to pass one day, when he had set aside enough shillings and pence to invest in a going venture, that he was visited by the spirit of enterprise in the person of one Sid Slymes, a rich American with a large head and a beaver hat who took the lad under his wing and convinced him to open the first business in England catering exclusively to the lame and the halt. "Cratchit's Crutches" was the result, and within ten years son Peter and his partner were a household name in the handicap trade.

But it was the other son who draws our attention—and concern: little Tiny Tim, the subject of our tale; little Tiny Tim, bereft of a patron by the death of Scrooge; orphaned at twenty-six by the flames that consumed his parents; forgotten and ignored by his surviving brother.

"Dear brother, you should be honored," Peter told him late one afternoon while counting the day's receipts. "You were the inspiration for my business . . ."

"*Our* business," said Slymes, standing by his side, his eyes bulging from a sallow face as if too big for the sockets. One of these orbs had a will of its own, darting about uncontrollably in his head while its twin fixed itself intently on his partner's calculations. Slymes was leaning on his walking stick, made, as he proudly averred, of good old American "elum, the hardest, most sturdiest wood on this here globe." His smile was tight, stiff, resembling a gash that made the rest of his countenance seem immobile.

"Yes, of course, our business. But why do you complain, brother? Haven't I used a tin-type of you as a trademark?"

And that was true, to a point. It was, in fact, this American partner who first suggested Tiny Tim as a fitting model for an advertising campaign. Incorporating the techniques of the new-fangled photographic process, it featured a smiling Tiny Tim, standing on his one sound leg, supported by the strong, the reliable and the cheap Cratchit Crutch.

"Why, God bless us, everyone!" exclaimed Tiny Tim. "I should never complain about anything my loving brother does for me out of the goodness of his heart. But such an honor, though well-worn on the outside, ill warms me on the inside. I can't eat it, and I'm hungry."

The American cut a thin slice off his smile. "I reckon this gimp's a might ungrateful."

Peter put his hand on his heart, sighed and looked to the heavens. "Oh, how sharper than a serpent's tooth . . ."

At this Slymes looked around him in alarm, his floating eye bobbing about in waves of panic as he flailed the air about his feet with his stick. "Didn't guess there was any snakes crawlin' about in Lonnun."

Peter did not answer. How crude, how savage these Americans. He shivered when he reflected that though they were still now only at the gates, sooner or later the barbarous Yankees would make themselves comfortable in one's own parlor and even—the thought made him ill—even show up one day for the rent.

But all of this is by the by. Neglect both of body and spirit at the hands of his brother Peter was one thing; enough by itself, certainly, to turn even an innocent boy like Tiny Tim into a sour, disillusioned youth. It was quite another matter, however, to be known as Tiny Tim when you were a grown man pushing thirty, had no visible means of support and were in love.

Aye, there's the rub. Now we are on to it. And all of what has gone before must be completely understood if anything wonderful is to come from the tale I am about to relate.

Tiny Tim was in love. Her name was Agnes Freake, and he had first seen her coming from a milliner's shop on Fleet Street whence he had taken up his usual corner spot, setting down his ratty blanket and box beyond the lurching spire of St. Dunstan's.

Christmas Eve it was, a light snow powdering the ground, though Tiny Tim's position was dry as toast. He had been installed here only a month, ever since his brother had given him half a crown and a one-way coach fare to Dover, and already he had become a member of the world's second oldest profession—that of beggar—recognized by pedestrian and constabulary alike as a harmless twit who greeted everyone with a vapid smile and a clutched palm. O, into what depths of despair and physical abasement can a good man plunge in so short a time! A plain, timid, insecure personage so marked at the outset by innumerable disadvantages of body and kin, so bemired in self-pity and disillusionment that the world of beggary seemed, in contrast, a life of quiet independence!

Yet there was Agnes! Though she herself could hardly be aware of this lost creature gazing at her from across the street, the mere

sound of her name brought to Tiny Tim visions of sweetness and
light. If only she knew of his love. Now especially at this season of
giving and redemption, now especially at this season of forgiveness
and hope, if she could return only a mote of what he felt for her
by a simple glance in his direction, by a mere passing notice or
vague regard, he would surely feel the odious chain of disaffection
dropping away, healing this cruel severance between him and the
world at large.

In the meantime, there was not the slightest recognition of Tiny
Tim by his angel. Even when she crossed the street and seemed to
be approaching him, he was abashed by her indifference. Even
when, burdened by overflowing parcels, she dropped a package
at his foot and he hopped on his crutch to stoop and pick it up,
she merely took it from him and hurried off in silence, wiping her
hand on her coat. It took him several minutes to recover from
her brusque repulse, but his spirits rose when he noticed several
copper pence hastily tossed on his blanket.

"Here now, what's this?' said a familiar voice.

Tim turned to see Sid Slymes.

"I thought you was in Dover by now, Mr. Gimp." Here he bent
down and picked up the coppers, putting them in his pocket.

"Don't do any thinking for me," said Tiny Tim. "Save all your
thoughts and advice for my dear brother Peter."

"Well, what I'm thinking now," said Slymes, his eye rolling
about. "What I'm thinking now is that you're bad for business.
People know you. People see you and they say to themselves, 'Aint
he the chap what's on Cratchit's Crutches, and shouldn't he be a
rich man by now what with his being on all them cards and labels
and things?' So what I'm advising now, Mr. Gimp, is that you use
that ticket to Dover or it won't be long before you won't need no
ticket or no crutch, neither, and that's the best and last advice I
give you, and it's for free."

Slymes had removed his beaver hat while he was conferring
such advice, brushing the brim gently with his fingers and blowing
on it. All the while his wayward eye scanned every point of the
compass, flurrying about aimlessly like a wind-blown ash. Then
Slymes fixed the beaver on his head, broke his face in a smile and
sidled off.

By the end of the day Tiny Tim had amassed two shillings, six
pence and a ha'penny, not counting the coins Sid Slymes had
swiped. It was enough for dinner and a mug of ale to wash it down.
It being Christmas Eve, there were few patrons at the Warty Toad

and Tiny Tim finished his shepherd's pie quickly and just as quickly dispatched his ale. A short walk took him back to his blanket and box, both neatly stowed under an abutment rich in shadow. Here Tiny Tim made himself comfortable settling in for the night. He watched the lamplighter make his rounds and observed how one by one the shops grew dim as the proprietors closed up and went home to wives or lovers.

Evening deepened, and Tiny Tim grew sleepy. He heard, or thought he heard, the clock of St. Dunstan's tolling midnight and now he felt himself falling gently like the snow into a deep, peaceful quiet, a quiet broken suddenly by a quickening backwards fall, as if off a cliff at the bottom of which vague creatures gathered. As he fell, reaching out his arms, he saw a roiling mass of dust and light, then a vortex of menacing shadows, then a vision growing more vivid as it rounded into form. He recognized in the gathering swirl the eyes and then the whole face of his erstwhile benefactor, the angry, severe, admonishing visage of his "uncle" Scrooge . . .

Stave 2: Night Journey

Most unsettling to Tiny Tim about the vision before him was that he saw himself sleeping. There he was, looking down at himself breathing rhythmically, odd gusts of wind blowing random snowflakes onto the folds and creases of his blanket while his sleeping self snuggled beneath. And the figure of Scrooge was real, not the transparent incorporeality of spirits he had heard about who shriek and carry chains and locks around their bodiless waists. This Scrooge, he felt certain, was tangible, a creature of three dimensions, hardly the sort of wraith called up from a bad piece of shepherd's pie or a mug of raw home-brewed ale. Yet there was something wrong with the vision. Scrooge was scowling, for one thing, an expression few had seen him wear since that remarkable Christmas Day not yet twenty years ago when the leopard of the old Scrooge had, indeed, miraculously changed his spots. This being was not his benefactor. This was the old Scrooge, unrepentant and unloved who now stood over the sleeping Tiny Tim as observed by the wakeful Tiny Tim beneath the beetling tower of St. Dunstan's.

"Hello," said Tiny Tim. Even while saying it he knew the greeting sounded absurd, disconnected, the perfect inanity of the dream, though as I've said, Tiny Tim was sure he was wide awake.

"Humbug!" said Scrooge.

"What's a humbug?" said Tiny Tim.

"A musical insect," said Scrooge. "But not for you, not for you."

He watched as the old Scrooge suddenly and quite naturally sprouted gossamer wings and began to float above the ground humming 'God Save the King'.

"Why is it not for me?" asked Tiny Tim, crying, bawling, yet putting his hand to his mouth, not wanting to wake the sleeping Tiny Tim. "Why is it not for me?"

"You're not the king," said Scrooge, descending.

"I am the king," said Tiny Tim. "I'm the king of the gimps. King Gimp. Who's going to save me? I want to be saved."

"Gimps, whether they're kings or not, cannot be saved, ever," said Scrooge.

"What? Never?"

"Well, hardly ever," said Scrooge. "And besides, you're not a king. You're a humbug."

"Hello," said Tiny Tim. "What's a humbug?"

"You're a humbug," said Scrooge. "Humbugs really don't want to be saved."

"God bless us everyone!" said Tiny Tim. "You're not my loving uncle Scrooge. You're the humbug."

"And you're not my gentle Tiny Tim," said Scrooge, now suddenly eating the roasted leg from a Christmas goose.

"I'm hungry," said Tiny Tim.

Scrooge went on eating, pausing only to hum a few bars of 'God Save the King.'

"Ask the beaver, ask the beaver," said Scrooge. "Peter and the beaver. Makes a good advertisement, don't you think? Peter and the beaver. They'll save you."

"You know they won't," said Tiny Tim. He began to cry again.

"Of course I know," said Scrooge. "The question is, do you?"

"I'm not a humbug," said Tiny Tim.

"No," said Scrooge. "You're a gimp."

"Why are you so unkind?" asked Tiny Tim, (who, of course, was wide awake).

"I? Unkind? That was the old Scrooge, not your uncle Scrooge."

"Which Scrooge are you now?" asked Tiny Tim.

"Which one do you think?" said Scrooge. "Let me give you a clue."

He smiled, and suddenly gold coins began flowing from his ears and nose, covering the ground everywhere except the bare patch on which Tiny Tim was standing.

"I saw nothing of the money, if that's what you mean," said Tiny Tim, picking up a few coins and throwing them on the blanket of his sleeping self.

Scrooge scowled again and resumed his Christmas goose. "I made provision for you in my will but foolishly depended on the good faith of your family to see it through."

"Then you are my good uncle Scrooge, after all. But I'm still hungry."

"None for you, none for you," said Scrooge, sticking the leg into his britches, like a pirate his pistol. Once again he started to hum, ascending just above Tiny Tim's sleeping self.

"You mustn't eat," said Scrooge. "The coach for Dover awaits."

"Let it wait," said Tiny Tim.

"You're on the road, nonetheless," said Scrooge.

"I don't want to go to Dover."

"God save the King!" said Scrooge.

"Besides," said Tiny Tim. "I'm a gimp. I can't make it."

"The coach!" said Scrooge.

"No coach and no Dover," said Tiny Tim.

"You're on the road, nonetheless'" said Scrooge.

"But not to Dover."

"Climb on my back," said Scrooge. "As in the good old days when you were little Tiny Tim."

"And you my good uncle Scrooge."

"You're on the road," said Scrooge. "But you can't eat yet. Pity it is, too, for this is the best goose in London. It's Cratchit's goose, do you remember?"

Tiny Tim began to cry again. "I remember," he said. "Somehow I knew it was you who sent it."

"And how did you know?" asked Scrooge. "I'll tell you. 'Twas your heart that spoke."

"And now it's Cratchit's Crutch," said Tiny Tim. "What shall I do with it, uncle Scrooge?"

"Throw it away, dear child. You won't need it this journey round. Better yet, bequeath it to the beaver. Let's be off."

Tiny Tim saw himself suddenly on Scrooge's shoulders. It occurred to his wakeful self that such a climb would have been fraught with terror and shame. He would have had to give Scrooge his crutch, then holding onto his waist, Tiny Tim would have had to swing himself round, hoisting himself onto Scrooge's back, reaching for his dead leg and throwing it over Scrooge's right shoulder. Then he would hoist himself further up onto Scrooge, easily slipping his good leg into Scrooge's hand which held his ankle securely. Then Scrooge would reach back the crutch to Tiny Tim, who would slip it round his arm. "Hold on, now," Scrooge would say. "Hold tight," and Tiny Tim would have been out of breath and ashamed at all the trouble he was giving. But now he saw himself so easily astride his benefactor, his ascent so effortless, so graceful, so secure, that for the first time he began to suspect the vision to be a dream.

Yet the ride on Scrooge's shoulders was just as he remembered it. Surely that couldn't be a dream. Nor could he be imagining the rush of wind in his face, and the occasional whimsy of snow playing about his eyes and ears. He could not be dreaming about the gentle bounce as he rode, or the sound of Scrooge's easy, careful tread, or his cold, visible breath or how he bent low, his face almost in a line with Scrooge's, as they went under an archway or how he tightened his grip and closed his eyes as Scrooge pretended to be heading directly into a wall.

"Where are we going, Uncle Scrooge?"

"To Banbury Cross to ride a stout horse."

"Where else, Uncle Scrooge?"

"To Paddington Station to hear an oration."

"Where else, Uncle Scrooge?"

"To Dover, to Dover, to die in the clover."

"Why Dover, Uncle Scrooge?"

"That's where the king is," said Scrooge.

"What king, Uncle Scrooge?"

"Why, Tiny Tim, the First."

"The first what, Uncle Scrooge?"

"The first gimp, of course. Tiny Tim, King of the Gimps."

"I don't want to go to Dover, Uncle Scrooge."

"You're on the road, nonetheless."

"I want to get down. I want to get off," said Tiny Tim.

"Hold on, now. Hold tight."

Scrooge was running, quickly gliding past shops and houses and courtyard gates and Tiny Tim was amazed how smoothly they went. He didn't feel the bounce or the wind; he needn't have held tight, for somehow his uncle Scrooge was being propelled by a force indifferent to the rules of gravity.

In as short a time as it took for the sleeping Tiny Tim to snuggle more deeply under his blanket, the wakeful Tiny Tim saw an ugly brick building looming just ahead. Years of wind and rain and London soot had darkened its walls and windows. Its overall gloom depressed and saddened him and he felt afraid.

"What is this place?" asked Tiny Tim.

"A place you've never seen but in which you've been living these many years." Scrooge pointed to a sign just above the gated portal and Tiny Tim could barely discern the faded inscription: "Dover Workhouse, Gimps Welcome."

"I don't know this place. I don't live here," said Tiny Tim, crying once again.

"You know it," said Scrooge. "You live in every room and sleep in every bed."

Suddenly the outer walls dissolved and they were within the dismal pile. Tiny Tim could see but indistinct shadows. Smoke billowed from unseen vents and noxious, acrid smells seared his lungs. He heard the squalls of colliding iron and the hollow thumps of wood on wood. His eyes watered, and the skin beneath his clothes began to itch.

He wasn't atop Scrooge's shoulders now. Scrooge in fact had vanished, but in the gloom Tiny Tim could just make out the crooked shapes of young boys hobbling about on crutches. Several were crawling along the floor picking up nails and bits of unknown refuse. Some sat wretchedly on high stools, their arms and hands covered with black as they smeared labels onto bottles of boot polish; some stood at low tables separating strands of rope. Tiny Tim heard a low groan, and turning his head saw a group of four small boys, nearly naked, sorting out shards of bones which periodically fell from a chute. Some began chewing them to get at marrow, while others simply pounded away at the shards with hammers too heavy for them.

"I don't live here," protested Tiny Tim.

"You do," said the voice of Scrooge. "You consigned yourself to its precincts long ago when you abdicated your self-respect and made peace with self-pity and cowardice."

"I don't belong in this place," cried Tiny Tim.

"In mind and spirit you are as much in thrall as they who labor here," said the voice.

"But what can I do?" said Tiny Tim.

"Why ask of me?" said the voice. "You are the King".

"I don't want to be king anymore." Tiny Tim was crying again.
"Come to terms," said the voice. "Come to terms."
Tiny Tim felt a chill. He looked about him, but the crippled boys and the workhouse, like Scrooge, had vanished, and suddenly he was looking upon his sleeping self twisting and turning in the blanket and he heard a bell toll and gazed upwards to see the snow falling and the lurching spire of St. Dunstan's and he realized he was awake and didn't know what time it was . . .

Stave 3: A Beggarly Enterprise

How long before or after midnight it was, Tiny Tim could not reckon. The street lamps gave off a smeared, cloudy glow and only an occasional lone figure hurried about, hunched and swaddled against the snow and gusty wind. A black dog gamboled aimlessly across the street, stopping once or twice to sniff the ground before moving on. The mongrel passed Tiny Tim without even looking up and our young man felt lonely. Sleep now would offer little solace this Christmas Eve. Urged by the solemn need for companionship, Tiny Tim took up his blanket and made his way past St. Dunstan's to what he perceived as a brightly lighted space just ahead. But as he hobbled toward the spot the bright light seemed to recede. For every step he took toward it, the light appeared two paces beyond; for every three steps, six, until Tiny Tim paused to catch his breath.

As he stood, fixing his crutch, the light suddenly shone in his midst with a brightness that forced him to shield his eyes. But in a trice the brightness dimmed and Tiny Tim looked about him to see a small, ramshackle structure that squatted crookedly before him. Oddly, the place itself seemed dark and brooding, but Tiny Tim could see flickering candle light in one window and he moved towards it. If he had expected the warmth of a friendly face or even the gladdening presence of a stranger, he could not have been more shocked and surprised at what he now beheld.

Seated at a long table facing the window brother Peter was thumbing a sheaf of papers. Standing beside him was that American with the beaver hat and the unruly eye, Sid Slymes.

"I'm tellin' you," Slymes was saying. "Tomorrow's Christmas, and puttin' dozens of cripples on every busy street would give us the jump on them charity people."

"You go too far, Mr. Slymes," said Peter.

"And you not far enough, Mr. Cratchit. That's why I come along when I did. "It's Providence, that what it is. A real act of Providence. Consider me sort of your guidin' spirit, meant to grease you through that tight little hole you call your conscience. I always said you was far too finicky, the kind of feller what makes "too fine a point of things."

"Scruples you mean, Mr. Slymes, scruples. I daresay, I mean to raise a few in this matter."

Slymes narrowed his eye; the other typically disobeyed and scampered about in its socket.

"You can't lay no scruples on a financial venture like this, my friend. As I sees it, it's whole hog or the manure pile, one or the other. Some men is born natural enterprisers. That's me. And some is born natural scarey cats. That's you."

"I don't know," said Peter, wavering. "It just doesn't seem right."

"All them pounds we put in the bank last week," said Slymes. "Didn't they seem right? Who did we kill? Nobody died and nobody knows nothin' to complain about."

Slymes watched as Peter made busy shuffling his papers. But as his partner said nothing Slymes thrust home:

"Tell you what," he said. "Let's trot them out here now. See how they do. And if you don't think they're good enough to put on the street tomorrow . . . "

"All right, all right," said Peter. "Let us proceed."

Slymes smiled and patted Peter on the back. "All right, fellers," he shouted. "Come out here and line up."

A door opened behind them and in filed dozens of boys, as if engorged London had spewed them out like so much refuse. All were small, perhaps eight or nine years old, and all seemed underfed and ill-used. Most were dirty ; none wore shoes.

Slymes gathered them in line. Then he stepped back and sat on the edge of the table, folding his arms.

"Now then," he began. "Who's for making half a quid tomorrow?"

"What's half a quid?" asked a very little boy in the front with a sooty face.

Slymes almost smiled. "What's your name, boy?"

"Fezziwig, sir. Winthrop Fezziwig."

"My, my," said Slymes. "What a precious fancy name. Where did you get a monicker like that?"

"I guess I was born with it, sir," said the boy, hanging his head. "They give it me at the orphanage."

"Here, here," said Peter. "Nothing to be ashamed of. I remember being told about an old Fezziwig family that used to be in business many, many years ago. Are you any relation?"

"I don't know, sir," said the boy.

"That don't matter," said Slymes. "Looky here. What do you weigh?"

"About three stone, sir."

Slymes turned to Peter. "How much is that in American?"

"A bit over 40 pounds," said Peter.

"Excuse me, sir," said the boy. "My old master said I was the best chimney sweep in all London. I could do it for you sir, even if I don't know what half a quid is. I never seen half a quid."

Slymes tried to smile but produced only a sneer.

"That don't matter, none," he said. "We got no innerest in chimineys. Can you gimp?"

"Sir?"

"Can you hobble? If I give you this here crutch, and you tuck it under your arm . . ."

"Left or right, sir?"

"That don't matter, neither. All you need to do is stick this here crutch under your arm, hobble around a bit and then when you see some folks passin' by on their way to church or dinner just stick out your hand and tilt your head and cry, ' A guinea for a poor lad, sir? Shillings for the orphan?"

"Here, that's too much," shouted Peter.

"What now, Mr. Cratchit? Another bout of scruples?"

"I only meant the guinea, Mr. Slymes. It's too much to expect a chap to give a guinea."

"Why, it's Christmas, Mr. Cratchit. Have you no faith in your fellow man?"

"I have faith," said Peter, "But not for a guinea. A shilling, perhaps."

"OK, OK," said Slymes, resorting in his desperation to the use of that ghastly American expression. "Let's say a shilling. Look, Fezzi, watch me."

Slymes pushed away from the table. Grabbing a special Cratchit crutch which he had brought for the purposes of these training exercises, he placed it under his arm—the left one, of course—and proceeded to hobble along the floor, occasionally wincing in mock pain, his maverick orb drunk with play. Every six or seven feet he thrust out his hand and twisted his head, looking up at an envisioned passerby. "Please sir, something for the poor. Merry Christmas, sir. God bless you, sir."

Even Peter was impressed.

"Now," said Slymes to little Fezziwig. "You try."

The little boy took a little crutch—the Cratchit #4—and hobbled around the room.

"Too fast," said Slymes. "Slow down a bit and give off a few more winces."

The boy did well, even improvising a few stifled groans. Slymes was well-pleased.

"Be here tomorrow morning at six," he said. "And don't eat breakfast. It'll look all the better." All the better, too, for Slymes, who had no intention of offering any.

"Who's next?"

"I know what half a quid is, sir," said a thin boy at the end of the line.

"Is that so?" said Slymes. "Tell me, what's your trade?"

"Newsboy, sir."

"Fine," said Slymes. "Go peddle your papers. Next!"

Through the window Tiny Tim watched as one by one the congregation of boys was interviewed, tried and chosen, a most bedraggled and hopeless group as he had ever seen. Slymes gave each of them a farthing which they most greedily snatched at and ordered their return next morning sharply at six.

"By the way," he said, as they were leaving. "No Christmas gear tomorrow. Don only your worst-looking duds."

He needn't have worried, of course, for the boys, one and all, had only the rags they wore over their bones.

When they were gone Slymes sat at the table with his partner and sighed.

"Tomorrow bodes well," he said. "What do you think?"

"I think my brother would be ashamed of us," Peter said.

"Your brother is well out of it now," said Slymes. "Or better be. And anyhow, he's the one what oughta be ashamed, the puppy. If he was young enough he'd have made an extra boy tomorrow, and a good one, for nothing like the real thing when all is said and done. Then again I wonder how good he'd really be. The trouble with your brother is that he 'aint a beggar by trade but inclination."

"What do you mean, Mr. Slymes?"

"I mean he aint got no pride in his work. You take these boys here. They aint beggars because they want to be. But they beg with all their natural strength because it's what they gotta do. Your brother really believes he's a beggar; he wants to be a beggar; he acts and feels and thinks like a beggar; he enjoys being a beggar. No point in being ashamed of yourself Mr. Cratchit, compared to the likes of him, your brother. Why, with all these gimps on the streets tomorrow the charity business will prove a noble trade. Us who get, it makes rich, and them who give, it makes holy. And so we both of us prosper. The sound of coin on one end and the odor of sanctity on the other; you can't do no better than that for a business! Why, old Queen Vic herself should give you and me thanks and guarantee it with a knighthood."

"I wonder where Tiny Tim is now," said Peter.

"Don't fret none," said Slymes. "He's better off feelin' sorry for himself and stayin' out of the way. Think of all the money we'll fetch tomorrow. By the way, Merry Christmas."

Slymes laughed heartily, and his rampant eye became delirious.

Suddenly the candle light went out, as if quenched by an invisible hand, and the window fell dark.

"I'm not a beggar at heart!" shouted Tiny Tim through the window. "I'm not a beggar! I'm not!" But by now even the shack had disappeared and he heard only a low sob of wind. In the next instant all was darkness.

Stave 4: An Angel

Had any passerby been within earshot of Tiny Tim's desperate cry, "I'm not a beggar, I'm not," he may also have been close enough to hear our hero mutter, "and I'm not a cripple, either!" But the stern reality was that when Tiny Tim opened his eyes to daylight he found himself as of former times: there he was under his blanket by St. Dunstan's, and there was his box on the bottom of which lay a pence or two; and there was his crutch leaning against the wall. So nothing had changed. Nothing except the bells, pealing with what seemed to him an impertinent insistence all over the city. The day was overcast, yet the bells rang out happily. People rushed by with smiles on their faces and lightness in their gaits. One fellow in shiny new boots and ruddy cheeks gaily tossed a sovereign into Tiny Tim's box, and the dog that only yesterday had loped indifferently passed him now licked his face as he lay. Even at this early hour the street was full of life and good cheer.

Then it struck him that it was Christmas Day and the utter despair of his life came home to him in a flash. "But I'm not a beggar!" he said to himself, and yet, in all candor, he could hardly convince himself that he was not. The vision of Slymes and his school for professional beggars festered overnight in Tiny Tim's mind, leaving him shaken and angry, uncertain of a course of action. He realized that all the affirmations, and all the declarations and all the self-proclamations born of insincerity and doubt were not enough in one's lifetime to alter the shape of even a single snowflake. Yet he was determined to a course of renewal. If he could do nothing about the lameness of his body, was there not a way by which he could at least minister to the palsy of his mind? And so the process by which all men and women eventually come to themselves now began to take shape for Tiny Tim.

But there was another shape, as well, tangible and real, like the morning. It loomed at first as a vague, indistinct verge of color and movement, and he saw it gliding quickly among the passersby, walking with deliberate speed as if certain of its destination. His heart beat rapidly as a seed of recognition sprouted, and as the figure crossed the street and seemed to be approaching him, his throat caught in joy as he watched his beautiful angel pause beside him and smile timidly. Agnes! Agnes Freake! It was, indeed, she!

She stood before him in all her ravishing beauty. Her golden tresses curled luxuriously from below the edge of her bonnet; her eyes shone a clear deep blue and her lips were full, framing a face of calm determination and spirit. What kindly fate could have directed her steps to him? How could she possibly have known of his love for her? He had told no one, keeping her name and her holy image locked in the tabernacle of his heart. Certainly Agnes herself could not have divined his secret, for how many times had she passed this very spot beneath St. Dunstan's tower and went quickly away, as if here were some repellent creature without a soul, without longing, without feelings. Even that day when he stooped to assist her with her parcels, she had simply hurried on, indifferent, offering no thanks, tendering no comfort or encouragement. He remembered thinking then that even her scorn would have served as some small, halting recognition of his existence, giving him the blessed guerdon of hope.

And yet, here now she stood, his Agnes. O, if there were a power of redemption in the gaze of female eyes, in the touch of female hands, then surely his own salvation was nigh! She would be the instrument of his restoration!

Tiny Tim straightened his rags and brushed back his unkempt hair from his face. Agnes looked at the ground nervously. Several moments passed between them in silence. Tiny Tim felt it his place to begin.

"Welcome!" he said, clearing his throat.

"I've no money," Agnes said, her voice a silken thread.

"I'm not a beggar . . . anymore." said Tiny Tim.

"I'm gratified to hear you say so," said Agnes. "Perhaps appearances are deceptive."

"No," said Tiny Tim. "Not deceptive. But changeable."

Agnes was clearly uncomfortable, reluctant, and Tiny Tim was never so aware of being ashamed as he was now, watching his angel accommodating her feelings to whatever necessity had brought her to him. He sensed an urgency behind her visit.

"I have come on a specified mission," she said.

"I wish you had said that you came by the promptings of your own heart," said Tiny Tim.

"You are impertinent, sir. I do not know you. The promptings of my own heart have little to do with my mission here."

"So much the worse for me," said Tiny Tim.

"I think not, sir. You will at the very least come away with a good meal."

"Ah, another benevolent soul engaged in the charity business," said Tiny Tim. Almost immediately he repented his sarcasm. Never could he associate Agnes with the shams of Slymes and company. And Agnes certainly sensed Tiny Tim's struggle between the poles of trust and incredulity.

"Why do you doubt anyone's good intentions? Why do you so doubt mine? You claim to be a beggar only in appearance, but your cold heart is real enough."

"My heart was warm when I was a child," said Tiny Tim. "My benefactor was a kindly man, and a generous one."

"Then why do you doubt anyone else could be so?"

"My benefactor died some years ago," said Tiny Tim. "And since his death I have seen only a world of greed and meanness."

"It has not been my world," said Agnes. "I feel sorry for you. But I can say no more. I offer you an opportunity. Will you come?"

"An opportunity for what?" asked Tiny Tim.

"Will you come?"

"Why me?"

Agnes did not answer. Quickly she thrust a card into Tiny Tim's hand, then abruptly turned, crossing the street and disappearing into the crowd now filling the square.

His angel was gone! As quickly as she had come to him she vanished, taking with her those few moments of felicity. He gazed at the card, regarding it with an awe akin to a knight's wonderment at the holy grail. His vision seemed to falter as he read the inscription: "Thaddeus Osbourne Freake, Esq., A.B, M.A. LLD., KCB, KG, KCI E,

KCSI, CVO, OM
Chuzzlewit Court
Gads Hill"

Tiny Tim puzzled over the inscription. Who was this Thaddeus Osbourne Freake? Her father, perhaps? Her guardian? Was she, like himself, perhaps, an orphan, adopted by this man of many initials? And why did he seek out, through the agency of Agnes, a poor beggar such as he, and a cripple to boot? At that moment Tiny Tim remembered his avowal that morning. He was not a beggar! Despite circumstances, despite appearances, his dream of Scrooge, his vision of Slymes and this present visitation from his Agnes, all confirmed him in his resolve to change those things that could be changed, to alter those conditions of mind and spirit that could be altered. He would do it, and he would start now, this instant!

The process began, oddly enough, with still another appearance. As Tiny Tim gathered up his box and folded his blanket, his gaze took him across the street where the figure of a pitiful little lame boy hobbled about. It was Winthrop Fezziwig, and he was begging with all the ingenious pathos as prescribed by Sid Slymes. He grimaced, he groaned, he pronounced "God bless you, sir" with studied but convincing sincerity.

Here, indeed, was an opportunity. He could begin his personal reformation by helping little Fezziwig retrieve his own. If charity begins at home, thought Tiny Tim, certainly redemption continues into your neighbor's yard.

Picking up his crutch, Tiny Tim made his way toward little Fezziwig, noticing as he did so that for the first time he could remember his bad leg seemed somehow stronger, less cumbersome.

"You there, Fezziwig!" beckoned Tiny Tim.

Fezziwig hobbled over, his Cratchit Crutch #4 as serviceable as ever.

"A little something for the poor, sir? A shilling? A quid? God bless you, sir. Merry Christmas."

"Fezziwig," said Tiny Tim. "You've learned your art too well. Are you so deeply schooled and so tender of age as to be incapable of shame?"

"I'm too hungry to be ashamed," said Fezziwig. "And too tired. And now I know what half a quid is."

"A poor bit of knowledge in exchange for the loss of dignity," said Tiny Tim.

Was this the same fellow who but a few hours ago held forth below the steeple of St. Dunstan's? Was this the same whose own dignity was smothered amid self-pity and indifference?

"Walk-er" said Fezziwig.

"If it's hungry you are," said Tiny Tim, "I know a place where you can eat to your heart's content, and it'll cost you little of your self-respect."

"Mr. Slymes, will he be there, sir?"

"I hope to God, no," said Tiny Tim. "Your tutelage to that rascal is at an end. This place we are going to is not for men like him."

"Where is it? Will they give us half a quid?"

"Neither you nor I are beggars anymore", said Tiny Tim. "Never again! Drop your crutch, Fezziwig, and follow me."

Stave 5: The Feast

The Christmas Day sovereign thrown into Tiny Tim's box by the gentleman in a shiny new boots was just the thing. It purchased for Tiny Tim and his little ally a temporary rehabilitation in a form of a hot bath for both of them and an additional shave and grooming for Tiny Tim. The barber had to be cajoled into opening his little shop above which he, his wife and brood crowded about each other in their expectations of Christmas cheer, but he was a charitable soul in all seasons, and especially generous at this time of year, so that the sovereign was enough even for the refilling of the tub after the first bath and for an extra dollop of pomade.

"I smell like flowers," observed little Fezziwig.

Gads Hill was on the other side of London, but it might as well have been on the far side of the moon. Tiny Tim had never seen such an elegant configuration of brick, stone and glass, sitting on the crown of a hill, enclosed by an iron fence and embowered by concrete urns and naked fauns. Once inside the gate he and Fezziwig were let in by a frowning manikin in a white powdered wig and green silk who conveyed them to a room bright with mirrors and candelabra and a blazing fire in the hearth. The mantel was strewn with holly, the walls festooned with wreaths. A towering evergreen glimmered with a thousand candles in the middle of the floor. Tiny Tim had heard of such a tree being installed in the palace by the Prince Consort to good Queen Victoria, but this paragon of light and cheer was like nothing he could ever envision.

And then Agnes appeared, wafting in with a rustle of silk, the most beautiful creature that Tiny Tim had ever seen.

"You and your friend are welcome," she said.

She led Tiny Tim past the tree and through a pair of richly paneled doors which opened to another room. From here they proceeded through another, and still another, Tiny Tim all the while feeling stronger as he followed closely upon the heels of his guide. Finally Agnes paused before finely gilded portals. Entering, Tiny Tim and his little friend beheld a magnificent space, a dining room set for a banquet, the table piled high with the delights of the season. There was a great piece of Cold Roast and there was a great piece of Cold Boil. There were turkey and goose and jolly mince pies and pyramids of apples and pears. There were bunches of grapes hanging from silver hooks and figs regaling gold-rimmed platters and brown-throated filberts piled in bowls filigreed in pearl. Negus steamed from china mugs and oranges garnished a ruby punch housed in crystal. And there were multitudes of confections in all shapes and sizes and colors, and cakes and gingerbread and honeyed tarts.

You may well imagine Tiny Tim's stupefaction. Amid this rich, delicious treasure, he felt like the thief in Ali Baba's Cave. And most astonishing of all, presiding at the head of the table, smiling broadly, was Ali Baba himself, the gentleman of the Christmas sovereign, he of the ruddy cheeks and the shiny new boots! So this was none other than Thaddeus Osbourne Freake, etc., etc.

As if in a trance Tiny Tim sat at the table. To his delight Agnes chose the seat beside him, while little Fezziwig was invited to sit next to Ali Baba himself. Can you conceive, reader, with what delicacy, with what refinement Tiny Tim engaged the feast ?

In his life as a beggar, Tiny Tim had often confronted hunger as a monstrous beast, and now it fiercely clawed and mauled at him as one by one the dishes made the rounds of the table. But hunger no matter how wild, hunger no matter how savage, was not enough to tear apart the image of himself he sought to present to Agnes Freake. And so he picked, he tasted, he nibbled, he chewed delicately with politic, dignified grace, like a member of parliament supping with the King. He wiped his lips after each bite and patted them dry after each sip, keeping his napkin folded by his side.

Agnes, meanwhile, was not indifferent to his reserve. As if she understood and deeply appreciated his restraint, she ate more heartily than he, showing him the value of candor and natural honesty. Tiny Tim began to feel at ease. He noticed how little Fezziwig was eating voraciously, gobbling up the feast like a miser his gold, while Thaddeus Osbourne Freake, etc. etc. laughed lavishly and showed him how to use a fork.

"Your father seems to be taking an interest in my friend, Fezziwig," Tiny Tim observed.

"As he has taken in you. Did you see him early this morning?"

"I did," said Tiny Tim. "He walked quickly by without a glance, leaving a sovereign, and I thanked him in my heart for his generosity."

"You yourself mocked generosity like his when I first spoke to you only this morning," she said.

"I was wrong," said Tiny Tim. "Not so much about your father's motives in particular. My life has been hard, but I realize now that my hardships were the result of my own self-pity."

"Is that what you meant when you said you were not a beggar anymore? That you could change?"

"I have changed," said Tiny Tim. "And from today on I shall try to prove it."

"To my father," said Agnes.

"To your father, yes. But more especially to you"

"You can prove it to me by justifying my father's faith in you."

"In me? Who is your father?"

"He is a great man," said Agnes. "Like you he was once a cynic, trusting no one, believing that life was a sordid affair. He served the queen in India for many years, regarding his native charges as grimy little beasts. But then he came under the influence of Swami Baharumi Patel-Singh, a man of wondrous powers and as virtuous a heathen as there ever was. Swami taught my father the value of even the most wretched life. No man is worthless. Not even a fly is worthless. Father said that Swami told him once that a man might have been a toad in a previous life, or a mosquito, and that the same man might become a dung beetle or a genius in the cycle to come. I don't know if I believe that. I don't know if Father believes it. But the fact that a heathen like Swami could value life in any form was enough to change Father for good."

"I know I have changed for good," said Tiny Tim. "It was a heathen of sorts that brought me to my senses, though he was American."

"Was he the benefactor of whom you spoke?"

"He was not, thank God. But I dreamed of my benefactor last night, a horrible dream, though it did me some good, I daresay. He, too, though long dead, has brought about the beginning of my reclamation."

"And Father, let us hope, will assist in that endeavor. A great example he learned in India, as I started to tell you. Swami had a habit of inviting two of the most scrofulous beggars to his table. I believe the Hindoos call them the Unclean, or the Unwashed. Swami was poor. He had nothing. But once a year he invited the most miserable of beings to share whatever he had. It was a lesson in virtue that impressed Father immensely, and after he made his fortune here he set aside Christmas as his Day of the Two, as he likes to call it. This year he asked me to pick the most disgusting creature I met with, and naturally I thought of you."

"Thank you, very much," said Tiny Tim with a smile. "But I suppose before today I was the most likely candidate for such an honor. Yet I see only myself here, and Fezziwig whom you did not invite. You spoke of the 'Two'."

"Yes," said Agnes. "I suppose you can call that part of it a test. We invited you alone but you did not think only of yourself. You brought another, thus effecting his reclamation as well."

"But how did you know I would bring him? And how can you know the purity of my motive?"

"We didn't and we can't," said Agnes. "But we had faith. And anyhow, does it really matter in the end? As I said to you this morning, at the very least you would have had a good meal."

"And so now it appears I have more than that," said Tiny Tim.

More than that, indeed! And, Dear Reader, what more is there to be said? Tiny Tim had changed, proving his reformation as much in deed as in word and proving his love for Agnes as well. Like all true reformations, a change in his heart and mind effected an improvement in his body, and his leg began slowly to grow stronger until that day he walked down the aisle with Agnes, for the first time in his life needing only a cane. He read law with his new father-in-law and in the course of time became a barrister and finally a judge, seeing his children's children and becoming in his will benefactor of a new handicapped children's hospital.

As for little Winthrop Fezziwig, he became the ward of Thaddeus Osbourne Freake, A.B, M.A., etc, etc. and when he came of age went to Paris, learning to become a chef, eventually buying a restaurant in Monmartre which he named Chez Fez.

And what of Sid Slymes? With the help of his father-in-law, Tiny Tim brought the American to justice. He was sent back to the States where word has it he settled in the wilds of Arkansas and became an itinerant preacher, discovering to his delight that religion paid almost as much as crime. He took with him his old partner Peter Cratchit, but we know little else about his fate.

But let us not concern ourselves with the fates or destinations of those for whom Christmas has little meaning or the season little value. Let us, instead, rejoice in the true spirit of the holiday. Let us celebrate it, as had Tiny Tim and Scrooge before him, as a time for good fellowship, a time for miracles and dreams and wonderment, a time for hope, peace and love.

Finis

How an Emperor Helped Lorenzo Da Ponte Get to America

This one foreigner come aboard. Navigating by starlight, you might say. Only a hard paper box cocked under one arm, the other hand clutching the damnedest cane I ever saw. Worth his passage by itself, I reckoned, though naturally I didn't let on at first. The head looked to be solid gold. He treated it with such landlubberly tenderness. I knew right off this must have been his first time at sea, else he would have stowed it with his other valuables—not that he had much, as I was to find out—so that it wouldn't get ruinous salty when we run into rough water. Made me suspicious, like he wasn't quite respectable. Respectable passengers on my ship stow their goods below and never wear their fancy duds on deck once we leave sight of land and it commences to blow. But this foreign fellow was different. He wore this one outfit every day, clean but mended all over and kind of old.

But it wasn't just the stick or the clothes or his gear that made me take notice. And it wasn't his scared, uneasy look. The quick reason was that he wasn't on the passenger list. The agent had informed me of only nine passengers. There was a liquor merchant, a widow and her dead husband—he came in a box stowed in the hold—and half a dozen regular gents who make this cross twice a year to take a sounding of their investments in New York. But there was no poet on the list. That's what he told me he was, a poet.

"Well, Mr. Italiano," I said. I forget his name now, but whenever he came on deck afterwards, I always called him Mr. Italiano because of the raggedy, female-like English he talked in. "Well, Mr. Italiano, how do you expect to find quarters aboard when I don't have you down on my manifest, hey?"

He bowed, looked me straight in the eye. Told me he hadn't time to bespeak his passage from the agent. Said he had decided quickly to go to America because there was no opportunity for good poets in Europe now, especially in England. He would take his chances in the new world. I don't recollect if I believed him. He didn't look like the kind of fellow who took many chances, only the right ones. I never knew nobody crossed the Atlantic on a whim unless he was a fool. And this fellow was no fool, though he must have thought I was, as you'll learn.

"You can't sail without the fare," I says. "I'm not running a fugitive ship. If you have spite against England you'll have to settle it ashore. If not, it'll cost you forty guineas."

He puts down his box and then glances about for a secure place for that stick of his. He leans it against the taffrail, then fetches about in the box and takes out what appears to be a letter or some official-looking document. It had a fancy ribbon on it and was written pretty.

"Look here," he says, as if he's about to recite something. "This is a proclamation from your President."

And sure enough, he commences to read, like one of them actors in a play:

"To whom it may concern and greetings: The bearer of this is an honorable man, a poet and esteemed gentleman, inured to the comforts, delights and privileges rightfully bestowed on his person by gracious majesties in sundry European courts. I shall consider myself deeply obliged if you show him all the courtesy and respect due a man of his extraordinary parts. Yours, Sir Thomas Jefferson, President of America."

He looked confidently at me, as if expecting I would fall at his feet and beg him take my cabin. But I came upwind of him and hit him broadside:

"And what am I supposed to think of that, hey?" I say. "Thom Jefferson can heave full sail across his own seas, but I'm the President of this ship!"

"But this is your own President!" yammers Mr. Italiano, waving the document, making sure I could see the seal and ribbon.

"Even the President needs forty guineas to take passage, my friend."

I reckon that if President Jefferson himself ever did board the Columbia I would carry him for free, just for the honor of the thing, you understand. But this Italiano fellow riled me, so confident was he that I could be so easily gulled. He had better learn that documents of this sort—"oblige me and bow, etc."—may work in Europe, but they don't amount to a skiff's ballast over here. I expect Mr. Italiano will find that out soon enough.

Mr. Italiano shook his head and muttered something in his native lingo. Then he fetches up another letter with more pretty writing. "This is from the Emperor," he says.

"What emperor?" I say.

"Joseph," he says, like I had done him some grievous wrong. "His Majesty, Sovereign Ruler of Austria and the Holy Roman Empire."

"Ah," I says. "*That* emperor! Forty guineas, if you please!"

Still another letter bobs up, from some duke or other, commending Mr. Italiano to my good will.

"Forty guineas," I say.

Italiano was working up a sweat now, and I'll admit I was beginning to enjoy his discomfort.

"I suppose you've tried all this on Mr. Priestly,"—he was the agent—"It didn't work with him, neither."

"Captain," said Italiano. "I regret that men of such high repute like me command so little respect from men like you. I must get to America, but I shall not grovel. I haven't got forty guineas."

"What have you got?" I said. I had already decided to put him off, but was having fun watching him squirm. I hate these foreigners who lack humbleness and think they're better than us, especially fellows like this who want to pay with their useless education instead of with good hard cash. Just then my eyes went to the taffrail where Mr. Italiano had reposed his walking stick. The fellow must have seen me looking at it because he spoke right out: "I cannot part with that."

"That's hardly worth forty guineas," I says, shrewdly.

He stood quiet, fixing his eyes on the rigging.

"Well," I says. "What's it to be? Either you've got forty guineas worth of goods or it's England for you."

Italiano snorted in disgust, shook his head and reached inside his coat. Fetching a faded green purse, he opened it and counted out six coins in his palm.

"I can spare only these," he says. An ill assortment of Austrian, French and English pieces, they was. I suspect he was trying to confuse me with their different values. I sensed that he had more real money about him and told him so.

"What little I have is for America," he says. "I need to live, to start a business if need be. These you may have."

"That's white of you, Mr. Italiano. Give them to Sir Thomas when you see him. What else you got?"

Into that paper box again. This time he takes out a couple of books, holds them up, looks at me. I look back at him, say nothing. He puts them back, scrabbles around, brings out a handkerchief folded over. It looks like pure lace, all fancy work around the edges. I remember seeing one like that on some English milord who made a crossing several years ago. Brought six traveling cases aboard, so help me, all stowed in his cabin, so I don't know where he could have slept. But that was his pleasure, I'd say, since he paid his fare and didn't try to unload some flotsam on me like Mr. Italiano here.

He begins to unfold the handkerchief and holds up a medal, not real gold, but with a nice red and green ribbon.

"This is from the Emperor himself," he says. "A testimonial to my poetic gifts."

I take a good gander at it but it don't look like it's worth no forty guineas so I give it back. "I guess it's England for you, my man," I say.

"Listen," he says. "I won't be humiliated. I am a true poet. Unused to this kind of haggling, I see now that you have your own code. If I'm to thrive in my new life I'll have to learn it."

"There's no 'code', as you call it," I say. "Pay as you go. It's forty guineas and no haggling."

I had just about had my fill of Mr. Italiano and was about to ask the mate to put him off when he plunges into his box again and fetches up a red case. At first I think he's tying to bribe me with a box of fine see-gars, seeing him caressing the case, like it was a pet.

"This is my final treasure," he says. "My only tangible claim that the world once acknowledged me as a great poet."

"It had better be worth forty guineas," I say.

"'O Tempora! O Mores!'", he says, shaking his head.

He holds the case like he was about to present me with a choice see-gar, like I said. But it turns out that when he raises the lid all I see is half a dozen tiny spoons staring back at me.

"The Emperor Joseph, may he rest in peace, personally presented me with these," he says.

I guess he must have seen my sour expression because he quickly adds, "Solid silver."

Now I didn't want to appear too anxious to jump at his offer. I wasn't so sure at this point that the spoons were worth the price of passage. They were too small to be of any use, unless you were only three feet tall and had a head the size of an apple. On the other hand, they may have a certain draw for Mr. Peale's collection of curiosities. In the next instant I calculated that the spoons would bring forty or fifty guineas in England, maybe more in America.

"Well," I says. "How do I know they're real silver?"

"Do you doubt a personal gift from the Emperor would be anything less?"

"I never knowed the Emperor," I says. "And how can I be sure that the Emperor himself knowed they were silver?"

Oh, Captain Grunge, I says to myself, you are a sly one, you are! No landlubber could steal upwind of you!

Just then Mr. Italiano slams down the lid and makes to go.

"You are a caffone," he says.

"Tell you what," I say—I knew I had him—"I'll give you passage in exchange for these spoons, but you're a few guineas short. Throw in that walking stick and I'll settle the difference with the owners."

I see Mr. Italiano widen his eyes and turn down his mouth.

"I cannot do that," he says. "This was given to me by a man whose genius was very nearly equal to my own. His gratitude and affection for me sprang from motives of respect that you could not possibly appreciate."

"Take it or leave it," I say.

"I will leave it," he says. "There must be at least one ship for America with no pirates at the helm."

"No use getting mad," I say. "Business is business. I'll give you passage for the spoons. You can keep your stick, but if you want victuals it'll cost you extra."

Here Mr. Italiano just about gives up. I watch as he reaches into his coat pocket and pulls out his purse. He opens it, grabs my hand, and empties the purse into it. Then he shakes the purse once or twice to show me his money's all gone.

"You've ruined me!" he says.

"Here," I says, giving him an Austrian coin. "I'm not a mercinous fellow. Welcome aboard!"

*   *   *

Da Ponte's Tale: The Story of the Masked Lady, A.D. 1770

Have you seen Venice? She is a beautiful city, though at the time of which I am speaking she was wrapped in the chills and damps of November. I was a young man, brash and full of myself, and one drizzly evening after midnight found myself shivering beneath a light blanket I had hastily thrown over my shoulders while making my escape. I see by your face that you are puzzled, but allow me, please, to tell this in my own way.

I was standing, then, by the canal, a faint mist falling. In the darkness every sound was amplified by the water, the mist, and the stone walls of the prison behind me. One of those sounds was of a gondola; I could hear it breaking the water in my direction, and though I couldn't see clearly I waved frantically at it. The gondolier no doubt would have ignored my distress and kept on, but I heard a man's voice from the boat telling the gondolier to head in.

"What is the trouble, signore?" the voice called.

Under the circumstances I thought it wise to be honest rather than discreet.

"The State Inquisitors," I said. "But I am innocent."

"Of course," said the voice. "Get in."

Quickly I wrapped myself in the blanket and leaped, so lustily, I admit, that the gondolier had all he could do to keep the boat from tipping. Taking a seat opposite my rescuer I sat in silence as the gondola made its way down the canal toward, of all places, the old Jewish quarter, the Ghetto. For a few minutes neither of us spoke. I huddled in my blanket, against the chill, while my rescuer, wrapped in a hooded cloak and wearing a cocked hat, looked off toward the looming black mass of the old synagogue to our right.

Suddenly he said, "Damn the Inquisitors. I can drop you anywhere along the way."

Still I kept quiet. What was I to tell him? I had lost my rooms, had little money and had no immediate prospects. If the truth be told, I had had so little success in the world that I would have floated down the canal indefinitely.

By now the haze and mist were starting to lift and I began to make out another figure sitting under a canopy alongside my rescuer. Elegantly swathed in a fur-lined cape and wearing a mask was the form of a woman. Even in the speckled darkness amid the glimmering water-lights that glinted about her, I could guess that she was young and perhaps beautiful, though as for that, her beauty was as much the result of the mystery that surrounded her as of my own emotional tumult. In any case, I saw her smile and suddenly tug at my rescuer's sleeve. To me, at that moment, her voice, when it sounded, was honeyed gold:

"Uncle," she said. "He is rather young to be of concern to the inquisitors." And then to me: "Are you a poet, young sir?"

You may be sure I was astounded. How had this creature known that I, this bedraggled fellow, shivering beneath a prison blanket, was a poor, unknown poet? Was she a witch, a sorceress for whom the night was like the day to ordinary mankind? I must tell you that Venice half a century ago was in many ways a most unenlightened state. Unlike here in America, which is too young and too busy to invest in delusion, Venice was a city ripe with fantasy. Superstition floated buoyantly in the very canals, and the most learned magnificos were afflicted with a belief in magic and all sorts of mystic mummery. Like a kind of malaria, it infected everyone.

"Poets are the current interest to the Council of Ten these days," the uncle said. "We are just returning from the opera and one of those sharing our box spent the better part of an hour describing the elaborate plotting—or it plodding?—of the council in tracking down loose tongues and indiscreet versifiers."

I spoke now only to protest: "I suppose I should be flattered that they regard me as important enough to warrant their interest. But I have no politics."

"Everyone's got politics in Venice. That doesn't matter in the least, my good fellow. Young poets like you are good object lessons. A few months, a year or two in prison, and you are let go, shriven of your unclean verses forever."

By now we were arriving at my rescuer's destination and I was quick to help the niece out of the boat. I recall how firmly she held my arm, as if long used to such courtesies. I was already imagining myself standing awkwardly outside the palazzo while they bid me good night, perhaps slipping me a ducat or two as they went about their business and henceforth putting me out of their minds. So you could readily conceive my astonishment when I saw the niece whisper something to her uncle and heard him invite me into the house.

I need not describe the faded grandeur of the place. In retrospect, I should have noted the significance of their not having any servants to look after us; my suspicions should have been aroused by the aura of dust, the vague atmosphere of decay that hovered about. Even the location of the place itself, just outside the Ghetto, should have schooled me to be wary. But I was too excited, too impressed, and, yes, too young, to have any mundane observations spoil the adventure.

Indeed, no one came to assist us with our cloaks (though I had an old blanket, you'll remember) except a humped-back beldam who walked with a limp. She it was who must have lit the fire which was blazing in the hearth. During all this time the beautiful niece continued to wear her mask; even as we warmed ourselves her face shone eerily behind her vizard of plain green silk embroidered about the eye slits with what appeared to be black serpents

But if I was surprised that she still hid her features from me, imagine my consternation when, without ceremony, she took a candle and grabbed me gently by the arm. "You must be tired, signor. Let me show you to your room."

Truly, I was fatigued, but now that I had felt the air of freedom and the warmth of a fire, I was beginning also to feel the pangs of hunger. I could hear my stomach snarling, and I almost would have put myself back into the hands of the inquisitors for a cup of hot soup. It was not to be, however. I followed my benefactress up the cold, narrow stairs into a room as chilly as my prison garret. Like my cell, the room had only one small window that looked onto the face of a blackened synagogue.

"I am sorry there is no fire," she said. "Get into bed quickly and you'll keep warm. Good night." When the door closed behind her I found myself in deep darkness.

The next day I was awakened by an unceremonious hammering on the door. I had slept fitfully, just below the verge, dreaming of my masked creature, clutching the bars of her cell—my cell in the prison—and singing a song about a cold fire and a lame old hump-back. It was, to be sure, the old woman who had been knocking, and my first thought, oddly, was how the wretched creature could climb those stairs to awaken a stranger.

Downstairs, the man whom I recognized as my savior—the uncle—was sitting on the sunlit edge of what passed as a balcony off

a little room facing the canal. He was seated at table, eating some
bread smeared with what I first thought was a kind of preserve but
which I soon discovered was olive oil, slightly rancid, sprinkled
with black pepper. He was sipping chocolate. Looking back now,
some forty years ago, that little dejeuner, poor as it was, seemed a
kingly sup!

He beckoned me to sit. He offered, and I ate. We talked little,
and I had the distinct impression that he was waiting for me to
finish—or, perhaps, for the entrance of his niece. I had just finished
my third piece of stale bread and my second cup of chocolate when
the niece made her appearance.

I had been wondering about her during breakfast, picturing
what she would look like, imagining how her beautiful eyes would
sparkle in the sunlight. But I was to be disappointed. She came
before us in a modest dressing gown, somewhat frayed about the
shoulders, but carefully brushed to look fresh. She was smaller,
more delicate, frailer than she had looked the night before.

But what was stranger yet—she was still wearing her mask!

What was the perverse secret she was trying to hide? What
hideous disfigurement lay behind the green mask of embroidered
serpents? Was she indeed a witch to whom the light of day was a
poison? Or was she—a possibility even more exciting to a young
man's sensibilities—a cruel coquette, proclaiming a novel, lurid
postulate to the arts of love?

"I hope you slept well, signor," said she, advancing to the table
where an empty chair marked her place, out of the sunlight.

Without waiting for an answer, she sat and ate quickly, like
Cinderella expecting at any moment her coach to vanish. The old
lady brought another pot of chocolate. We sat for some time in
awkward silence before my masked lady spoke again. She asked my
name, and when I told her she declared herself to be Constanza
Varesi, niece of Domenico Varesi, her guardian. Then, as if to shift
attention:

"I know this mask puzzles you," she said. "And displeases."

"I am as displeased as any man has a right to be who is forbidden
to look on the face of an angel," I said.

I can well credit your smiling at this response, but you must
remember that I was very young. As one who featured himself
a poet, I was naturally also a gentleman and irresistibly gallant.
Under the circumstances I should expect to be forgiven such
foppery. Besides, under those same circumstances, what was I to do?
Should I be discourteous to my rescuers by insolently demanding

she remove the mask? Even more stupidly, should I take insult and storm out? No. Young as I was, foolish as I was, I understood my obligation to allow a woman in her own house to determine her own conduct.

"You know," she said. "The followers of Mohammed believe that a woman should hide her face from public eyes."

"You are, then, a follower of Mohammed?"

She smiled. "Like you, I am a Venetian. But I want you to understand that things are not what they seem."

I recognized in this a jibe at my own situation. "I am an honest man!" I said.

"Then let's be frank with one another. I sense that you are, indeed, an honest, trustworthy man, not easily disconcerted by the unusual or the inconvenient. You will abide by your promise."

Let me confess that I was beginning to suspect that my masked beauty was about to unmask something less attractive than her face.

"I've made no promises to anyone," I said.

She looked at her uncle now, who, during this conversation, was pretending to gaze out on the canal but whose eyes were looking inward and whose ears were hearing all.

"I think we can rely upon him," he said.

"So," she said, grabbing my hand. "I will unmask if you will agree to a bargain. But first, tell me. How long were you imprisoned, and how did you escape?"

Now surely you must deduce that I had finally come to that proverbial fork in the road. On my left was the possibility that this bewitching creature was, indeed, an agent of the Inquisition. This whole charade—the mask, the rescue, even the frugal hospitality—was, in fact, an insidious snare laid for me by the diabolic forces of the State whose stratagems in the art of entrapment could easily accomplish such things. On my right lay the supernatural, the mythical, the superstitious. Smile if you will, but I have already admitted that we Venetians were a superstitious lot. It was the times and the illusory quality of the city itself, its maddening beauty, age and venality. Could this masked lady, then, be the personal incarnation of the Medusa, a kind of poisoned maiden? Would not this house, this whole adventure, be the mythical but true bower of bliss; and both she and this house the living instruments by which I would easily be led to slide into the very jaws of Cerberus?

In the end I closed my eyes, as it were, and trusted my masked lady. I told her how I was accosted on the street by men who claimed they were from the state inquisitors, was forced to take them to my lodgings which they searched, throwing my books into the fire and ordering me to follow them to the Leeds, the notorious prison. Never did they tell me what I was charged with. They didn't answer my questions. They simply presented me to the jailer and locked me in an upper cell just below the roof of the building.

You can imagine the forbidding quality of it all! The only light to my cell came from a small window, merely a slot, which looked out over the tiled roofs of the smaller buildings beyond. Escape looked impossible. The floor, walls and ceiling were stone; and the window, as I said, was but a slash into the rock and too high, at any rate, to risk falling from, even if I were to manage getting to it and squeezing between the bars. What was I to do?

"I would like to tell you that I carved my way out with my fork or that I broke through the window and then let myself down with bed sheets. But the truth is I walked right out the door! My jailer had somehow forgotten to lock it after leaving my food—perhaps he was drunk—perhaps he pitied me—I don't know. But when I didn't hear the turn of the lock I knew that miracles could still occur. I waited till about midnight, grabbed the blanket from my bed, opened the door and walked out. No one was there to stop me. You know the rest.

"I'm not surprised," broke in the uncle. "That was their way of letting you go. You've served their purposes. You are now sufficiently chastised and de-clawed, a walking warning to any freebooting poet."

Before I was able to speak again the lady smiled, and bringing her hands to her face, removed the mask. I swear to you now that she was indeed beautiful but at the very moment of her unveiling I admit to being somewhat disappointed. I can compare the experience as akin to that of being in a dark room for many hours and then having the lights brought in: for a few moments the room looks smaller, if less forbidding; commonplace, if less perilous. There was no exhilaration, only a dropping of the spirits. The lady Varesi struck me at first as merely ordinary; her eyes suddenly losing the luster they had behind the mask. But gradually, as we talked—and over the ensuing weeks and months—I grew to admire the delicate lines of her face. Forty years later I can still see those fine features.

Perhaps seeing the look in my face, the lady said. "Do you think me fairer, then, behind the mask?"

Embarrassed, "No, certainly," I said. "I'm waiting for you to continue. You spoke of a bargain."

She drank a cup of chocolate, sat back in her chair, like the empress she was, and looked at her uncle. He had turned from gazing at the canal and now moved his chair closer to his niece and me.

"My niece has infallible instincts," he said. "And I, too, am certain that we can come to a mutually rewarding arrangement."

In my youthful self-esteem, I suddenly imagined the uncle was proposing an "arrangement" between his niece and me, an alliance, I assumed, to which the niece was arduously, passionately committed. My physical charms, my wit, my supposed reputation as a poet dangerous to the state, these qualities assuredly inflamed her with a natural amorousness. I was to be sacrificed on the altar of love! Besides, I had read many books about the fatal attractions of men and women, and I was, after all, still a Venetian.

The lady now took my hand. So. It had come to pass at last. She was about to give voice to the arrangement, and I was mulling in my mind how to accept her offer to become my mistress. But suddenly a startling, subtle change came over her. Her eyes took on a glaze and her grip tightened on my hand, then relaxed. I watched in horror as her eyes rolled back in her head, only the whites showing as the lids closed and fluttered. Then her whole body collapsed, as a puppet's bereft of its strings. I must have sat there, an imbecile, unable to act, frozen, as she slumped in her chair, dropping into a sleep beyond sleep.

We carried her to a couch. I remember her uncle's saying nothing, conducting himself as if he were a workman or a shopkeeper, going about his business with an automatic ease. I would not have been shocked to hear him whistling as he tended to her. "Give her a minute or two," he said. "She'll be all right."

And, indeed, a minute later the lady opened her eyes and slowly sat erect on the couch.

"It has happened again?" she said to the uncle. His silence was answer enough.

"Then we should make our agreement quickly."

She looked into my eyes and continued.

"Signor Da Ponte, I was hoping we could discuss a business proposition as equals. Now I fear you have the advantage of me."

"How can I be of service?" I said, ever the gallant.

"Even if you agree just out of sympathy for my condition, that would put the arrangement largely in terms of charity."

"But Lady, we are not Mohammedans, as you say. As a Christian alone I would be pleased to serve you, provided that I am in no danger of losing my honor." (Let me confess to my shame that I was still playing the gallant, coining a formula for acquiring a lover. We read so many silly books in our youth, so many silly books.)

We had moved back into the sunlight, though the November weather, always fickle, cast a chill about our little terrace. If I had been momentarily shocked by her seizure, I was no less oddly disappointed to learn that the arrangement she had in mind did, indeed, involve no dishonor, for it was clear that I was not to be her lover. Worse, her attachment to me was hardly physical and worst yet, her scheme ignored the fact that I was a poet and obnoxious to the Council of Ten.

"I want to be your pupil," she said. "I must make a confession. I am ashamed to admit, Signor Da Ponte, that I can neither read nor write."

The thought had never occurred to me that my lady, with as fine a figure and bearing as any princess, could lack the rudiments which I had all my life taken for granted. I had never known anyone who could not decipher even a simple letter. I had been brought up virtually in the womb of the Church; the learning of letters was as natural as eating and drinking. And so my first thought was of how the lady had managed to thrive in society without knowing how to read or write.

The answer was forthcoming, for she had no trouble reading my mind. "What can I say?" she answered. "I've learned to read people."

"And to use a quick wit," continued the uncle. "She has nothing to be ashamed about. My niece is remarkable at anticipating and reading situations. And besides, not everyone in society is clever. We know some particularly stupid people."

"But I am a simple poet," I protested, refuting the belief in my own genius in the hope of escaping a chance to prove a failure.

"I can't hide my ignorance forever," she said. "In whom among my friends can I confide? They know only that I've been raised by my uncle, and they naturally assume he taught me my letters."

I turned quizzically to the uncle. He simply shrugged. "I can read situations, too," he said. "But it is getting harder, more difficult as the years go on."

"But have you not had schooling?" I asked the lady.

"Schooling?" the uncle sneered. "You mean purgatory. When the child's parents died I brought her to live with me and soon learned how the world deals with its ignorance and prejudice. She was taken in by a convent of praying nuns on Burano. They didn't understand her sickness, were afraid of it, saw it as a sop for the devil. She was soon treated as a leper, washing and cooking and doubtless polishing their rosaries which they put to ill use, praying for the poor dead souls instead of tending to the good live ones."

By this time I had walked over to the window to breathe in the palsied sunlight. If the truth were told, I was almost sick amid this scene. My gallantry had worn off and I imagined some vague contagion swarming about the place where the lady sat. I was ashamed and wanted only to leave. But again, the lady gave proof of her ability to read the import of the occasion.

"You aren't afraid," she said. "I can see that."

The last assertion on her part was meant, of course, to embarrass me. But she did not press her advantage. She was too kind, too gentle, and too wise for that. Instead, she took my hand once again and looked me directly in the eyes. She told me that because her seizures were becoming more frequent, she realized that she had no time to waste and must become literate as the first step in getting a husband. Suitors there were, apparently, but none was suitable. Naturally, she was intent on marrying well, but from what she told me, and as I was to observe over the next few months, she had a mind of her own and dismissed them all as so much dross. More about them in a while. In short, we concluded a bargain: I was engaged as her tutor for a period of three months, in exchange for room, board and the "invaluable" contacts with society that the uncle's influence could win me.

I was soon to learn, however, who really got the best of the bargain. My room was acceptable enough—I was quartered on the second floor, next to my lady, and not in the servants' spaces below where I understood many in-house pedagogues were often remanded in the houses of the rich. Not so here. In my lady's house I was an equal. As for the board, well, that was the leaky part of the ship. Our breakfast, always taken as on that first morning on the parapet of failing sunlight, was as invariable as it was paltry: hard bread softened in oil and washed down with chocolate. To give credit, the chocolate was excellent. Generally we had no lunch, but we supped early on weak soup, a broth that was as limpid as water, and probably as nourishing, and a meat course, very little, to be sure, but enough.

The limits of our bargain were tested even more rigorously on those occasions when I became nurse as well as tutor, for as the days grew darker and chillier my lady's spells became more frequent. I had begun to develop a kind of sixth sense as to when she would get an attack, much like they say animals can sense the onset of an earthquake before it occurs. We would be reading aloud, she following me with her text. Suddenly she would pause, as if wrapped in thought; her eyes would flutter, the book dropping to her lap, and she would fall into an immediate sleep. It was as if she were cut off from the world, from life itself. The whole process was oddly quiet, painless. When I saw it coming I would rise and stand beside her chair, holding her hand. I daresay it made little difference to her, but the gesture made me feel better and somehow made the whole experience less terrifying.

All in all, she was a remarkable pupil, a remarkable woman. She learned quickly and had the good sense and the manners always to permit me to decide when to begin her lessons on a particular day. There were some days, for instance, when I preferred to be by myself, to read or to write or to think. She never coaxed, never insisted, but bided her time with patience and dignity, so that those times during the day when we studied together became a balm for the both of us.

No. It wasn't love then, although as I look back on it now I suppose it could have, should have, been. But I was young, well, if not wisely read, and I cherished certain notions of what constituted love. What was I looking for? Forty years ago, who knows? If one can be forgiven youthful indiscretions, then surely one may be absolved from youthful omissions, too. No, I didn't love her, not then. Then it was just an adventure, a young man's journey, if you will, into his own capacity for self-delusion. She didn't love me, wasn't interested in me as a lover or husband or suitor. It was simply a business transaction, and after a while in the interest of my self-esteem I forgot all about love.

Besides, there were the suitors. The first one, I remember, was at the opera. We had gone—the three of us (in public I was to be a friend or some such distant alias)—as the guests of one of the uncle's "connections". Such connections were growing more attenuated with each passing month of unpaid bills and unrequited dinners. The famous castrato Cafferelli was singing.

Now old, he still had a voice of astonishing sweetness. His notorious disposition had not mellowed with age but had ripened into ferocity. In the middle of his aria from "Dido Abandoned" he stops, glares into the orchestra pit and struts to the edge of the stage. Glowering at one of the musicians, he takes the shepherd's crook he was holding, taps the man on the pate and declaims, "Heinous boor, I will christen thee!" Whereupon he spits on the poor fellow, resumes his place on stage and continues his aria. My protégé, Wolfgang Mozart, had seen Caffarelli on occasion. As fate would have it, the young composer was in that very house on that very night, or so I was told. But Mozart was unknown to me at that time, and I assumed the prodigy to be nothing more than that season's current pet. I discovered Mozart, did you know that?

But I was telling you about the suitors. There were many, like this fellow at the opera. He had obviously set his cap for the lady, and somehow before the evening was ended, had managed to get himself invited to dinner the next night. We soon discovered that it was dinner he was courting, not the lady. Poor as the fare was, he consumed it with a voraciousness that went beyond mere appetite and betrayed him to be more beggarly than us. Poor fellow, I rather admired his gall.

I remember another fellow who arrived with the uncle one day while my lady and I were engaged in her studies. What this uncle did for a living, by the way—or, rather, how he spent his daylight hours, for he certainly had no living other than cadging loans from an ever—decreasing pool of "connections"—how he survived, I could never make out. But on this occasion he came in with a most unlikely prospect, a large, florid-looking man whose pigtail was dyed a monstrous shade of green and who wore a patch over his left eye. He had the annoying habit of asking a question and not allowing anyone to answer it. "Do you like me? Yes, of course you do. What is your opinion on the price of cheese? Yes, it's outrageous. Is not mauve a perfectly hideous color? Most assuredly." Up to this point, I had credited the uncle to be a shrewd, clever, worldly man, an apt accomplice in securing a husband for his niece. But this bizarre cavalier whom the uncle had offered up, presumably as a last resort, was almost enough to force me to reconsider my assessment.

I say "last resort" because the lady showed herself to be indifferent to all the suitors that eventually made their appearance at the Ca Varesi. True, there were some scoundrels in the lot, and some hungry and tedious boors. But there were a number, too, who were charming, polished and moneyed, and her rejection of these made me wonder what she was really looking for in a husband. Certainly it must not have been love. The practical nature of the compact she had made with me gave proof that love was irrelevant. On the other hand, what was the point of making such a bargain when the goal of the agreement—matrimony—was delayed, forestalled, denied, rejected, shunned, ignored or otherwise put aside? Perhaps she had, in the pursuit of a husband, ridden to the edge of the forest of doubt and was unsure what she really wanted. Perhaps she had been in pursuit for so long that she grew fond of the chase.

In any case, it was clear that her survival, in whatever form it would take, was an issue that she knew she had to confront.

As for myself, as I have intimated, my contacts with society—the fruits of the uncle's "connections"—were merely tangential. I was like a waiter at a banquet, a poor one, to be sure; I could smell the food, even taste it when the guests were unheeding, but I could never sit at the table.

The three months were passing quickly. From me my lady had learned the rudiments of her letters and her natural intelligence did the rest. In short, my contract had been fulfilled and three months to the day of my rescue I left the Ca Varesi and never saw my lady again.

"Six months after leaving the Ca Varesi I was browsing at one of the bookstalls off the Grand Canal when I saw the uncle passing. He looked a bit thinner than when I had last seen him and I came to the conclusion that he was still cadging acquaintances and perhaps a meal. That impression might have been unkind of me, the result of my having a few scuderi in my purse from a benefactor who had taken a liking to some sonnets of mine. The Inquisition hadn't scared me off, you see. The uncle recognized me at once and we began to chat. He told me that he had been living alone for the last few weeks and I suddenly became frightened at the thought that my lady had died.

He smiled. No, he said. The lady was now a Madam James. She had met Mr. James at a ball. He was an American, it seems, and had an inordinate attraction to royalty of any sort. Himself unmarried, in Venice only en route to the south, he was thoroughly bewitched by this Italian "princess" who could not only read and write—his own letters apparently being of the meaner kind—but whose malady was one with which he also was afflicted. She had taken a seizure, it seems, in the course of one of his visits and the gentleman knew precisely what to do—which was, of course, nothing—and stayed to offer comfort and to share with her the secret of his own sickness. It was a match from the very beginning, one which, indeed, the lady had been waiting for all her life.

*   *   *

Mozart's Rabbi

What prompted me, Lorenzo Da Ponte—poet, scholar, friend, collaborator to the great Wolfgang Mozart—to hazard at the age of 60, a new life in America? Yes, I think it was that last visit to my old friend Jacques Casanova. He was wearing, I remember, a gown of brocaded silk, a parrot perched on his shoulder, but the bird seemed to prefer pecking at Casanova's crystal earrings than the morsel of wine-sopped bread my friend was offering it. He was so happy to see me that he abruptly thrust the bird into its cage, covering it with a cloth.

"Lorenzo!" he smiled.

I'd been hearing rumors about Casanova's habit of dressing as a woman. There was talk that the old man was dying a slow death in Bohemia, whispers afloat that the pox had done its grisly work all too well on its host. Even Mozart had mentioned to me something about Casanova's bill from the milliners. But Wolfgang was always joking—as he did about most things except his music—so I'd put down the remarks as jealous gossip.

Jacques must have sensed my uneasiness. It was difficult to ignore the change in him. His once smooth, glossy skin was marred now by a yellow pallor. From time to time he brought a lace handkerchief to his face and daubed at a running sore on his cheek.

Directing me to a chair next to the table on which lay a disordered pile of books, he took a seat across from me and scratched his balding scalp.

"It's so good to see you after so long a time. What are you doing these days?"

I cleared my throat and told him of the few projects for which I had high hopes.

"Prospects, high hopes, they don't put food on the plate, Lorenzo. You of all people should know that."

"I've never been lucky enough to have a generous patron."

"Yes," said Jacques, sweeping his arm as if to take in his surroundings. "You mean all this. Luck had nothing to do with it. I've a nice set-up here, I'll admit. My patron is a discerning man; he recognizes and rewards my genius. He knows nothing about books, of course. But he likes the looks of them. Tooled leather bindings fascinate him. Sometimes I think the very sight of them arouse his erotic ambitions. The hardest part of my being librarian here is toting the damn things and cataloguing them."

Jacques picked up a dark, ponderous volume and grunted as he let it fall.

"I shall have to recommend some pamphlets," he said. "By the way, how is your little friend, Signor Mozart?"

"Dead," I said. "Four or five years ago."

"That's too bad. I liked the little fellow, though I found him a bit surly about taking suggestions."

"He was my protégé, you know. I was his great champion. I took him under my wing. My operas . . ."

"Yes, yes, I know. Your operas. I should tell you, Lorenzo, that after all these years I'm still annoyed with you. That opera, *Don Giovanni.* I remember distinctly making suggestions and handing you my brilliant text for it. I spent a great deal of time on it but saw nothing of my work in the finished production."

"Jacques, you said yourself that Mozart hated taking advice. You know how stubborn he was about his music."

"If you were such a godfather to him, his rabbi, as you put it, he'd have listened to you. You used to go around strutting like the cock in the hen house about your protégé, your jewel, your kindred spirit and all that. Maybe it was you who thwarted me. There's only one genius in this room, my friend."

I had put my walking stick—the one Mozart had given me—on the table and for the first time Casanova took notice of it.

"What did he die of?" he asked suddenly.

I replied that I didn't know but that Mozart himself thought he had been poisoned.

"I'm not surprised," he said, daubing the sore. "He never took care of himself. A glass of nitrate water once a day for six weeks would have flushed out all those poisons. By the way, I want you to listen to something I've written."

I hoped my friend would not notice my squirming in the chair. Perhaps Jacques was a genius after all, but the shock of seeing him the way he was and the doubts I had about my own future at the time made me vaguely fearful of enduring one of Casanova's bouts of inspiration. He walked over to a side table beneath a gilt mirror and took from its case a violin. He began to saw a little tune, hopelessly atonal and dispatched in less than a minute. I wondered what Mozart would have thought of it.

"Well?" he said.

"I heard you were working on your memoirs."

He cast me a scolding look.

"My memoirs are not for posterity, Lorenzo. They're for me, to keep from going crazy. In fact, I've been scribbling some notes just before you came. I calculate I've slept with at least a hundred twenty women."

If Jacques was waiting for my reaction he must have been disappointed. The truth was I didn't know what to say. But in the next moment he freed me from the obligation to say anything.

"That's not an exaggeration, Lorenzo. The truth is I hardly loved any of them. Women, by and large, are vicious beings, vain creatures incapable of loving anybody but themselves."

He rose and walked over to the side table, placed the violin gently in its case, then began examining his face in the mirror.

He came back to our table, took up a quill next to a large volume and began to write something, quickly crossing it out. He looked up, sighed, then throwing down the quill sat back in his chair.

"You mentioned prospects, Lorenzo. 'High hopes', you said. What kind of prospects?"

"A book for a new opera," I told him. "Mozart would have been able to do magic with it. But the people today . . ."

"You're wasting your time. Mozart is dead. The Emperor is dead. All the people who knew anything about art or music or love, they're all gone, except for you and me. How do I look, Lorenzo? Do I look all right?"

"You'll outlive all of us."

"About those prospects. I have a suggestion for you. There's nothing here. You know that. But I've heard there are some rich pickings in America. The Count and his friend were talking one night a few weeks ago. I overheard them from the scullery where I was trying to entertain a young lady. She wasn't very young and I had some serious doubts about her being a lady, but let's not get into that. I heard this friend telling my patron about his adventures in New York, a wild, raucous place, he said, where everybody rushed to make money, cursed in different languages and watched the pigs wallowing in the main street. Naturally, I was intrigued. My first thought was that there must be some beautiful women there."

"But none for you," I joked. "No countesses. No one of royal blood."

"Nor of peasant stock, I hear. Everyone is equal there, you know. It must be a dreadfully boring place for geniuses like us."

With much effort he reached across the table and slid from the pile one of the great books, an ancient atlas in deep decay, held together by leather straps. I heard him breathe heavily as he dragged the thing toward him and with unsteady hand began turning the pages.

"There's a map of America here," he said. "I've looked at it many times."

He opened to a place he had marked and together we sat staring at a page purporting to show a land mass of unfinished definition and vague, undetermined boundaries, surrounded by the words "terra incognita," punctuated by puffing dragons, spitting gorgons and cartouches of dire omens.

"This tells us very little," I said. "How do we know it's America?"

"It's America, all right. But it doesn't tell us anything. I've asked the Count to acquire a book about it. It makes me feel like I'm doing my job. He says 'Of course, Jacques, of course,' but I know he's only appeasing me, and pretending to do his. Besides, what does one know of any place from a mere map? Even Europe is 'terra incognita' if you haven't seen it for yourself."

"America doesn't look very promising from all this. Maybe there's nothing to see, after all."

"Still," he said. "I'd like to know something of the place. Those prospects we've been talking about. I'll wager they're growing on trees, sprouting from the very dirt under your feet. Yes, I've thought a lot about America. Only a few years ago there was little keeping me from going. But now there's the Count, and my duties here."

He closed the book abruptly, hefted it, looked at the spine, then rose, carrying it as if it were made of heavy iron to a smaller table beside a bookcase. He was proving to me that his duties were real, his devotion to them sincere.

"In any case," I said. "It's a dangerous trip . . ." I was going to add "for old men" but caught myself. Casanova, though, was not fooled. He laughed. "Ah," he said. "You haven't read my memoirs. I enjoy danger. Thrive on it. There's a sensuous, almost erotic pleasure in putting oneself at hazard. I've risked danger at least 120 times."

For a while we sat quietly, I pretending to be gazing out the window, Casanova gazing at himself in the mirror.

"You're right, Lorenzo. You're absolutely right. I'm too old to pluck the fruit from the vast American groves. But you should go. And pluck some for me."

We sat again in silence for a while. Then he carefully closed the book and sat back in his chair. "You've said it yourself, Lorenzo. You have no patron here, no real prospects. And with your protégé, as you call him, dead and buried, what's the use of answering the beck and call of a thousand mediocrities?"

I remember that final meeting so clearly. After all these years I realize that the difference between us was as wide an expanse as that "terra incognita" on that ancient map. I've made good here in my new country. My family, my career, most of all my reputation and the respect of my fellow citizens. Unlike poor Jacques, I've refused to rust away under the pitiless countenance of an idle patron or an indifferent race. Although I didn't know it at the time, Jacques had taught me that inertia is death. There was no future in Europe for Casanova. He was right about there being no future in Europe for me, as well. All I had to look forward to, as he had warned, was answering the beck and call of a thousand impatient fools.

Yes, that was it. My visit that day in the Count's library taught me the need for seizing opportunity, which was only another word for courage. If one door closes, you open another, even if it fronts "terra incognita".

*   *   *

Ozymandias II

In the weird, iconic wit of dreams I see him, thin, frail amid shadow, receding down a corridor of palm arched in sepia, his back to me, his face turned to stone, pharaoh-like, his cartouche floating above him like a dialogue bubble in a cartoon, middle finger poised to meet a sneer, as if by gesture to proclaim futility: "No use trying to catch me now, I'm gone forever and ever." He was gone, as sure as Ramses, the mongrel he himself had named that day it followed him home, wet, delirious, the cur and he obviously recognizing in each other the absent, the vanished, the forlorn.

He had not lost his full identity then. There were at first the worried looks, the blank refusals of favorite meals, the repeated questions, the odd, panic moments of laughter. There were the angry repetitions of actions that used to be second nature to him, boring into him now like irritating cankers. He was first only disturbed, then frightened by the strangely familiar faces of students he should have recognized. Bits of verse came and went, mere mangled fragments of poems he could once recite with the joyful ease of love. But the time came when the campus police brought him home, too tired and scared to be ashamed or even angry as he often was during those early days when memory fled and his stubborn insistence played quarry to doubt.

"He's gone," my mother says, but in the dream I see only her frontal eye and feet, harried consort to his mindless divinity. "He yelled and screamed, said he was going for a walk. I grabbed his arm but he shook me off. He's too strong even now."

"There he is," I say in the dream. "He's walking by the pyramids."

"Ramses is dead," she says. "Maybe that's why."

"Why what?" I say.

"You know. You see the way he is."

"Did he hurt you?" I ask, standing suddenly by the river.

"He doesn't realize . . ."

"I'll go after him," I say.

"No use. I know he's gone. You should have been here."

"I couldn't," I say. "I was building my empire."

"He forgot the lines. He never forgot the lines."

I know I'm dreaming, cajoling my slumbering self to go on, play it out, see it through. Recall instead my sitting in his office. He is grading papers. Beyond his window bombs are exploding, mummified bodies swaddled in bloody sheets hover, then crumple into sarcophagi.

"The students can wait," he is saying.

"Yes," I say. "But I can't. I'm gone, too."

"I get it," he says. "But is it really worth it?"

"A man must do what a man must do."

"I see your point," he says. "But still. Is it really worth it in the end?"

He is showing me a student's paper: "Remember Shelley's 'Ozymandias?'"

"You've recited it often enough," I say, gazing at the pyramids along the Nile.

"My name is Ozymandias," he began, "king of kings: Look on my works, ye Mighty, and despair!" You know the rest. Maybe this kid's got it right, even at his age. All things are vanity sayeth the preacher."

"Even so, I'm gone, too," I say. "Maybe I can keep the statue from crumbling."

"By God, I hope so, son. But I couldn't save the statue when I went to 'Nam."

"You went. You tried."

"Yes," he says. "And the statue crumbled anyway. Good men fell whose bones now pave the walkway to the beach." He grabs my arm. 'Go if you must. Just for the record, though. You are my most sublime work. Never have I ever despaired of you, never."

And then mother, too, is holding my arm. She is wearing black.

"Yes, yes. Go after him if you must. But I know it's too late."

I am running after him, down the corridor of palm. The trees are alive and my own body glides, floats, as if impelled by wind. Before I'm out of breath I reach him. I stretch out my hand but cannot touch him.

"Who are you?" he says.

"Your best work," I say. "Let's go home, Dad."

I grab for him, but he stands firmly outside my grasp, beyond my reach.

"Come," I am saying. "I'll take you home."

"All right," he says. "But where were you all these years? I can't remember the lines."

"I know them", I say, raising my hand. "I know them, I know them now."

"Tell me," he says. "I must see to my tomb."

I begin: "'Look on my works, ye Mighty, and despair!'"

"And the end?" he says. "Finish it. Go on to the end."

So I finish it, waking to its spell, hearing it as if in speech:

> "Nothing beside remains. Round the decay
> Of that colossal wreck, boundless and bare
> The lone and level ands stretch far away."

*   *   *

The Wash-Out

"You wanted to see me, Fred?"

The man in the immaculate white shirt and firmly-knotted tie sat at his desk. A photograph of himself as young Marine Gunnery Sergeant Frederick Dick, in full braid and ribbons, smiled bleakly at his elbow.

"Have a seat," he said.

The man in jeans and open collar stood for a moment by the door, noting Dick's omission of his name. He took a chair and sat stiffly as Dick leaned forward, opened a drawer, shuffled a few papers, then slammed it shut; he swiveled in his chair and then sat back, folding his arms.

"I suppose you know why I sent for you."

"I've an idea. You're going to give me hell." The man offered a hopeful grin.

Dick suddenly rose, as if remembering something, and walked into the bathroom just off the office. He began washing his hands, slowly, methodically. He pulled six or seven paper towels from the dispenser, dried his hands, drew another five or six, drying them again.

"How many times have I given you hell?" he said, returning to his chair. The younger man squirmed. "Fred, I do my best."

"I know you think so. Look, you're young, bright, energetic. I like you. I really do. But you're just not cutting it."

"You're getting complaints?"

"It's more than that. It's the way you carry yourself. The way you leave yourself open. It looks bad."

"What do you mean, 'leaving myself open'?"

"The image you project. This 'hail fellow, well-met' persona of yours."

"Persona? You mean I'm putting on? Look, Fred, this is the real me. What you see is what you get."

"But that's what I mean. Your calling me 'Fred,' for instance."

"You've never objected before. It seemed natural from the very beginning to call you 'Fred'."

"Have you ever asked me if it was all right? Have you ever said, 'Can I call you 'Fred'? I've never granted you the right to call me 'Fred'."

The younger man crossed his legs, draped an arm over the back of his chair.

"Well," he said. "I suppose I should have called you 'Dr. Dick' from the start."

"In the office it's different. The fact that I personally hold a Ph.D. doesn't enter into it. But in public, on the road, with customers, I don't think you should refer to me as 'Fred'. Our Columbus client mentioned to me more than once that you call me 'Freddie.' He said you often laughed, laughed out loud."

"If this is why you sent for me . . ."

"It goes beyond that, beyond respect. It's your attitude that sucks."

"My attitude?"

"Your attitude toward the job, the profession. You don't seem to give a damn about our reputation. You don't seem to realize that Sleep-Well Caskets is an industry leader. We need reps who are dignified, elegant, compassionate. The days of a rep telling jokes to potential clients, like one of the good old boys gathered around the cracker barrel, they're gone."

"Well, Dr. Dick. Can I call you 'Dr. Dick'? I've placed a number of good orders recently. Like that Columbus client. They're well aware of our reputation. I've unloaded eight of our Slumber Box Elite models."

Dr. Dick straightened his photograph in its brass frame, giving the man opposite him a better view of it. He rose suddenly and walked into the bathroom. Again he began washing his hands, tumbling them over and over, drying them with a sheaf of paper towels. He came back, still wiping, dropping the towels into the waste basket by his desk. He sat back, making a teepee with his fingers and bringing them to his lips.

"Am I supposed to be impressed? If you cut out the jokes, dress soberly, show some respect, you could've have sold ten times those eight."

"The Columbus client was dressed in shorts and a polo shirt. I was the one who was over-dressed. He told the jokes. I was the sober one."

"You're reaching. Reaching. Sid Botch has placed three times as many orders to your one."

"Good for Sid. He's got a larger territory."

"And better manners. You don't see him approaching the Pleasant Abode people in jeans and a grin.

"Sid Botch is Sid Botch."

"Yes, Sid's a good man. And do you know why he has such an outstanding record with them, the biggest pet burial service in the world? He has dignity, bearing, class. You wouldn't see him entertaining his clients with crummy jokes."

"You don't unload eight Slumber Box Elites that easily, Doctor. Let me see him unload eight Slumber-Box Elites and then we can talk about class."

"Sid knows how much people adore their pets; how loving and caring they can be about their doggies and their tabbies and their widdle tweetie birds. Personally, I think these people are whackos. Sick. I've got no use for them. I'd flush them all down the toilet like so many goldfish. A good D.I. would have these wimps soiling their shorts. But that's another story, another life. To each his own. Don't ask, don't tell, that sort of thing. In the meantime, business is business, and I've always been one to separate business from personal feelings. In 'Nam we had a guy who adopted this dog. The scrawny mutt just showed up one day and Tyrone fed it and the mutt became a sort of mascot. That dog could smell a landmine from a dozen yards until one day he missed his mark and got blown to hell. His guts rained down on us like so much chopped meat. Tyrone cried like a baby, all of us did, except me. I thought it was kind of funny to see chopped meat scattered about Tyrone's fatigues, guts dripping from his helmet. That's how I learned to separate. That's why I've been so successful. That's why Sleep-Well Caskets is so successful. You might say we're really going to the dogs."

Dr. Dick repressed a smiling tribute to his wit.

The younger man uncrossed his legs and leaned forward. "Doesn't Sid have a pet? A ferret, isn't it?"

"Don't ask, don't tell," said Dick. "Sid does his job."

"So you're saying I can't do mine?"

"That's exactly what I'm saying. You don't separate one thing from another; you don't distinguish. It's all one long game to you."

"I don't try to compete with guys like Sid Botch. I like to have fun."

"But not at the expense of Sleep-well Caskets, mister. Not on my watch."

For a moment neither spoke. The younger man straightened himself in his chair, Dick flicked open a folder and scanned the data. He reached into his back pocket, took out a handkerchief, and wiped his hands.

"No," he said, not looking up. "Sid Botch could easily add your territory to his. I wish I had ten more Sids. I like you, I really do, but I'll have to let you go. The usual severance. If you need a recommendation I can get you one. That's all."

The younger man rose to leave. As he turned, he noticed Dick walking into the bathroom.

"By the way," the younger man said. "Sid's ferret is named 'Freddie'. "Did you know that, Freddie?"

Dr. Dick didn't hear the laugh, nor did he see the younger man flipping him the bird. By now he had turned on the water in the sink and was washing his hands.

*   *   *

Plato's Cave

"Now then," said Wister. "Let's see."

He scanned the preliminary questionnaire, making with his pencil little checks after significant items. Then he looked across the desk at his client.

"What is your professional objective?"

The client was a dwarf with a large nose. His eyes protruded from his ashen face, and the few hairs on his head were combed neatly across his scalp.

"Well," said the dwarf. "I think I'd like something in public relations. That always seemed like the kind of thing I could do."

Wister swallowed. "I see. But your background here, Tad, doesn't really qualify you."

The dwarf looked puzzled and a little nervous. "Isn't that what you résumé people are supposed to do? Qualify me? The agency guaranteed I'd be satisfied."

Wister did not answer but continued perusing the form.

"What about my circus experience? Can't you use that?" asked the dwarf.

"We could if you were applying for a job with another circus. We could possibly aim at an acting job, maybe a few commercials."

Tad grimaced and waved his hand, throwing it at Wister and then bringing it back again, his arm still attached, to its original position on his right thigh.

"Nah," he said. "I'm through with all that. No more being a freak for me. The circus is O.K. when you're first starting out, but I'm not a kid anymore. I'm thirty-five years old, and I want a good job and good money, something with a little respect."

Wister could not see below the level of the desk, but he could imagine the dwarf's misshapen legs dangling a few inches below the seat of his chair.

"I understand your situation," said Wister. "But do you know anything else besides the circus? Do you have any skills, any accomplishments? Anything at all that would impress an employer?"

"Just the circus. I know the circus inside out. That's dealing with the public, isn't it? Making them laugh, relating to them. Isn't that public relations?"

"We need an angle," Wister said. Out of Tad's view, he began doodling in the margins of the questionnaire.

"My job with the circus was pretty different. You know the kind of stuff you usually see, with us coming out of little cars or boxes and things? Well, that's not for me. I don't do that kind of stuff. I have a class act."

Wister waited for the dwarf to continue, but Tad just sat across the desk from him and thrummed his fingers on the imitation wood-grained top. So Wister succumbed.

"And that is?" he asked.

"I come out in a cap and gown, like those guys at Oxford, and I begin to read poetry in a gorgeous English accent—not mine, of course. It's on tape, and I just lip-sync to it. As I get half way through the poem, something about this monster named Jabby Wock, my associate comes out from behind and tears my gown right up the back, showing my underwear—only sometimes I'm not sporting any underwear, you know what I mean?"

"That would be difficult to put in a résumé," said Wister.

"I could give you some good references," said the dwarf. "I get along good with people; that's why I think I can handle it. I wouldn't expect anything big to start, of course, but just something to get my foot in the door. A man can't spend the rest of his life in a circus, you know what I mean?"

Wister had been working on a fine parallelogram with radiating lines struck from the center. Now he leaned forward in his chair. "Yes," he said. "I think we could help you, Tad. Tell you what. Give me a few days on this, and we'll call you."

"O.K., great," said Tad. "I'm not looking for any miracles. Just a stepping stone."

"'Entry level position with medium-size firm offering opportunity for advancement.'" Wister was writing this on the paper as he recited it to his client. Tad nodded approvingly.

Wister dotted the period with a flourish, slipped the paper into a folder and closed it. He shook his client's hand. "Call you in a few days," he said.

When the dwarf had gone, Wister looked at his watch and saw that his present workday with Redounding Résumés was over. As always, he stuffed his briefcase with half a dozen questionnaires, including the last, intending to do some work on them that night while at his second job. Tonight was his early shift, and he would just have time to eat dinner at his favorite Italian restaurant before reporting in.

Over his dish of osso bucco, Wister remembered his uncle—his mother's brother and the only father he ever had. As a boy, Wister would sit with his uncle in front of the window of his fish store and listen to him pontificate on the economic situation of the country, always with yesterday's Times folded on the wire-backed chair next to them, a bludgeon for the flies, large, green and pesky, that continually swirled and buzzed about the pop-eyed, pucker-gaping heads of the bluefish. His uncle had never been to high school, but he read the Times daily, and his discourse was thus an odd mixture of the erudite and the preposterous. Wister remembered his uncle taking his hands and turning them over, as if they were a pair of flounders.

"Bonehead!" he would say. "Don't be a bonehead. You'd better be smart. These hands—they're not for fish. They're for books. Get a good education. Make a lot of money with your head, not your hands. You want a position with respect, too."

Wister quickly finished his meal and hurried to his second job. A short bus ride from Redounding Résumés, the warehouse for Beauty Bod Cosmetics was in a spectacularly ugly part of the city, and Wister sometimes imagined he had gone through a time-warp and had gotten off the bus somewhere on Uranus.

In the locker room, a paint-peeling, plaster-gouged cubbyhole lit by a naked twenty-five-watt bulb, Wister carefully transformed himself from a dacron/polyester executive to a flannel/khaki night watchman. He closed his locker, picked up his case and walked into the night room. On the wall was a clipboard with a check-list of assignments. Taking down the clipboard, Wister began making his rounds. On the first floor he checked the cartons of eye shadows, hair rinses, and lipsticks. There was a forklift in the corner, a pallet of cosmetics still on it, its two steel arms raising the pallet in a grotesque offertory to the wall. The second floor housed the skin creams and mascaras, highly prized by women everywhere, so went the ads, because they had just the right amount of pH ingredients.

His Ph.D. had brought him to this. His uncle had not lived to see him get it, and at first Wister was sad about that, but now as he skulked about the perfumes and body rubs of the third floor, he was glad of it, for his uncle would not be able to understand how a man with a Ph.D. in America—a man trained to use his head and not his hands—was forced to guard the nation's female paint supply by night and help secure by day the economic well-being of the restless, the ignorant, and the incompetent.

With a cursory glance at the depilatories, Wister concluded his tour and returned to the night room. He sat at a large old desk. Shared among the other watchmen, it contained a number of unused drawers, one of which Wister had appropriated because it had a lock on it. Carefully now he inserted the key and opened the drawer. From it he took a black, speckled composition book, placed it on the desk and opened it to the first page. Taking up a pen, he began writing:

PLATO'S CAVE
a Novel of American Education
by Rocco Wister
Chapter One

A young man then, fresh with a Ph.D. and a seamless notion of myself. I was teaching my first course and was still sizing up the class, getting used to names, faces, and intellects.

Wister paused and read the first sentence aloud, just above his breath. He murmured his approval and began writing again, but half way through the sentence he struck out the passage and started over. Again he paused and read what he had written. This time he inserted a phrase and deleted a word. He read it again and this time struck out the entire passage. Then he ripped out the leaf from the book. His mind began to wander. He ought to do the résumés, after all . . .

He looked at his watch. In two hours his shift would be done. But tonight he was aware of being vaguely fearful of going home and to bed. He remembered now the interview that awaited him the next day with the chairman of the department at the college to which he had applied weeks ago. Wister felt his stomach tighten. He knew it would be difficult if not impossible for him to sleep, although the letter calling for a meeting with him was no different in tone or in degree of commitment from the scores of others he had received since graduating. He could picture his uncle, N.Y. Times bludgeon in hand, swatting flies and telling him not to worry, the bastards needed him, would hire him on the spot if they knew how smart he was: "You'll do fine. Just remember, you're a doctor. A doctor, not a fish peddler." Wister could see swimming before his eyes his uncle's bygone fish store, now a beauty parlor where handsome ladies daily glorified their bodies over the very spot where his uncle once battled flies amid the crabs, the eels, and the bins of baccala.

Outside chairman Manfred Orm's office, Wister was sitting in an odd, straightback chair, his knees together, as if he were waiting for a bus. Dressed in his best suit, he was pretending to read The Chronicle of Higher Education, but his eyes stared blankly at the print while his mind played at composing a picture of Orm and at fitting together words for the forthcoming interview. In front of him a plump, middle-aged secretary in a brown frock typed casually from her notes. When her phone buzzed, she reached over, picked up the receiver, listened, and glanced at Wister as she did so. He knew this was Orm asking for him, and Wister could see from the corner of his eye as the secretary put back the receiver and swung her chair around to face him. But almost with the beginning of her voice telling him to go in, he was up and opening the door.

"Ah, sit down, Rocco," Orm said, rising from his desk in the middle of an office that looked like a storage room or an air raid shelter. Orm was holding out a large, long palm, and Wister took it, thinking vaguely that it resembled one of his uncle's flounders.

Orm was a tall man with an elongated, pockmarked face and a wide, aggressive nose aflame with thin red lines running across its tip. It seemed to Wister, as he tried not staring at it, as if the nose were quietly smoldering, waiting for the first combustible opportunity. Orm returned to his desk and sat back in his chair, putting his hands together like a slotted teepee.

"Now then," he said. "Let's see. I'm glad we could get together. I see by your résumé that your field is Renaissance poetry. We happen to be in the market for a Renaissance man at the moment."

He looked at Wister, perhaps expecting a response, but Wister shifted in his chair and crossed his legs in studied nonchalance.

"Wister," Orm continued. "That's English, isn't it?"

"Welsh, really. My father, of course . . . "

"Of course. And Rocco.' Your mother . . . "

"Italian."

Orm smiled and gave off a quiet snort, like a man recalling a joke. "What more fitting background for a Renaissance man. That's rather an unusual combination."

Orm smiled, tilting his head, his eyes nearly closed, his mouth almost in a pucker, his nose smoldering. For a minute neither one spoke, and Wister could hear only the coldly distant sound of typing beyond the door.

"What was your thesis, by the way?"

"'Illusion and Reality in Spenser's The Faerie Queene,'" Wister said proudly.

"Hmm," said Orm. He straightened his head and looked back into Wister's résumé. "You may be able to get a fairly creditable article from that. My thesis, now, was quite original, you know."

At this Orm sat back and put his hands behind his head, as if showing Wister how relaxed he could be.

"Although I'm not a Renaissance scholar, as you are, my studies do have some peripheral relationship to yours."

There was another interval of silence, and Wister suddenly realized that Orm was waiting for him to pursue the subject. In another second, however, it was too late, and Orm had to throw out the line again.

"You've heard of Cotton Mather, of course," he said.

"Of course." Wister tried smiling.

"Yes, well I did a rhetorical study of his Wonders of the Invisible World, a marvelous work, really. It's a long time ago, but I've mined quite a number of good things from it. I'm sure I don't have to impress you, Rocco, with a litany of all my responsibilities here. They eat away at my time. Frankly, it's a tough, demanding job. Still, I turn out my three or four papers a year. I don't see anything published by you here, incidentally."

Caught off guard, Wister shifted in his seat. "I've got high hopes," he said, and then felt foolish when he thought he detected a trace of a smirk on the chairman's face. He quickly considered mentioning his novel in progress, but hesitated, feeling rather ashamed, as if he were somewhat queer to be engaged in a work of fiction. He was superstitious enough about it as well, to believe that revealing his secret project would make it stillborn. He felt superior to Orm, regarding him as too much the philistine to appreciate his ambition.

"I was only twenty-three when my first paper on Mather was published," he heard Orm say. Wister watched him open his desk drawer, look in quickly and tenderly withdraw several pages of printed text. Orm handed them across to Wister.

"That's an author's copy," he said. "I've others. You might want to use it somewhere. Page four is particularly good, I think. That's where I deal with Mather's style as a correlative to his sincerity. Mather was not the madman many people make him out to be, you know. He was really quite reasonable, quite compassionate, a good, honest man."

Orm leaned back in his chair, giving Wister time to study the text. Wister was aware of Orm's awkward breathing. Pretending to scan the pages, he had time to note a hurricane of convoluted prose. He heard a grunt. Looking up, he saw Orm gazing at him, calmly swiveling in his chair like a judge passing sentence.

"That is an odd combination. Welsh and Italian. Did your mother speak any English, by the way?"

"My folks were both born here. I'm second generation."

"How's your Italian? Speak it well, I guess."

"Not really, no," said Wister, thinking now of his uncle who spoke Italian only when he did not want the customers to understand his contempt for them. "Watch this woman," he would say in some dialect. "She commands like the Queen of England, but all she buys is a buck's work of whiting."

"It's a shame, isn't it?" Orm was saying, his head tilting again with half-closed eyes and erupting nose. "We Americans don't value our heritage. Did you know I'm related to Cotton Mather?"

The image-making apparatus in Wister's mind quickly developed a picture of Orm in black Puritan gown, the split-tongue collar of the cleric and the scholar about the neck. Wister could picture Orm sitting at his desk, one hand on the hilt of a sword by his waist, the other on the Bible before him, an ineffable smile on his face.

Orm took his hand from his sword and now suddenly there was a pipe in his mouth, the littlest Wister had ever seen: small, delicate burled; it resembled a palsied mushroom. Orm was jamming the bowl with his finger, passing a match over it, taking long, energetic puffs, sucking the flame eagerly into the pipe, his cheeks collapsing and inflating with each puff. He reminded Wister of the stuffed, alien creature on the display case of his uncle's fish store. About the size of a soccer ball, it was brown, speckled and spiny; its glazed eyes reflected the light from the case, and its mouth formed a perfect pucker as if it were preparing to bestow a kiss. "That's a blowfish," he heard his uncle explain. "Tiny little thing puts up a big show. Blows itself up to three, four times its size when scared. Not much of a fish—not a good, honest eating fish."

Orm was sitting back, blowing smoke rings: "On my mother's side we go back to one of the daughters of Cotton Mather. On my father's side, well, 'Orm' is actually French, probably Huguenot. I've been doing some work on my father's side and I can tell you, Rocco, there are some interesting old Yankees all along the way. Your father was Welsh, you say?"

"Welsh, yes. But I don't know how far back beyond the coal mines we can go." Wister had made the remark as a joke, to slacken the taut formality of a genealogue, which rather embarrassed him.

Orm merely cocked his head and smiled within tight, pouting lips. "Perhaps farther back than on your mother's. The Welsh are a race of kings. Ah well," he said, coming erect in this chair. "All this has been fun, but not what we're here for. Tell me. What can you give to Lemming College?"

As if he had asked a trick question to an intimidated undergraduate, Orm narrowed his eyes and peered into Wister's face. Wister, in fact, had anticipated the question. It was the one basic inquiry he had been rehearsing an answer to for days.

"What can I give to Lemming?" he began, remembering the words. "Nothing but my dedication. I love my work, and I know I'll do a good job."

Orm was unimpressed. He grazed bovinely over Wister's file. "Yes, that's all very nice. But I don't see here any mention of previous experience. How can you say you love your work when you haven't done any work of the kind you love?"

Wister felt the drop in his stomach and sensed a peculiar form of betrayal. "I should have said 'if given the chance.' I guess I was being a bit rhetorical. I forgot that you are an expert in rhetoric."

Wister was patronizing now, and he wondered if Orm would take the bait. He smiled amiably, but Orm gave no indication of biting, of even being amused at Wister's hook.

"Frankly," he began. "Your lack of experience is not necessarily a drawback in getting this position, you understand. One must start his career somewhere. The problem, Rocco, is not so much your lack of experience as my own excess of it."

He waited for the remark to register on Wister's understanding. "You see," he continued. "I've seen so many bright young men like yourself begin with the highest dedication and the deepest love for the profession, only to end up after a year or so as sour old buzzards. For one thing, we don't pay very well."

"Oh, the money's not the important thing right now," Wister said quickly, earnestly.

"It never is, in the beginning. But aside from that, we've got to be very careful. We can afford to be, you know, with so many Ph.D.'s looking for work, even in Renaissance poetry." Orm was smiling, head cocked, eyes nearly closed. "For instance, how do you interpret academic freedom? Is it liberty to teach the best way you can or license to teach whatever you want?"

Wister did not answer. He was trying to decide whether Orm's question was meant to test him or was merely rhetorical from a man who prized rhetoric above all things.

"How do you feel about women, by the way?" Orm asked suddenly. "What I mean is, how would you feel if I were a woman? Would you be able to work under me?"

It was a question Wister had not expected; he felt pressured into answering it quickly, carefully.

"If you mean would I feel uncomfortable with a woman as a colleague . . . "

"Or a superior."

"Or a superior. No, I don't think it would bother me. Women are every bit as good as men in many things." Wister felt hypocritical, qualifying the answer so as to be safely outside the net of Orm's opinion.

"Oh, we have women on the faculty here, of course. But I feel it only fair to tell you, Rocco, that there is a woman also being considered for this position." Orm smiled, his eyes closed as if he had gas.

"I am what I am," said Wister.

"Personally," Orm said. "I'm not a libertarian. I haven't really dismissed her from consideration yet. I have to tell you, though, Rocco, she's very, very good. A Woodrow Wilson. And pretty."

Again Wister was silent, sensing this time that anything he would say now would somehow be demeaning. Orm relit his pipe. "Why do you want to teach, anyway?" he said. "You seem to be quite good at what you're doing now. And what exactly is it that you do?"

Wister felt his face redden. He heard his uncle urging him to tell Orm to go to hell; that he, Rocco Wister, didn't need him. "I guess you can say I'm in public relations," he said, finally. 'I sell people to the right employer."

Orm widened his eyes and motioned with his mouth, as if impressed. "Pays well?"

"It's not teaching," Wister evaded.

"Ah, yes. A bright young man with dedication and a love for the profession. Did you know we once had an Italian gardener, by the way? Charming man. Just off the boat, but he could get anything to grow."

As Orm continued, Wister could detect signs that the interview was coming to an end. Once or twice Orm glanced at his watch. Carefully he closed Wister's file, putting it neatly under a stack of papers. He tapped his pipe several times on the palm of his hand before slipping it into his jacket pocket. Swiveling in his chair, he spoke quickly now of his illustrious colleagues. He spoke of "what a lovely man" the dean was and of his own overriding pressures to whip the department into shape. He spoke of the provost, who was also a lovely man. He spoke of the vice president, a lovely, lovely man. He spoke of his personal friendship with the chief trustee who, in addition to being a lovely man, was also a great human being.

Orm ended by rising, extending once again his flounder-hand and suggesting that Wister take lunch, as arranged, with a Professor Augont, whom Orm praised merely as a great guy.

"You'll be hearing from us in a few days," he said.

Professor Augont was a small, elderly, barrel-shaped man who taught philosophy and whose head looked the wrong size for his body. It was large, shiny, and hairless, and the forehead protruded like an ice-age boulder over wide, pop eyes. The only faculty member free at the time, Augont had met Wister, unsmiling; had taken him to the cafeteria, unsmiling; and was now sitting across the table from him, still unsmiling, listlessly pushing a blob of tuna fish across a brown-edged field of lettuce.

Wister, too, had little appetite, thinking of the interview with Orm. "It's good of you to take this time with me," he said.

Augont glanced up at Wister from his plate. "No problem. Are you joining us this term?"

"I hope so," Wister said.

"Hmmm," Augont said. His tuna had been shoveled across the lettuce and was now making a return trip.

"Does that mean 'good'?" Wister asked.

"I guess it does for you. I don't really care. I wish you well, I really do. I remember when I was your age. Couldn't wait to get to class every day. Now I don't give a damn. I'm getting out."

Surprised, Wister felt oddly uncomfortable, embarrassed by Augont's sincerity. "If you mean you're retiring, congratulations," he said lamely.

Augont snorted, his shoulders quaking as he hissed air from compressed lips. "Hell," he said. "I've been retired for years. That's the way they do it around here. It's getting to be like a goddam business. If I'm going to work for a business, I might as well get paid for it. I've got my résumé out to a few places. I'm not too old, and I've got a lot of experience."

"What are you looking for?" asked Wister, oddly professional.

"Public relations, maybe. Or counseling. Something dealing with people. I've simply had it with education. Look, thirty-five years ago when I started, it was a great profession. But something happened. It's become a supermarket, different brands, different prices. These kids take whatever's on sale."

"It can't be that bad," Wister said, trying to smile.

"It's bad enough. Some of the professors around here create a whole routine just to keep the kids happy. One fellow in Modern Cinema shows skin flicks all term and has the kids write papers on their redeeming social value and the symbolism of sex. That fellow has a full class every term. I tell you, it's a regular Barnum and Bailey."

"Is that what you'd call 'academic freedom'?" Wister said, remembering Orm's interview.

"It packs the house. I suppose it's academic business. Nobody wants to learn anything anymore. That's hard work. Today they want to be entertained. It's bread and circuses."

"Well, I can't very well show films in Renaissance literature," said Wister, laughing. "I'll have to rely on my knowledge and my love of the field."

Augont left the tuna stranded in the middle of the lettuce, dropping his fork with a dull tinkle against the plastic dish. He looked directly into Wister's eyes.

"In that case, my boy, you'll be teaching to empty seats in three weeks and out on your rump at the end of the year."

"If I get the job, I'll give it my best," said Wister.

"I'm sure you will," said Augont. "Here, let me show you something." He reached into his back pocket and pulled out a battered wallet. Opening one of the flaps, he withdrew a soiled, dirt-veined piece of paper. Unfolding it carefully, he said: "Years ago this was the greatest profession on earth. You didn't make a lot of money, but you had fun. I remember we used to trade funny stories about our students and their glorious mistakes that nobody could make up. One time, I remember, I was lecturing on one of Plato's Socratic dialogues. It was the Meno. That was the one you remember in which Socrates demonstrates the existence of innate knowledge by questioning a slave boy on the common-sense principles of geometry. The boy was unschooled, knew nothing of geometry, but the whole point of the experiment was that Socrates gets the boy to give the right answers simply by asking the right questions."

Here Augont handed Wister the paper. "I spent an entire class explaining the experiment. Next period I gave a quiz. That's one of the results. Go on, read it to me."

Wister read aloud: "Socrates was an ancient Greek philosopher who experimented on boys."

Wister smiled, but Augont was as sullen as when they first sat down. "You can laugh at it, yes," he said. "Well, God bless you. I used to find it all so funny, but I don't anymore. You're the first person I've shown that to in years. Why don't you keep it? Anyway, I wish you luck. Maybe you'll do all right. Something will come along for me any day now, so let me wish you the best and say good-bye here."

Augont rose, a few flecks of tuna sticking to his wrinkled pants. They shook hands and Wister watched as Augont, sad and stoop-shouldered, swam slowly away, like a salmon upstream.

At Redounding Résumés the next morning Wister was tired. He had tossed all night, seeing in his fitful catnaps Orm's smile and Augont's deadpan face. It was nearly dawn when he finally dozed, awakened then by the cruel alarm and the vision of his uncle's body lying behind the counter, his hand still clutching the apron he had just started to take off when his heart suddenly stopped. Wister's elbow was now on the desk, his fist propping up his head. He was doodling, dreading to get at the day's work. In a while he heard the quick tread of heavy elevated shoes and sensed that Tad was standing near his desk.

"I know you said you'd call me," he was saying. "But I wanted to come in to tell you personally."

Wister looked up, straightening himself.

"The troupe's moving out," he continued. "Just got the word yesterday afternoon. We're all going out to California, isn't that great?"

"Wonderful, Tad," Wister said, trying to show interest. "It might be better for you out there. The weather's great most of the time, I hear."

"Oh hell, Mr. Wister, the weather don't interest me. An old flame of mine's out there with another circus. I don't know why I didn't think of her before. Good old Tinkerbell; that's her professional name. Maybe we can team up. Get in the movies, maybe."

"But I thought you were through with the circus?"

"I am, I am. This is only temporary, don't you worry. Something better will come along. Tinkerbell's got connections. The two of us are going to hit it big out there, you watch."

Wister took out Tad's résumé. The dwarf looked guiltily at him. "I'll pay you for what you done so far," he said. 'But I finally got it settled in my head. The circus is only temporary, you watch. Well," he said after a pause. "So long."

"So long," said Wister.

He watched as Tad made his way out through the canal of desks, his false-bottomed shoes striding boldly. As Tad disappeared through the door, Wister saw the mailman enter, a letter in his hand. Someone was directing him to Wister's desk, and Wister's stomach dropped.

"Rocco Wister?" the mailman said. "Registered letter. Sign here please?"

Wister scribbled his signature on the yellow slip and stared at the envelope, knowing already its contents. It had been postmarked yesterday afternoon. Not even the courtesy of a seemly delay, he thought. Not even the courtesy of sending it home.

"After careful consideration of your credentials (it began) the committee must regretfully inform you that the position for which you applied has already been filled . . . "

He did not need to read the rest of it, though his eyes saw the print and paused briefly over Orm's illegible signature. When Wister looked up again, there was a walrus of a woman standing over him, eating a candy bar.

"I need a résumé," she said.

*   *   *

The Dancing Barber

Our Love of Spectacle

So you go in to get a haircut. The place is not your regular shop, but you're early this morning and have been emboldened by that third cup of regular coffee to explore brave new worlds. The old-fashioned insignia, a pole of red and white stripes swirling into themselves, declares that this new world, if not brave, is at least masculine. Several men are sitting about, quietly reading the papers. One fellow, not reading, is sitting with his back to the wall. He is wearing work boots and checkered shorts held up by wide, navy blue suspenders. You take a seat next to him. The lone barber is just beginning on a bald man who insists that the hair in his nostrils be cut first. It's going to be a long wait.

But just as you're ready to leave, something extraordinary happens. He's thin and wiry, this barber, wearing not the usual white smock but dapperly attired in a lime green silk shirt and matching tie. On his wrist a gold bracelet matches his cuff links and he's sporting a rubber glove on his right hand; the other is naked except for a gold pinky ring, the size of his knuckle.

Having taken care of the nostril hair, the barber cocks his head, looks into the eyes of the bald man and smiles broadly, as if in prelude to something imminent.

The fellow in the checkered shorts nudges you and gestures with his head, as if to say "Watch what he does now."

You watch, but at first you see and hear only the skim and snip of the comb and scissors as wisps of hair fall about the sheet on the bald man's shoulders. But then you observe the barber's legs beginning to quake and instantly his feet become alive. Almost before you can gape, the feet are beating a rhythmic tattoo, a toe-tapping counterpoint to each snip of the scissors. The barber is dancing now, but virtually still in place, and the bald man's final grooming is done. The performance culminates with the barber's tossing his comb in the air and arching his body so that the comb plops neatly into his breast pocket.

Now you're late. But there is something in the experience that keeps you from leaving, even when you discover that the barber has yet another set ready for the next customer and another still for the one after that. By the time he gets to the man in suspenders and checkered shorts you're hooked, trapped, caught up in what novelist Joseph Conrad called the fascination of abomination.

But Conrad's despairing cry at mankind's capacity for evil is a moral distance from your own attraction to this barber and his antics. Fascination, yes. But abomination? The only evil here is the loss of time, precious enough in our finite lives but important only if experience is to be judged by its quantity rather than its quality. And so you stay, transfixed, like Coleridge's wedding guest in "The Ancient Mariner", gladly swapping a portion of eight hours labor in the vineyard for an hour or so of harmless worldly amusement.

Forty years ago Luigi Barzini noted in his book, *The Italians*, that one of the characteristics of this vibrant race is its love of spectacle. Italians, he observed, live in a world of appearances, thrive on the essence of illusion, willingly suborn themselves to the effect, the gesture, the paradoxical act of deliberate spontaneity, what the Renaissance Italians called *sprezzatura*. (It is hardly coincidental, by the way, that opera, most spectacular of the arts, was born in the Renaissance. Where else but in Italy could the contradictions and excesses of the human imagination, the very essence of spectacle, be at perfect ease?) Barzini was on to something, though he was hardly the first to notice. Orson Welles, whose film *Citizen Kane* was not without its own spectacular effects, is reputed to have remarked that there were fifty million actors in Italy, the worst of them on the stage.

Not wishing to subvert the opinions of scholar Barzini and showman Welles, I would maintain that the love of spectacle is inherent in all of us. Whether or not your barber is Italian, he is endowed with that irresistible sense of theater, that unique human faculty which makes us rubberneck on highways, peoplewatch on beaches or sympathize with Hamlet or De Niro. All of us need the spectacular in our lives, not only as an antidote to the mundane, but also as a kind of innate response to that last great adventure inevitable for us all. Why else would we build cenotaphs and monuments and mausoleums like the pyramids? Ladies and gentlemen, welcome to the greatest show on earth, a three-ringed world bounded only by your powers of observation, participation and appreciation. Like Caesar in Gaul we mere mortals must learn to recognize and seize the essence of experience, armed mainly with a willingness to engage and an unshakeable resolve to give no quarter to the ordinary.

But the "spectacular", from the Latin meaning "to look", does not necessarily entail the grandiose or the violent. Your barber makes clear that point. Making a spectacle of yourself is not always a bad thing. It may, in fact, be a corollary to wisdom. Benjamin Franklin, when American ambassador to France, officially appeared before the court of King Louis not in ermine or silks but in plain brown broadcloth. He understood that spectacle, properly seasoned and applied, had a seditiously democratic allure, not so much humbling himself as bringing down the King to a more human scale, making his Majesty a mere mortal, gawking in wonderment and admiration, just another guy waiting for a haircut.

The force of spectacle when turned upon itself sometimes breeds unwilling participants, victims unaware of their captivity to illusion. Many of us can cite friends or relatives who, for better or worse, live solely in a private world. My Sicilian grandmother is a case in point. In her eighties, an immigrant no longer able to keep house or make bread, Nana and her mind settled into a life of daytime soap opera, keeping track of the baroque goings-on from one show to the next, talking to the screen, purring "figlia mia" to the heroine, cursing and spitting at the villain whom she generically named "disgraziata". In one particular episode the villain deceitfully apologized to the heroine.

Nana's eyes narrowed, her lips tautened. Her left arm shot into the air, as if angrily opening an umbrella.

"No usa be sorry," she hissed. "I killy anyway."

My grandmother's surrender of what we would call reality was, at bottom, not an escape but a kind of catharsis. Her days passed in a complete emotional freedom, allowing her to sympathize, to love and to hate; to believe or to disbelieve, to regret and to forgive, all with her humanity intact. What more can one ask of the power of spectacle to redeem? And make no mistake. There is a redemptive power in our embrace of the spectacular. Spectacle saves us from the ugliness of the world, frees us from the useless dregs of doubt, despair and the quotidian hassles of modern life. "We live in an old chaos of the sun," wrote the poet Wallace Stevens. But all he needed was a good show to lighten his heart.

And so, your workday done, feeling spiffy with your fresh haircut, you decide to have dinner in town, trying one of those new eateries in the Plateau Mont-Royal. It's already getting dark, and the restaurant is lighted only by a few simulated lanterns and electrified sconces that flicker in precision from walls made to look like stone battlements. Your table is by a window, mullioned and grated, a rusty padlock swinging from one of the bars. Your waiter arrives in tights and motley, hands you a parchment from which he takes your order, a King Arthur with a side of fries. You have a glass of wine—dubbed a Merlin—and after a few sips you're in the swing of things.

The first of two musicians appears. She is accoutered in a wimple and, for good measure, a conical cap, a veil fluting from its peak. She begins to tune her dulcimer and is soon joined by a squire in plastic chain-mail and cardboard greaves. He is straddling a viol da gamba. They are billed as the "Jackanape and Jill" and together they begin to play a selection of galliards and airs from the Saxon Miscellany.

Getting used to the darkness, you can just make out, sitting in a deep recess near the kitchen, (labeled "ye olde scullery) the form of a man. In modern dress, he looks somewhat out of place. You notice he is wearing a shirt and tie, but his suit jacket is feathered over his shoulders like a cape. Unmoved, expressionless, he is peering out from behind dark glasses. On his head, perched at a rakish angle just above his brow, sits an immaculate white fedora. You learn from Master Geoffrey, your waiter, that this fellow in the shadows is Mr. Nino, the owner.

"Mr. Nino likes to keep an eye on the place," he says. "Pretty much stays out of sight. "Doesn't want to be noticed."

"Yes, of course," you say.

You're on your way home now, and you feel good. That spectacle within a spectacle has lightened your spirits. You are full, satisfied, almost ebullient. The air is clean and crisp and you breathe deeply. Life has, somehow, taken on a rare opulence. The King Arthur was the best burger you've ever had. You must tell your barber about it.

*   *   *

A Yankee Doodle Fantasy
or,
Manicure, Pedicure,
a Pound of Baccala

When the British surrendered at Yorktown, effectively ending the American Revolution, tradition says their band played "Yankee Doodle", a version of "The World Turned Upside Down". For the losers the tune was an apt, ironic commentary on their political fortunes. For me, the song has become a kind of nostalgic ghost, a recurring haunt humming through the corridors of my memory, particularly on those occasions when I revisit scenes of my youth and discover that the look, feel, even the very smell of those places have disappeared forever. This ghost is a shrewd, playful sprite. It is capable of calculating the most subtle degree of atmosphere, of sorting through the mere accident of detail and homing in on the true pulse of experience. Then it arranges its tune, measure for measure, cadence for cadence, as the mood strikes it.

Sometimes the tune is a dirge, as when I see what was once a grove of oaks now become a fast-food joint, rife with golden arches and garbled voice, innocent of any sexual innuendo, asking if I wanted to "super-size it". At other times I find myself whistling "Yankee Doodle" in three-quarter time, as I drive along a street lined with Victorian houses, all gingerbread and lace, and recall the girl who sacrificed herself as my first date.

Her name was Ludmilla, and she looked just like her name sounded. But she was mine, picked by lot from among girls who had no looks or charm but needed a date. She could not have known that my name had been picked from a hat because I, too, had no looks and less charm and needed a date. It wouldn't have mattered if she had because I was sure she would never see me again after I had gotten sick on the dance-floor and threw up on her shoes.

The tune dissolves into a triumphal march when I push my cart through the aisle of a local supermarket and bump into a fellow who had bullied me all through high school. He had been on the football team and a letter man. Now when I glance into his cart I see muesli and suppository creams and a can of Soup for One.

An ominous note, introduced by a low register among the cellos—for by now my ghost has become a master of orchestration—sounds in my head when I wander into the corner deli to buy a newspaper. The place used to be a candy store, a "Sweet Shoppe", as it was archly dubbed by its proprietor. He was a short, frog-faced man constitutionally unable to smile, whose teeth dimly glinted in all their enameled verdigris as he snarled, "Yeah, so whaddya punks want?" We kids used to go into the store just to rile him, one of the highlights of a dull, thirteenth summer. By the time I was fourteen and had put away my candy-store days I learned that "Froggy" had been indicted. The coke he sold had not always been a soft drink.

Even the neighborhood parks render themselves into a cadence, meaningful in rhythm and timber only to me. My ghost arranges "Yankee Doodle" now as a kind of scherzo as I remember a summer job with the city department of parks. I was the youngest of a crew of three, nicknamed the "G" team, and assigned the garbage detail. Two of us were to follow the truck and empty into it the pails straddled among picnic tables and barbecue pits. The driver was an Englishman in his late forties who always rode with a brown lunch bag next to him. His lunch was a pint bottle of hooch, but he looked us straight in the eye when we began our run and swore solemnly that he would "take a short dram" only when we came upon a cluster of overflowing pails and would be stopped there for a spell. The other fellow, my partner, also old—as everyone over sixteen was—constantly complained about his aching feet. During lunch he would take off his shoes and socks, massage his feet, grunting in pleasure as he rubbed between his toes, then unwrap his egg sandwich and proceed to eat it. To this day I am nauseated at even the sight of a chicken.

Now the oboes and bassoons come in and "Yankee Doodle" emerges as a sprightly air as I pass the old movie theater where I spent many a Saturday afternoon. I remember little of the films, but as "Yankee Doodle" gallops along in my brain I see poor Matron. We never knew her name, though I'm sure she must have had one, like Mrs. Grundy or Mrs. Twaddle, or perhaps Miss Folderol. During one summer she was hired by the incompetent manager, charged with keeping order among the nasty boys who tried to sneak into the balcony or the even nastier ones who put their feet over the backs of the empty seats in front of them. A small, bespectacled thing in a white uniform, she patrolled the main aisle like a wraith, seeking vengeance on wayward youths. She had an uncanny talent for beaming her flashlight into our aisle at the most exciting part of the movie and exclaiming, "Get your feet down!" or "Watch what you do with that gum, mister!" Her days as a Fury were numbered, though, and by August we did not see her anymore. One wag spread the rumor that she had gone insane, becoming a flaming idiot when someone stole her flashlight, but he was doubtless one of the nasties squatting in the balcony. The truth was more banal, as truth often is alongside rumor. The owner of our theater, and father of three, had simply fired the manager and Miss Folderol in one fell swoop.

Of late my ghost has out-Heroded Herod. I have called it shrewd, and correctly, for it seems to know the exact tempo at the right time in the right place. But I also declared it a capricious, willful being. No clearer example of its whimsy occurs to me now than one day recently when I caught myself humming "Yankee Doodle in a kind of syncopated lilt, something of a cross between a jig and a polka. It was a strange revelation, not in the manner of déjà vu, exactly, but nonetheless pleasant and comforting, as a return to one's roots ought to be. I had been passing along a street in my old neighborhood when suddenly I recognized a building that had once housed my Uncle Vito's fish market. I remember working there during the holidays when demand for fish, especially at Christmas Eve, entailed all of us in the family to pitch in. Even my Uncle Angelo helped, though he couldn't stand the smell of fish, much less the taste, his throat closing up, he told us, whenever he came within a stone's throw of the ocean. Standing erect and dignified behind the counter, his jacket caped neatly over his shoulders (like a "padrone", the family used to say), he took down the customers' orders, writing them on the wax wrapping paper and passing them along to the less courtly of us handling the flounder, haddock, mussels and shrimp.

My job was the one nobody wanted—doing execution to the eels. In the cellar, lit only by a fifty-watt bulb, they lay at the bottom of a large tank, filled with only enough water to keep them alive. I would fetch one, grabbing it with a gunny sack, and bring it upstairs to show the customer it was still breathing. Then I would beat out its brains, slamming it on a cinder block, always under the customer's close inspection. If he liked my work, the customer would grant me the privilege of selecting a nice piece of baccala. This was a singular honor, you must understand. It took a fine, practiced eye, an even finer sense of discernment, not to mention an extraordinary finesse of fingers that must be able to feel the ideal stage of readiness. During this procedure, as serious to some as the selection of an engagement ring, Uncle Angelo turned his back, pretending to stare at the wall calendar which declared "Eat Fish, Live Longer". His face was ashen.

All of which brings me back to my ghost, capricious, indeed, but amazingly apt.

For this store is now a hair salon. On the very spot where Mrs. X is languishing in the luxury of a manicure sat the execution block. And over there, where Miss Y is enjoying a pedicure and the refurbishing of her toe-ring, lay the bin of baccala. And please to note that Mrs. Z is delighting in a hair rinse where once my uncle disemboweled the porgies.

The lesson in all this, if there is anything to be learned from the vagaries of memory, is that the past, despite the opinion of philosophers and historians, is not always prelude to the future. It is, as modern cosmologists have it, its own contained universe, parallel yet independent, tideless and immutable. What's done is done, we say. No use crying over spilt milk. But what we are acknowledging in those wise sayings is our very faith in the past as certainty, and there is settled warmth and comfort in certitude, even when, as my ghost has pointed out, the memory of one's personal past often turns the world upside down.

*　　*　　*

A Busy Late Summer Morning

My front steps were pulling away from the house, I remember, and if I didn't take care of them soon someone would get hurt—the postman or the paperboy, any visitor using the front door. Additionally, the two pillars supporting the porch were settling after all these years and needed attention. Keeping up an old house, I've learned, is more than an act of love: it's a longstanding relationship, a bargain and sale contract the terms of which must be lived up to. I knew this even before I bought the old place. My wife and I fell in love with it, as we fell in love with each other, almost at first sight. But we realized that owning it would take work and tireless patience.

So I was out front this Saturday morning ripping off the old bull nose stepping. I was surprised at how the aged nails came away so easily, how they sank quickly through the rotting wood. I could hear screaming across the way at the Shipley house. Luther Shipley was at it again with his wife. I couldn't make out what it was they were yelling about, but over the last few months the screaming, especially on weekends, had grown more violent.

When it first started, the screaming had also come as a surprise because we had always seen Luther and his wife in church on Sunday, and afterwards they would come over to us, holding hands.

"Frank, you've done wonders with that old place," Luther would say, meeting us outside St. Jude's. His wife was not looking at us. "You're really a handy guy."

"Not really, Luther. I just work at it a lot harder."

"Well, when you finish your place, come over and do mine," he laughed.

"Ours," his wife said.

"Right! Ours. I can't seem to get anything done and everything needs work."

Mrs. Shipley pulled her hand from her husband's.

172

"I keep telling Barbara that the best thing to do would be to call in a professional. But they're so doggone high, who can afford them? I'd do it myself, but you know my weekends are my only time off and I need my rest. I'm in the middle of a great book right now. Have you read 'Thinking Like a Million'? There are some great ideas in that book."

I thought I saw Barbara smirk. Luther must have seen her, too. He turned to her, rubbing his hand.

"Some of us might do better to develop our minds—and I don't mean by watching TV. That's for idiots—and kids."

"What do you know about kids?" his wife said.

This time I thought I saw a smirk on Luther's face. "We'd better be going, my love," he said deliberately.

At the mention of kids I saw my wife, Mary, turn aside. "Yes," she said, half to me, half to them, "we'd better be going."

Anyway, Mary was out shopping and there I was working on the front steps and hearing the screaming. It was difficult keeping my mind on the work. I was proceeding by trial and error, cutting out the forms for the steps by placing the original cuts over the fresh wood, using the original as a template, trying not to snap the blade of the electric saw as it cut through the new, thick wood.

I heard another shout and Shipley's screen door slam, and with it, oddly, the chirping of the birds. It was one of those noisy, buzzing, late summer mornings with a sense of nature's busyness in the air. Already the sun was beginning to warm my arms.

I was putting one of the cutouts against the house, assessing such things as height and pitch, when I noticed Luther walking toward me in a quick, forceful gait, as if by charging along that way he could more easily expend his anger.

I could sense his pausing in front of my house, watching me work. I was pretending not to notice him, pretending, in fact, that I had not heard the yelling. I didn't want to embarrass him, yet I was the one feeling embarrassed.

He was waiting for an opening, a pause on my part, perhaps, but I kept busy.

Suddenly he cleared his throat and scraped his shoes on the driveway and there was no point in pretending now. Glancing up from my work, I smiled and greeted him.

"Morning," he said. "Still at it, I see."

He came up the driveway and leaned against one of the columns. I had the strange vision of his crashing through it, like a blinded Samson, bringing the whole porch down about our ears. But the column held.

For a moment neither of us spoke, but now it was his turn not to pretend "I guess you heard us arguing again."

I shrugged.

"You know me," he said, "I've got a temper. Anyhow, I've read that it's no good to keep things bottled up. It causes strokes and heart attacks. In my case it's better to let it out."

"Maybe you're just honest," I said. In the next moment, though, I was ashamed of having patronized him. In my attempt to put him at his ease I had become cowardly and dishonest.

To drive off the feeling, I went back to work. I took the bull nose stepping and fitted it. It sat unevenly on the new cutout, so I removed it and set it on my workbench. I grabbed my plane and began to shave the edges. Luther was still leaning against the column and I was getting a bit self-conscious at being watched.

"She's a little crazy, anyway. I'm getting fed up. Last week in church, for instance. I was trying to be nice. I even cooked dinner for her afterwards but that woman is impossible."

I refitted the step. It sat much better on the riser, but it was still not quite right, so I took it off and sighted it more carefully, checking for imperfections.

"She's always talking about kids, you know. Never misses a chance to bug me with the subject. Kids are all right for some people. I like kids, but I can't see raising them. I was reading an article the other day. Do you know what it costs to raise one kid from birth to age eighteen? You wouldn't believe it if I told you. For some people, though, kids are okay, I guess. You don't have any yet, either."

I paused, but could not look up from my work.

"You and Mary, kids are all right. Have a thousand if you like. But for Barbara and me—kids are out of the question. And anyhow, what kind of world is this to bring them into? Pollution, inflation, wars. Is that the kind of world I want my kid to see?"

For a few minutes he stood watching me work. I had gotten the first step nailed down when I heard him say, "I guess you know it's all over."

"What is?" I said.

"We're finished. I've had it with her. That woman is a little crazy. Did I tell you she's got plants all over the house? It's a jungle."

His face grew hard; his eyes widened.

"I'll tell you," he said. "This isn't going to change my life. Nothing's going to change, not one bit."

It was then that it happened. A whiff of smoke, a vague sense of something burning as in a fireplace or as a quirk of wind and air on a busy late summer morning. Luther was not aware of it until he saw me look anxiously toward his place and then he sniffed it, too. I could see an open kitchen window, the shade partly drawn, squirming, bellying out against the flames behind it.

Both of us began running towards his house. I was running so hard I didn't see Luther in front of me until I caught him from the corner of my eye cutting across two lawns and crashing through a privet hedge bordering his yard. By the time I had run up his drive he was already in the house. Following him in, I could see the smoke, a grey and black smudge looking oddly peaceful as it flattened itself about the room, shattering against the kitchen ceiling. Then I felt as if I had swallowed pepper, my lungs burned and I started to cough as I heard Luther call out.

I smelled gasoline and as my eyes filled with smoke I thought I saw row upon row of potted plants. They were piled along the counters, on the stove, the table; dozens were on the floor so that I almost tripped over them. The stove was on fire and the woodwork and paint were blistering.

From a corner I heard sobbing and I could see Luther on his knees, shaking his wife by the shoulders. She was sitting on the floor, swaying back and forth, her hands closed under her eyes.

"Barbara," he kept yelling. "what did you do? What did you do?"

That night I told Mary about the conversation with Luther. She listened quietly, taking my hand and looking thoughtfully, it seemed, out the window. We sat quietly on the porch, listening to the buzzing of the night. Once or twice the light breeze brought the smell of charred wood from the Shipley place. Before turning in I looked across into their yard. I could see Luther and his wife sitting on the lawn amid the rubble of potted plants. They were holding hands.

*   *   *

The Only Game in Town

The Master sat cross-legged on the lawn, a hand on each knee, palms heavenward. Behind him, in the arbor, plumed peacocks strutted and the Carrara fountain plashed misty rainbows amid gazebo cages where preening birds-of-paradise, perched on one leg, clucked contentedly in the shade. From the second floor of the mansion, the Favorite Disciple descended. His sandals hissed on the dew-encased grass, making his feet wet. Approaching the Master, the Disciple sat at his right, ignoring the dampness. For his part, the Master seemed to be ignoring the Disciple. His eyes were closed, though not tightly, for the Disciple could see the lids fluttering as the Master's lips moved in silent prayer.

The Disciple waited, holding the paper on which he had written the hasty telephone message. The Disciple could hear the humming of the day and the plashing of the fountain. A peacock screeched and suddenly the Master's eyes opened.

"You look anxious," he said.

"News," the Disciple answered.

"It can wait if it is good. It is unimportant if it is bad."

"It could be trouble," said the Disciple, tendering the paper. "I don't know."

The Master looked to the sky, his face radiant in the sun. He breathed deeply. "Let it wait in any case," he said. "Trouble, like beauty, is in the eye of the beholder."

"Trouble could be twenty years," the Disciple said.

A bird of paradise, a silky, blue-and-green confection, tucked its sleek head beneath its wing.

The Master raised his right hand, two fingers forming a V. "First the lesson," he said. "A lesson on trouble."

The Disciple dropped the offering to his side and bit his lip.

And the Master began:

On the first of April, the Professor came down to breakfast to find his wife upset.

"The milk spoiled overnight," she said. "Something's wrong with the refrigerator."

"It's only a few months old," he said. "We haven't even finished paying for it yet."

"The meat's thawing, too. For tonight, do you want chicken, steak, hamburger or a roast? I've got to use it all now."

The Professor sat at the table, eating his cereal dry. It tasted like sugared sawdust.

"Damn American crap," he said. "What's happening to this country? Even this cereal. From America's heartland. Junk. Plain old junk!"

His wife sat at the stove, frying his eggs. She was holding the pan with an oven mitt, for the handle on the pan had but recently cracked and fallen off.

"Can you call the plumber from school?" she asked. "He'll listen to you."

"What now?" he said, pushing away the bowl of sawdust.

"I don't know what he did, but the sink downstairs still leaks."

"Isn't there anybody any more who takes pride in his work? Where's all that American craftsmanship?"

"The eggs at least are good," she said.

"Laid in China, I'll bet."

"You still do good work. The Dean said so, didn't he?"

"I don't make sixty dollars an hour like the plumber does," he said.

After breakfast he kissed his young wife, Faith, and started on his journey. On his way out he checked himself in the hall mirror and was pleased at how he looked in his new, snappy, American-made blazer. It was his one vanity that he took care at least to look, as well as to act, like a professional; to maintain standards in an age when standards were hard to locate; when his students, for example, dressed like vagrants while they drove luxury automobiles.

In the driveway he noticed his own late-model Buick with the velour seats and the $10,000 note. A piece of the vinyl roof was peeling, curling leather away from the windshield like the tongue of a discarded shoe. He shook his head. "Garbage," he muttered. "Garbage."

His office at the university was a mere cubicle, a partition little better than a makeshift fitting room in a warehouse. The desk lamp had never worked, but he was near a window so that on a sunny day the light was bright enough for him to read or grade papers; yet there was still sufficient shadow in the room so that he did not have to look at the imitation wood stain of the metal walls. He proceeded to grade one paper, a semi-literate affair from a student who made more money waiting on tables than he himself did teaching his students medieval history.

For some reason, this morning he had a headache. Leaving his cubicle for the drinking fountain he glanced at his digital watch. It had suddenly started blinking back at him, as if flashing a signal that it was ready to blow up. He tapped the dial and the face went black. "Garbage," he muttered. "Garbage."

Returning to his desk and his waiter's paper, he continued reading:

"The Peasants' Revolt of 1381 was a revolt by English peasants. They didn't like the tax that they had to pay and so they started a revolt, known as the Peasants' Revolt. The times was bad."

The Professor thought suddenly of the plumber. Putting the waiter aside he picked up the phone and dialed the number.

"I'd like to speak to Mike, please."

"Who's this?"

"Mike did some work for me yesterday."

"Yeah, okay, hold on."

There was an abrupt thud at the plumber's end, as if the phone were being thrown against a table. The Professor waited, continuing to read:

"It started when a bunch of peasants some of them not even peasants but noblemen too decided to revolt against Richard II (see Shakespeer) because he was not doing a good job . . ."

"Hello, you still there?"

"Yes, hello?"

"Mike ain't in. He's out on another job."

"When will he be back?"

"Couldn't tell you. Probably out all day."

"I see. How about tomorrow?"

"Hold on."

This time there was a muted sound, and the Professor heard inarticulate voices above the grinding turbulence of some machine.

"In the end they all got their heads chopped off, not the peasants but the politicians working for the king who was responsible for the tax (and for screwing up other things like farming and trade) which caused the revolt. This happened in 1381."

"He'll be out all day tomorrow," the voice said. "He'll be busy all this week. Try next week."

When the voice hung up, the Professor slammed down his own phone. Hastily he scribbled "D" on the waiter's essay, rammed it in his briefcase and left his office.

Walking to class, he heard music. Turning, he noticed student couples sitting in the shade, smoking sweet-smelling cigarettes and laughing. One student lay on his back, against his ear a stereo radio hammering out some folk-rock tune about how the times they are a-changing.

He arrived in class, still with a headache. His waiter was absent and as he looked about the room he felt oddly unimportant. What was all this for anyway? None of these students cared anything about the Middle Ages. It was as if, to them, the epoch of clear hierarchy, of station, rank and standards, never was. It never was, certainly, to his waiter, to Mike, to GM, to the men who sold him his watch and his refrigerator, and least of all to those nutritionists at Battle Creek.

Yet as he faced his class, pain pulsing at his temples, he knew that he, at least, was taking a stand. For if peasants could affect the beheading of noble men who acted ignobly, then he . . .

He thrust his hand into the pocket of his snazzy, expensive blazer. The feel, the texture of quality could not be mistaken.

And so, in the comfort of the uncompromised, the Professor began to pontificate. He felt the brilliance of his own words, savored the incandescence of his examples, the elegant structure of his historical proofs. But in the end he noticed two things. The first was that most students were not interested. Some looked at their watches, some were doodling; two or three were asleep. The second was that his fingers had unexpectedly run into trouble. They had encountered a hole in the bottom of the jacket. He could feel them falling through, dangling in the space of air the rent had opened. The jacket, everything, was coming apart at the seams.

But suddenly he realized that his headache was gone and he wondered in a vague calm if his students would notice him standing there, secretly smiling . . .

The Master ceased and turned his head to look upon the Disciple.

"So the Professor conquered his troubles, is that it, Master?"

"Or simply came to terms with it; made his peace with it. Life, like electricity, feeds on opposites.".

"I understand, Master," said the Disciple. "But I guess you've heard about the Mystical Prophet."

"The bad news you brought to bear against my peace?"

"They've charged him with sexual abuse."

The Master shook his head. "Sins of the flesh; sins of the flesh. The Mystical Prophet was a bold and careless man. A weak man."

The Master was silent for a moment. "It would seem, then," he said, "that we are, as the saying is, the only game in town."

"What do we do now?" the Disciple asked.

The Master closed his eyes. In the pause that followed, the peacocks screeched. From the woods beyond the mansion a crow sounded and another answered.

The Master sighed. His palms lay open, his fingers almost clutched.

"Do this," the Master said. "Pull all our people out, even our homeless specialists. Fill them in at all the places the Prophet's people were working. And one more thing: don't forget the airports and terminals."

As the Disciple rose, pulling the back of his pants away from his rump where the dampness had seeped through, the Master uncrossed his legs and drew his knees up to his chest, his arms embracing them. For the first time now, the Disciple noticed a pillow under the Master's rump.

The sun had moved across the sky, and in the gazebo cages, bars of light streamed in upon the smooth, unruffled, blue-green hues of the birds of paradise.

*   *   *

The Old College Try:
The Admissions Director's Nightmare

Mrs. Lemming, of the Lemming College Lemmings, sits in my office. She is wearing a crude broadcloth tunic and sandals. Her legs are rough, bowed and hairy, like a well-fed goat's. She is holding a shepherd's crook and her face is covered by a Greek theater mask, not smiling, not frowning, just a horizontal gash below dark eyeholes. I could see her eyes dilating in some wild conviction. The mask is too small for her face and her fuzzy ears protrude from her jowly cheeks. The mask is gray but her ears are pink. About them the air is shimmering, as if from smoldering heat.

At her feet the Ape, of the Lemming College Apes, is playing with an ashtray.

"As I was saying," Mrs. Lemming says. "Jocko is really a better student than his record indicates."

She looks down at the Ape, then reaches into the pouch at her waist and takes out a tiny book—the kind garnered as a prize from a box of Cracker-Jack. She reaches down and offers it to Jocko. The Ape smothers it in his palm, puckers up, lowers his face into the book, his gray, leathery lips curling in overbite and befuddled scrutiny. Accidentally his hairy fingers riffle the pages and the stick figures within writhe frenziedly. Jocko screeches and yelps.

"I wanted to meet the Admissions Director personally. And I wanted you to meet Jocko personally. There are some things, after all, that one cannot learn from a transcript."

Having tired of the book, Jocko is now humping the ashtray.

"I see what you mean," I say. "He *is* impressive when you see him apart from his record. It explains a lot."

For some reason I reach down to pat Jocko on the head but the Ape suddenly abandons his romancing and jumps into Mrs.

Lemming's lap, throwing his arms around her neck, knocking her mask askew.

"I'm dreadfully sorry," Mrs. Lemming says. "He is rather shy."

An awkward pause between us is marked by my picking up the ashtray and putting it in the desk drawer, against the possibility of Jocko's again becoming horny. Mrs. Lemming takes off her mask, keeping it at arm's length from Jocko. The Ape, though, amidst his rocking and keening, is too smart for her. Mustering a speedy erection, he impales the mask and brings it to his face.

"Oh my," says Mrs. Lemming, appalled. I notice now that she has one blue eye and one brown, and I realize that one of them is glass, but I can't tell which.

Jocko belts out a scream and settles to the floor. He pouts and mews, looks down and behind him between straddled legs, searching for the ashtray.

"Of course," Mrs. Lemming is saying. "The fact that my late husband founded Lemming College has nothing to do with my interceding for Jocko now. I wouldn't dream of exerting any pressure on the College. Milton was a good man in many ways but quite stupid on most occasions. I suppose one could fairly indict him as a man possessed by a singular form of idiocy, but he was my husband, after all, and Jocko is, as you must know, his adopted son. One must look after one's family, don't you know. I feel obliged to honor his final wishes. His last words to me were: Brunhilde, see to it that Jocko gets a Ph.D."

And Brunhilde Lemming begins to weep. Her tears flow hard, earnestly. They fall on Jocko; they fall on my desk; they overflow onto the floor. Jocko screeches, tries to dance beyond the tide of tears. Succumbs to the feel of wet feet and himself begins to weep.

I offer Mrs. Lemming a tissue from the box I keep on my desk to soothe desperate, pleading parents. Jocko jumps up, yanks the tissue from me, smells it, stuffs it in his mouth.

"There, there, Jocko, Mrs. Lemming says, coming to her senses. "It's all right. This nice man will straighten everything out." Then looking at me: "Won't you straighten everything out, Mr. Nice Man?"

I clear my throat. "It's really not up to me."

"Really," says Mrs. Lemming archly. "I don't quite understand. I've already spoken to Dean Shmuck and President Putz. Both of them knew and loved Milton, that crazy bastard. They both assured me that Jocko won't have any problems. He may even be awarded a scholarship."

"Well, . . ." I answer.

"Of course, if it's documentation you need—I know how committed you admissions people are to records and such—I have some supporting credentials here in my staff."

Mrs. Lemming takes her shepherd's crook, breaks it over Jocko's pyramid of a skull and withdraws from its hollow a scrolled paper.

"Here is all the evidence you need," she declares in high melodrama. "Lemming High—Milton's old alma mater—they changed their name after he gave the school a three million dollar endowment, that loony son of a bitch. Lemming High awarded Jocko medals in Foreign Languages and Athletics. He graduated with honors. See for yourself."

I reach for the scroll, though I know it is of no consequence in this particular scheme of things. I unroll it; I gaze at it. It is dirty. The brown grime of excrement is splattered amid the gothic print.

Mrs. Lemming rubs her bowed, hairy leg. "I'm sorry about the mess. When I told Jocko we were coming to see you he got very upset. Jocko develops strange bowel movements when things in this nasty old world tend to offset his basically lovable personality."

Holding out the document with the tips of index finger and thumb, I offer it back to Mrs. Lemming.

She glares at me. "What are you doing?"

"Doing," I say. "Doing?"

"Won't you be needing this to make an assessment of Jocko's status? Of his position in this year's class? Dean Shmuck—we've had him for dinner several times—I mean, we didn't eat him, of course. I mean we've had him over for dinner on several occasions. Milton and he were such good friends. Dean Shmuck said everything would be fine. See, even Jocko feels better now."

Jocko is now seizing a picture of my wife on the desk. He is studying it, puckering up again. Mrs. Lemming snatches the picture from him. For a moment I grow anxious, fearful that Jocko will beshit my desk. I'm relieved when Mrs. Lemming gives him a lollypop from her pouch.

"Yes," I say, getting up. "Everything, indeed, will be all right. I'll talk to the Registrar at once and we'll get Jocko accepted immediately."

"I know Jocko will love it here," Mrs. Lemming says. "It's so—how does one say it?—so bucolic."

"Yes," I say. "You're absolutely right. There are lots of trees."

*   *   *

Edwards Brothers, Inc.
Thorofare, NJ USA
May 26, 2011